Sophia was overtaken by her reaction to the earl.

Had she lost her mind? Not only was it assumed she would marry another man, but Lord Northbridge remained in mourning for his late wife. She should help him become closer with his children, not closer to her.

"Can we play draughts?" his son asked, pointing to an upper shelf. "I see a board right up there."

"Of course," Sophia said. "I will bring it over to the table, and we will set it up there."

Michael ran away, calling to his sister to come and play the game with him.

Sophia rose on tiptoe to take down the board and the round draughts. Her hand bumped into Lord Northbridge's as he reached for the board, too.

"I can get it," she said.

"I know you can, but allow me to do so in an effort to atone for my son's intrusion."

"There is nothing to atone for."

"For him or for me?" His low voice was almost as warm as his touch.

"Neither of you."

"I am glad to hear that...."

JO ANN BROWN

has published more than one hundred titles under a variety of pen names since selling her first book in 1987. A former military officer, she enjoys telling stories, taking pictures and traveling. She has taught creative writing for more than twenty years and is always excited when one of her students sells a project. She has been married for more than thirty years and has three children and two spoiled cats. Currently she lives in Nevada. Her books have been translated into almost a dozen languages and sold on every continent except Antarctica. She enjoys hearing from her readers. Drop her a note at www.joannbrownbooks.com.

The Dutiful Daughter

JO ANN BROWN

HARLEQUIN® LOVE INSPIRED® HISTORICAL

Recycling programs
for this product may
not exist in your area.

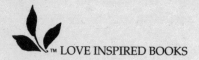 ™ LOVE INSPIRED BOOKS

ISBN-13: 978-0-373-82981-1

THE DUTIFUL DAUGHTER

Copyright © 2013 by Jo Ann Ferguson

www.LoveInspiredBooks.com

Printed in U.S.A.

Everlasting joy shall be upon their head:
they shall obtain gladness and joy;
and sorrow and mourning shall flee away.
—*Isaiah* 51:11

For Regina Scott

A dear friend whose books always delight me.

Thanks for answering all my questions!
I'm sure there are more to come.

And, as always, for Bill.

Chapter One

~

Meriweather Hall, Sanctuary Bay, North Yorkshire
September 1816

"He is here? *Now?*" Sophia Meriweather stared at Ogden, the family's butler, in dismay.

Ogden nodded, his silvery hair catching the light from the book-room window. Even though he had been in service in the house since her father was a boy, the butler was not bent with age. His black livery was perfect, as always, but she noticed the slightest quiver in his fingers. And why not? Everything was going to change from this moment forward.

That was not quite true. Everything had changed when Sophia's father took his last breath without a male heir. Without a brother or even a nephew. Only a distant cousin several times removed who had never visited Meriweather Hall on its promontory overlooking Sanctuary Bay. A distant cousin named Edmund Herriott who now possessed the title of Lord Meriweather and held claim to the estate and all it contained.

Including the previous lord's older daughter.

Not that she was property, but it was assumed by her mother and sister and by the residents of the nearby village that Sophia Meriweather would do her final, most important duty to her father and marry the new baron and give him a male heir to keep an unbroken line at the estate.

Sophia slowly rose from the rosewood desk in the book-room. If she did not marry the new lord, she and her mother and sister would be relegated to the dower cottage where nobody had lived for more than thirty years. Her fingers curled on the edge of the desk. Papa had assured her that once the war was over, they would travel to the places on the Continent that he had visited on his grand tour before the French Revolution and Napoleon's wars.

But her father was dead, and she was expected to marry a man she had never met.

Sophia raised her chin. She had promised Papa before he died that she would take care of Mama, her sister, Catherine, and Meriweather Hall. That was a promise she must keep. Therefore she would present Meriweather Hall in its best light and at its most welcoming. It did not matter that the new baron had not had the forethought to send a messenger ahead to alert them to his arrival so early in the day. Learning to live with how the new Lord Meriweather handled his household was something they must do.

Affixing a smile, she said, "Thank you, Ogden. I trust you had him escorted to the formal parlor."

The barons of Meriweather Hall had received guests in that room since the manor house was built in the 16th century. *But the new Lord Meriweather is no guest.* She silenced that perfidious thought. She had known this day was coming, and she had prayed to be prepared for it. Now she must trust God would help her be.

"They are waiting for you there, Miss Meriweather." Ogden's voice was calm.

Hers was not, because it squeaked when she asked, "They?"

"Lord Meriweather has not traveled here alone." The butler's face was placid. Only that faint tremble in his fingers revealed that he was as on edge as she was.

Sophia squared her shoulders. Greeting the baron and his traveling companions was her duty. Mother still was not receiving because she remained in mourning.

"Where is Catherine?" she asked, for she had not seen her younger sister that morning.

"Miss Catherine is in her private chambers. Shall I let her know of Lord Meriweather's arrival?"

"Do so, and have rooms aired for the baron and his guests." She added as the butler turned to obey, "Ogden, my mother need not be bothered now. I will inform her of Lord Meriweather's arrival after I have greeted him and his companions."

"As you wish, Miss Meriweather. But if she asks…"

"Tell her the truth that I have made arrangements for the baron and our—his other guests." She hoped she would not speak unwisely in the presence of the new baron. Meriweather Hall was no longer her home. It belonged to a man who was setting foot in it for the very first time today.

Sophia took a steadying breath as she walked into the corridor that lead to the front of the house and the formal parlor. A few lamps had been lit to fight back the gray dreariness of the rainy September morning. She did not need light to wind her way past tables and cabinets and the pictures that were lost in the shadows.

She knew each inch of the house, because except for a single visit to London for the Season, she had spent every night beneath its roof.

She heard the men's voices before she reached the formal parlor. The sound, deep and resonant, seemed out of place in the house. One man chuckled, and she wondered if she had heard a male laugh in Meriweather Hall since her father took ill.

Taking a deep breath as she paused by the wide staircase that led to the gallery above, Sophia murmured a quick prayer that God would put the right words on her lips. If it were only her future, she might find this easier, but she had to think of her duty to her family.

Beside the doorway stood Jessup, one of the footmen, who must have escorted the guests there. She smiled a greeting, but he looked hastily away. He probably wished to keep her from seeing how upset he was by the abrupt change in the house.

Her eyes widened when she saw three men in the chamber. All wore rain-drenched brown greatcoats and mud-splattered boots. Their tall hats perched on the circular window seat in the bow window. She was glad they had not thrown their coats on the yellow settee or the marble-topped tables. But mostly, she was pleased to see they were of above-average height. Her one Season in London had been humiliating, because she had not been able to ignore the whispers about how tall she was and who would marry such a Long Meg when there were many petite dolls to choose from?

If her distant cousin shared that belief, it could be disastrous for her family. So, which of the three men was Edmund Herriott?

Was he the redhead who stood with his hands clasped behind his back by the window that offered the best view of Sanctuary Bay? Or was he the light-haired man examining a painting on the chimneypiece? That man was at least five inches shorter than the man by the window, which meant he probably would stand eye to eye with her.

Surely the new Lord Meriweather must be the third man. He was also not as tall as the gangly ginger-haired man, but was well over six feet tall with broad shoulders. He stood in profile to her, so she had an excellent view of rugged features beneath his black hair. Well-shaped mouth, aristocratic nose, firm jaw. His greatcoat was whipped back on one side to reveal an unadorned black waistcoat with silver buttons. Dark brown breeches ended in his mud-stained boots, which he wore with the ease of a man used to a rough life of overseeing his estate and tenants.

Her gaze was caught by his eyes that were as dark as his hair. Heat scored her face when she realized he had been watching her appraise him with candid curiosity. In return he regarded her with cool detachment before looking away as if she were unworthy of his time.

If he is the baron, give me patience, dear God, she prayed. She had seen men with an expression like his in London. Men so certain of their place in the world that they disdained anyone else's. If she were to marry him... She shivered at the very thought.

"Good morning," Sophia said as she stepped into the room. She hoped her fingers did not shake visibly as Ogden's had. "I am Sophia Meriweather, and I welcome you to Meriweather Hall. I trust your journey here was uneventful. North Yorkshire autumns can be beautiful, even though today's rain and chill winds off the sea are dismal." She was babbling, but she could not halt herself as the three men focused on her. Wishing the new baron would identify himself, she decided she must guess. She turned to the dark-haired man. "We hope you soon will feel at home here as we do, Lord Meriweather."

His eyes narrowed, but she saw something flicker within them. She was unsure what the strong emotion was. "I am not your cousin," he said, then gestured to the light-haired man by the hearth. "Herriott, come forward and greet your cousin."

Heat scored Sophia's face. She wished she could leave and come back in again so she could avoid such a *faux pas*. Why had she assumed the man with the most powerful aura was the new baron? Her distant cousin had held no title before, and the dark-haired man exhibited the air of someone accustomed to deference.

Shrugging off his greatcoat, the new Lord Meriweather hurried to greet her. He was well-favored, but his face did not hold her gaze as the dark-haired man's had. Who was the other man?

She could not ask that now. She must greet her cousin—the new Lord Meriweather—prettily. He had an uneasy smile as his gaze swept over her. Was he shocked at her height as other men had been? He was, now that he stood in front of her, a bare inch taller than she was. She resisted the urge to pat her blond hair to be sure it had not loosened from its chignon. She realized she should have changed before greeting the gentlemen, because she wore a simple light blue gown that had no lace or ruffles on its hem. What must Lord Meriweather think of her receiving them in such a simple gown?

"Forgive me," he said. "I was captivated by the elegant brushstrokes in the painting and failed to keep an eye on the door to take note of your arrival." He bowed his head to her. "I am Edmund Herriott, your cousin. I trust I may address you as Sophia since we are family."

"Of course." How could she say no? That would suggest that she had no interest in truly welcoming him into the family. He could then assume that, in spite of everyone's expectations, she did not want to marry him. Even though that was the truth, insulting him now would be unwise. The dower house was in no condition for her mother.

"And you must call me Edmund. I know my proper address might be uncomfortable for you now." Her cousin gave her a lopsided smile. She was grateful for his understanding how unhealed the loss of her father remained, even though almost a year had passed. She realized that he was as nervous as she was. For the first time, she wondered if he had brought the others with him to avoid being alone at this first meeting. He straightened his shoulders, much as she had, before adding, "Allow me to introduce my two friends, both of whom served with me on the Continent. May I present Jonathan Bradby?"

The redhead stepped forward and gave a half bow to her. "A pleasure to meet you, Miss Meriweather. I must say your family chose the most desolate location possible for a house. I have never visited North Yorkshire before, but I now understand its reputation for putting even the strongest man to the test." He raised his head, making her tilt hers to look up at his smile, something she seldom had to do. His grin told her that he was attempting to put her at ease. "Crags and storms."

"But you cannot fault the view, Mr. Bradby," she replied, appreciating his efforts. "It is spectacular."

"I shall let you know once it stops raining." He

laughed, and she realized it had been his laugh she had heard earlier.

She would have enjoyed engaging Mr. Bradby further in conversation, but her gaze was drawn back to the dark-haired man. Unlike his now smiling friends, he remained somber. She wondered if she could ever be unaware of him when he stood nearby.

Her cousin glanced from her to his friend before saying, "May I also present Charles Winthrop, Earl of Northbridge?"

Sophia's breath caught as the earl lowered his head in a gracious greeting. Light played across his sharply sculpted face, and her eyes riveted on the white puckered line of a scar that ran from the middle of his left cheek to his temple before vanishing into his black hair. She could not regain her composure before he straightened and caught her reaction. Any hint of emotion vanished from his face while hers grew warmer with each passing second.

Oh, bother! She was making a difficult situation even worse by gawking at Lord Northbridge like an untutored child. Whether he had been injured in the war or elsewhere, she should not stare. Had she learned nothing from being stared at herself? She must say something to atone for her rude behavior.

She chose the first words that popped into her head, praying they would be the correct ones. "I apologize, Lord Northbridge, for mistaking you for my cousin. I hope I did not discomfort you."

His ebony brows lowered. "Quite to the contrary, Miss Meriweather. I would venture that you are the one who has been put to the blush."

"A most flattering shade it is," Mr. Bradby said with another friendly grin. He pulled off his greatcoat to reveal a peacock's attire. His green coat was worn over an eye-searing blue waistcoat and ruddy breeches.

Jessup rushed in to collect the coats. The footman's eyes almost popped from his head as he stared at Mr. Bradby's garish clothing. Then he recalled himself and held out his arm for the other men's coats. Cousin Edmund handed over his coat, but Lord Northbridge did not remove his. Jessup waited a few seconds, then took the two coats where they could be cleaned and dried.

"Allow me to add, Miss Meriweather," Mr. Bradby said, "that your home was a welcome sight on such a stormy day."

"We have rooms ready for you," Sophia said, her aplomb in place once again. "I trust you will find them suitable for your needs, and I can assure you that each has a splendid view of the sea." She allowed herself the slightest smile. "Or they shall once the sky clears. If there is anything special you require, please ask, and we will do our best to provide it."

"Thank you, Sophia," said her cousin, who then looked at the earl. "Northbridge, don't you have something special to ask of our hostess?"

Sophia stiffened, unsure what the earl would say. Her cousin had treated her with respect and kindness, but she knew none of these men. Would they hoax her for their amusement?

"I do have a unique request, Miss Meriweather." His face softened, and she was startled by the change in his austere expression. Something fluttered in her middle, something she was unfamiliar with. Something delightful, something that had appeared the moment his gaze held hers. "You see, I am traveling with my young son and daughter."

"Of course they are welcome here, as well." She

spoke the words automatically, still unable to look away from his mysterious eyes that seemed to hide so much.

"You are very kind," Lord Northbridge said, "when we have arrived without giving you a warning that the children would be with us."

Sophia blinked, breaking the connection between them, as she understood the significance of his words and looked around the room. Where were the children? She did not ask the question aloud, but the earl answered it as if he were privy to her thoughts. A most discomposing idea.

"I had your cousin ask the staff not to mention this to you immediately or to tell you that the children are being taken to the chamber where I will be staying," Lord Northbridge said. "I thought one shock at a time was enough for you."

Sophia nodded, not trusting herself to speak. Her cousin was already exerting his place in the household. No wonder Ogden had been aquiver. It was not his way to keep secrets from the Meriweather family, and he must have been deeply distressed to be put into such a position. Had Jessup been avoiding her eyes because he feared she would guess his part in the deception?

The staff was doing exactly as they had been trained. She should be proud they were making the transition to the new Lord Meriweather with such skill. She wished she could do the same.

Sophia forced a smile. "I shall have the nursery rooms aired out immediately, my lord. Your nursemaid and—"

"The children shall stay with me. There is no nursemaid." His stern words left no room for debate. "If you will excuse me…" He strode toward the door as if he were lord of Meriweather Hall.

The moment he opened the door, two small blurs rushed into the room. Jessup followed, then brought himself up short before he ran into Lord Meriweather. The footman started to mumble an apology, but Sophia walked to where two small children were clambering onto the curved window seat.

"Where is it?" asked the little girl, who appeared to be about six or seven years old. Her dark red hair was trying to escape from beneath her cap. "Where is the sea?"

"Want to see the sea." The toddler boy beside her, his hair as black as Lord Northbridge's, jumped up and down on the cushions.

Sophia put her hands on his waist before he bounced off and hurt himself. "The sea is out there all around us."

"Where?" the little boy demanded.

"In the rain. The rain is filling up the sea. Once the clouds are empty, you will be able to see where the rain-drops have landed." She sat beside the children who regarded her with uncertainty. "Then the sea will be as beautifully blue as the sky."

"Really?" asked the little girl as her brother popped his thumb into his mouth and regarded her with wide brown eyes.

"Really." Sophia smiled, relaxing for the first time since she had come into the drawing room. "My name is Sophia. What are yours?"

"I am Lady Gemma Winthrop," the little girl said with a dignity that seemed too old for her age, "and this is my brother, Michael. He is Lord Winthrop."

"I am a bearing," Michael said around his thumb.

Sophia silenced her chuckle because she did not want

to hurt the little boy's pride. "My father was a baron, too."

Michael lowered his thumb. "Like me?"

"Just like you."

He grinned and gave a laugh that seemed too deep for a young child.

Sophia wondered if he had inherited that laugh from his father as he had his coloring. At the thought of Lord Northbridge, she glanced over her shoulder.

The earl was staring at them with a taut expression. His eyes snapped with strong emotion. Anger? But what had she done to cause him to regard her with such an expression? Surely he could not be distressed because she had spoken with his children in hopes of making them feel welcome.

She was about to ask what she had done to incite his fury when, beside her, the children grew as quiet as Cousin Edmund and Mr. Bradby. She did not lower her eyes until the earl looked at his children and motioned toward the door. They slid off the seat and edged past him before following Jessup out of the room.

Lord Northbridge said, "The children are tired from their long trip. If you will excuse us…"

Sophia swallowed the questions battering her lips, not wanting to ask them when Gemma and Michael could hear. No one spoke as the earl let Jessup lead him and the children across the foyer. The heels of the earl's boots struck the stairs while he climbed to the upper floor. Sophia knew she should say something, but she could not think of a single word that would not reveal her dismay at Lord Northbridge's actions. She could understand his urgency in wanting to get his children settled in, but not why he had looked daggers at her when she had spoken with the children.

At a throat being cleared behind her, Sophia realized she had been staring after Lord Northbridge like a puppy eager for its master's return. Oh, bother! Why did she have to think *that?*

"Do not take his attitude to heart," Cousin Edmund said as he moved to where she could see his strained face. "He is gruff with everyone, including us. The road God gave him to travel since his beloved wife's death is not an easy one."

Mr. Bradby added, "But you will seldom hear him complain. Rather, he moves ahead like a stag racing through a wood. Woe be to whoever is in his way." His smile returned. "I would advise you, Miss Meriweather, to keep out of his path."

"We have learned on the Continent that is the wisest course, and I hope you will learn from our experience. If you will excuse us as well, I believe it is time for us to stop dripping on the rugs." Cousin Edmund started to walk away, then turned back to her. "Your kindness is more appreciated than you can guess, cousin. To own the truth, I was uncertain what welcome I would find here."

"You are Lord Meriweather." She fought to ignore the sorrow that clutched her heart as she spoke those words. Ten months were not long enough to ease the grief of her father's death. She should be glad that he was in heaven and out of pain—and she was—but she missed his booming laugh and the way he'd always teased her and her sister, Catherine, when they came in windblown from walks along the cliffs. And she missed the evenings when they would sit in his book-room and talk about the places they would visit once the war was won.

Cousin Edmund took her hand and bowed over it

politely. Yet she could not mistake the question in his eyes. He was curious if she was willing to do as everyone expected and become his wife. Did he feel the weight of duty, too?

What a pea-goose she was! Many marriages among the *ton* were based on matters that had nothing to do with love. She should be grateful that Cousin Edmund was treating her with kindness and not acting as if he would never consider marrying a woman who could look him directly in the eye. Another man might have tossed her and her family out of the manor house without a backward glance or insisted that the vicar have the first reading of the banns at the next Sunday service.

He released her hand. Walking past her, he went toward the stairs.

With a quick nod, Mr. Bradby followed.

Sophia remained where she was. Even as the two men spoke their warnings, she had heard their genuine admiration and friendship for Lord Northbridge. She could not help wondering what bound three such different men together and how their presence was going to change Meriweather Hall and everyone who lived within it.

Charles Winthrop smoothed the bedding over his children who were asleep in the large tester bed. Gemma, even at seven years old, showed hints of her mother's lustrous beauty. His three-year-old son resembled him—not just physically. Michael had inherited that stubborn streak that had led Charles into trouble too many times.

He walked into the sitting room where Bradby sat by the tall bay windows. His friend was pouring himself a cup of tea from the pot that had been waiting when Charles had arrived with the children.

"What are you doing here?" Charles closed the bedroom door partway, so he would hear if the children were awakened by his conversation with Bradby.

"You know I get bored when the only company I have is my own." His friend poured a second cup and held it out to Charles. "And Herriott is meeting with his new household staff."

Waving the cup aside, Charles went to close the green draperies. The wind off the North Sea rattled the windows as rain crawled down the glass. He paused and looked out through the storm at the volatile ocean. From the house's location at the edge of the promontory he could see the whole bay. Boats rocked violently in the waves crashing along the bases of the cliffs where huge boulders had fallen in previous squalls. Through the rain he caught sight of a small village perched almost vertically at the inner curve of the cliffs. The weathered stone buildings with their red-and-gray-tiled roofs clung close together on the steep streets, but offered scant shelter from the tempest.

In the open fields at the top of the cliffs, the parish church stood firm against the wind. Its square tower was almost the same color as the gray sky. Sheep grazed around it, oblivious to the showers. The stone outbuildings set closer to Meriweather Hall had been built to withstand storms, because the buildings slanted away from the wind, better to absorb its buffeting.

"Whoever named it Sanctuary Bay must have done so in jest," Charles said.

"I didn't come here to talk about the view." Bradby set his cup on the tea tray and picked up one of the iced cakes from a plate. Taking a hearty bite, he mumbled through his full mouth, "What do you think of Miss Meriweather? They raise tall ones up here in the north."

Charles frowned at his friend. "I prefer not to gossip about our hostess."

"I am not asking you to gossip. I am asking your opinion. Herriott is your friend, and you must have seen how shocked he appeared when she walked in like some mythical tawny-haired Amazon."

He had not noticed Herriott's astonishment because he had been struck by Miss Meriweather himself. An Amazon? No, he would not describe her that way. There was something ethereal about her golden beauty. On the other hand maybe Bradby was not wrong, because Charles had also sensed a will of iron. Her bright green eyes had met his gaze steadily, and he had found himself in the peculiar situation of being the first to look away.

He was not going to say that to Bradby, but he would not lie either. He continued to look out at the sea as he said, "I have to own that I was not watching Herriott or Miss Meriweather at that moment."

"All you think about are your youngsters. Maybe that is because you have an heir, and you are not worried about making a match as Herriott and I must be." His mouth twisted in a wry grin. "I know you never expect to find another woman like Lydia. Not even the heroic Major Winthrop can have a second once-in-a-lifetime love."

"No," Charles said, "I am not seeking for that." His hands clenched on the lush draperies. He yanked them closed so hard that he heard the material creak. Quickly he dropped his hands to his sides. He had not come to Meriweather Hall to destroy his friend's inheritance, but he wished Bradby would talk about something other than Charles's supposed heroics or his marriage.

Bradby instantly said, "I am sorry. I should not have mentioned Lydia. I know how memories of her must afflict you."

"More than you can know." Again he did not stray from the truth. At least the truth as his friends knew it. A truth no one else could refute, because Lydia had died from complications of Michael's birth.

Pushing away from the window, Charles sat in a chair facing his friend. He must let go of his past failures—all of them—and think of the future and the promise he had made to his children and to God. He had vowed to be the best possible father he could be.

If he had some idea how...

"As least the children seem to be putting their grief behind them." Bradby finished his cake and picked up his cup to wash it down. "I vow that, in the near fortnight we have been traveling north, I have not heard them laugh or talk as much as they did with Miss Meriweather."

"Yes, she seems to have a way with children."

"Maybe you should talk Herriott into letting you marry her. What a match you would be. Like out of an old children's story. She is a beauty, and you easily can play the beast with your temper."

"Amusing." Charles used sarcasm to defuse his annoyance that Bradby was sticking his nose where it did not belong.

His friend chuckled, then clamped his hand over his mouth as he glanced guiltily toward the bedroom door. "I meant it seriously."

"You? Serious?"

"This time, yes. Marry the inestimable Miss Meriweather, and then you would not have to worry about the children as you do."

Charles stared at the teapot. His friend was right on both counts. Somewhere on the Continent, Charles had begun to lose his once tight hold on his temper. Now it was always ready to strike out, no matter how he struggled to restrain it. The rage that served him well in battle could hurt those he loved. Thus far, he had kept it from bursting out at the children.

And Bradby was as on the mark about Gemma and Michael. They had been almost mute on the journey to Meriweather Hall. At first he had assumed it was because he and his comrades were strangers; then they'd met Sophia Meriweather and blossomed instantly within the warmth of her smile.

How had she done that? She was unquestionably lovely, so perhaps the children had responded to that.

As he had.

Dash it!

Hadn't he learned that a pretty smile could hide a greedy heart? He would be a beefhead to fall for such a scheme again.

Chapter Two

Sophia closed her bedchamber door and walked toward her mother's room. She owed her mother the duty of informing her about Lord Meriweather's arrival as well as their other guests.

When she heard rapid footfalls moving in her direction along the upstairs hallway, she paused. In astonishment she saw Lord Northbridge coming toward her at a near run.

"Miss Meriweather!" he called. "Exactly the person I hoped to find."

"Is there something amiss?" she asked when he stopped beside her. She knew the answer. The composed, controlled man she had met a few hours before had vanished. He wore his dismay vividly on his face.

"Gemma and Michael have vanished."

"I am sure they are somewhere in the house," she said, relieved that the only problem was mischievous children sneaking away when their father's back was turned.

"How can you be certain of that? If they wandered off, they could be in great danger." He gripped her arms in his powerful hands. His dark eyes burned into her like a pair of brands.

"Lord Northbridge!" She gasped, shocked by his actions.

The sound of his name seemed to bring him back to himself. He looked down at his fingers shackling her arms. He released her so quickly that she rocked on her feet. When he put out a hand to steady her, she edged away.

"Forgive me, Miss Meriweather." He lowered his hand to his side. "I beg your indulgence for this anxious father."

Sophia nodded, accepting his apology. She had to wonder if there was more to his distress than two impish children. There had been a wildness in his tone that astounded her. She reminded herself she knew nothing of the earl other than the few comments his friends had made. His aura of rigorous control over his emotions might be nothing more than an illusion.

"I will be happy to help you look for them," she said.

Gratitude eased the stress gouging deep lines into his face. "Thank you." He took a ragged breath and released it. His voice regained its previously cool tone as he said, "I suspect you may be correct. I doubt they would have gone outside. Michael might have, if his sister went with him. I think that is unlikely because Gemma complained when we arrived that her slippers would be ruined by the puddles."

"Then let us begin." She would explain to her mother later why she had been delayed in bringing news of Cousin Edmund's arrival.

"Which way?"

"If I know children," Sophia said with a smile, "they

will be looking for a sweet treat. The best place for that is the kitchen. Come with me."

Lord Northbridge walked beside her along the corridor. She tried not to glance at the family portraits and the painted landscapes that now belonged to Cousin Edmund. She had known that nothing in the house, save for her clothing and gifts she had received, would be hers once he arrived. Still, there was a vast difference between knowing that and experiencing it firsthand.

"Do you hear that?" Lord Northbridge asked, holding out an arm to halt her.

Sophia stopped before she could bump into it. Straining her ears, she heard the familiar creak of the house as gusts struck it. Then the unmistakable sound of a childish giggle came from her left.

"This way," she said, waving for him to follow.

As she reached an open doorway, she heard, "Michael, do you mind if I offer a sweetmeat to your sister first? It is the way of a gentleman to wait while a lady makes her choice."

She looked into her mother's private rooms and saw an astonishing tableau. On a bright gold chaise longue, Gemma and Michael perched. Her mother sat, facing them, and held out a plate to them.

Elinor Meriweather wore a pale pink shawl over her black dressing gown. It was Sophia's favorite because it flattered Lady Meriweather's coloring. Even though her black hair now was streaked with white, she had few wrinkles beyond the ones that crinkled around her eyes when she smiled at Gemma and Michael.

"You speak the truth, my lady," said Lord Northbridge from behind Sophia.

The children froze at his voice. Gemma's fingers

hovered over a piece of candied fruit, and Michael was half out of the chair in his eagerness to choose one.

"Are you Lord Northbridge, the father of these charming children?" Sophia's mother asked. "Forgive my informality. I am Elinor Meriweather."

He gave a half bow. "It is a pleasure to meet you, my lady. I am their father, it is true, but you are generous when you call them charming after they have barged in to disrupt your afternoon."

Sophia watched in silence. Her mother was dealing with Lord Northbridge with her usual equanimity, but Sophia could not help wondering what her mother thought of the earl. That thought bothered her. Why should she care what her mother's opinions were of Lord Northbridge? But she did care. Deeply. More than she was concerned about her mother's thoughts about Cousin Edmund. That realization disconcerted her even further.

Lady Meriweather urged the children each to make their selection. Placing the platter on the table, she said, "They did not barge in, Lord Northbridge. I invited them in when I heard them outside my door."

"As soon as I realized they had slipped out of the room, I went in search of them. I will keep a closer eye on them, so they do not disturb you again." He stepped aside as a maid entered with Lady Meriweather's tea. "Gemma, Michael, it is time for you to leave now. Thank Lady Meriweather for her hospitality."

"Must we go?" asked Gemma, looking from Sophia to her mother.

"For now," Lady Meriweather replied with a smile. "When you return, be sure to let your father know where you are bound."

Gemma and Michael exchanged a glance, then nodded with clear reluctance.

Sophia took each child by the hand and led them into the hallway. She released them, turning to go in and sit with her mother. Lady Meriweather shooed her toward the door as she had the children.

"You have guests." Lady Meriweather's eyes twinkled. "I can entertain myself, and Lord Northbridge could use your help."

"Mother, I came here to have a nice coze with you."

"And what would you have talked to me about other than our guests?" She waved toward the door again. "Go and help the earl get his children settled before supper. You shall need to use all your wits to keep those two lively children out of trouble."

Sophia knew arguing with her mother would gain her nothing. Giving her mother a quick kiss on the cheek, she hurried out into the hallway where Lord Northbridge was walking in the direction of his rooms.

The children lagged behind, and he looked back. His eyes widened when he saw her following. He halted to allow her and the children to catch up with him.

"Yes?" he asked when she reached where he stood.

Sophia bit back her sharp retort. He did not need to act like a martinet again now that the children had been found. When his gaze shifted, she realized he was embarrassed that she had witnessed his raw emotions earlier.

He was hiding something, something more than grief at his wife's passing. She was as sure of that as she was of her name. For a moment when he'd rushed up to her in the hallway, his eyes had been wild with fear. A fear that far surpassed what a father should feel when his children wandered away in an unfamiliar house.

She could not ask him about it. His cool demeanor prevented that, but she could pray that he would be able to come to terms with that fear and whatever else he was hiding.

"Miss Meriweather, did you have something you wished to say to me?" the earl asked impatiently.

"Yes." She watched the children's faces alter from unhappiness to tentative smiles when she said, "I do hope you will allow Gemma and Michael to pay a call on my mother each day during your stay at Meriweather Hall. I can see that they have brought a happiness to her that has been lost. Thank you." She locked her fingers together in front of her because her hands suddenly seemed awkward. She must not reach out to place a hand on his arm to express her gratitude as she might have with her sister or mother.

"I am glad she sees their exuberance as a blessing rather than as a burden."

"Is that how you see it?" she asked, shocked.

His brows lowered in a familiar scowl. "No. Don't be absurd. They are no burden for me. I am pleased to have them with me."

"I am glad." She was proud she had not let his frown overmaster her again. "Mother has asked that I offer to help you with the children while you are guests at Meriweather Hall."

"You don't need to do that."

"I know, but my mother believes that one's Christian duty should be acted upon, not merely spoken of."

"That is an excellent way to live one's life."

Sophia met his eyes steadily. "And do you live your life to that Christian ideal, too, my lord?"

"I try. I may not always succeed, but I do try." He looked past her as one of the upper maids came around a corner. He motioned for her to come over to them. "Please escort the children to my rooms..."

"Mary," Sophia supplied in a near whisper.

As if she had not spoken, Lord Northbridge continued, "And I would appreciate if you would wait there with them until I return, Mary."

She curtsied. "Of course, m'lord."

He bent toward the children. "Go with Mary. There are some cakes on the tea tray, but have a sandwich first. Remember to walk. No running."

"Running is better suited for the shore." Sophia was rewarded by wide grins from the two children.

"At the sea?" asked Michael as he rocked from one foot to the other in excitement. "Will you take us there, Sophia?"

"*Miss* Meriweather," his father corrected.

"Will you?" the little boy asked again.

Sophia hesitated, looking from Michael to Lord Northbridge.

The earl asked, "Miss Meriweather, may I have a word with you?" Not giving her a chance to answer, he added, "Gemma, make sure your brother heeds Mary."

"But Miss Meriweather didn't say if we were going to the sea," Gemma protested.

With a glower in Sophia's direction that suggested she had caused the whole of this on purpose, Lord Northbridge said, "Right now, I need to speak with Miss Meriweather. We will discuss tomorrow's plans later, children. Please go with Mary."

Gemma and Michael exchanged a glance as they had in Sophia's mother's room, then walked away, every step radiating with fury. Michael looked back, and Sophia gave him a bolstering smile. How sad that the children deflated like balloons whenever their father spoke to them! He was a daunting man, but he must love the children dearly if he had brought them north with him so they could have time together.

And how could she forget his raw fear for them when he discovered they were missing? He loved his children. She knew that, but she wondered if they did.

Sophia wiped her face clean of any expression when Lord Northbridge asked, "Is there a place where we might talk?"

"Yes." She understood what he sought. A place where they could speak without being overheard, but where they could be seen so there was no suggestion of impropriety. "There is an alcove at the end of this corridor by the window that overlooks the front garden."

"Excellent." He offered his arm.

Sophia put her hand on his sleeve and hoped he did not feel her trembling. The powerful muscles beneath her fingers contracted, and she thought he was going to pull away. Then they relaxed, and his stern face did, too, as they continued along the hallway toward the front of the house.

Her gaze traced his straight jaw. It was shadowed by a low mat of a day's whiskers. None grew around the scar along the side of his face. His hair was in need of a cut, for it dropped over his high collar. His clothing had been made by a skilled tailor. The coat did not pull at his shoulders, and his waistcoat fit well against his chest. There was nothing foppish about the way he tied his cravat. He was no dandy. She looked higher at his firm chin and his expressive mouth. He was a man of rapidly changing moods. She already had seen that in the short time he had been at Meriweather Hall.

When Lord Northbridge stopped, Sophia blinked. She had been lost within her appraisal and was astonished that they had reached the large Palladian window at the corridor's end. A tufted bench was set on one side of the window next to a mahogany longcase clock. The soft ticking of its pendulum matched the splatter of rain against the glass.

"I appreciate the offer extended by you and Lady Meriweather," the earl said, "but I do not want to add to your other duties by putting two rambunctious youngsters in your care."

"They have been kept closed up in your carriage during the trip north and now within the house because of the storm." As if to stress her words, the wind threw rain against the window. "Tomorrow, when the clouds have blown out to sea, I can give your children a tour of the grounds. There are many things that they will find interesting."

"You don't need to go to that trouble."

"It is no trouble, and I had already planned to offer the same tour to C-c-cousin Edmund." She hated how she tripped over her cousin's name.

"Miss Meriweather," the earl said, "please do not misconstrue what I am about to say. God has blessed me with two children, and they are a gift I never want to take for granted. I would like to be the one to show them the shore. I have not been able to spend the time I wished with them during the past few years, and I would like to make up for lost time."

She was taken aback by his words for a moment. Then understanding flooded her. Cousin Edmund had mentioned that the three men had been on the Continent together. They must have been fighting the French, a task that would have kept Lord Northbridge far from his family.

"Will you rethink having us open the nursery?" she

asked. "Up there, they can run around and play under watchful eyes. They will not be confined within your rooms, and you can spend as much time with them as you wish."

He considered her suggestion, and she wished Gemma and Michael could understand how he was trying to balance making them happy and keeping them from getting into trouble.

"I daresay you are correct, Miss Meriweather. Your reasons are well thought out, and I will give them consideration. I should have thought of them myself. You clearly have a greater insight into children than I do."

"I often help during Sunday School at the parish church, so I have learned much about children." She hesitated, then said, "Believe me, Lord Northbridge, I do not mean to interfere."

"It is not interference."

She smiled. "Ah, but it is. You will learn that we speak plainly at Meriweather Hall."

"Then I suspect I shall feel quite at home." A hint of smile tipped his stern lips. "May I speak as plainly?"

"Of course."

His gaze swept over her again. "You are a remarkable woman."

Sophia quickly withdrew her hand from Lord Northbridge's arm, abruptly aware of how alone they were. She had never guessed he would turn their conversation in such a personal direction.

"I have embarrassed you," he said.

She was tempted to tell him that *remarkable* was not always a compliment. In London words like remarkable had been used to describe her, and there had been no question about the speaker's intention to point out that such a tall woman was doomed to a life spent on the shelf. Not that they were right, for soon she might be Cousin Edmund's bride. It was not the dream of love she longed for.

Sitting on the bench between the window and the longcase clock, she said, "It is nothing. I am glad you are considering letting the children enjoy the nursery. They will have fun with the toys."

"Gemma may, but Michael will not be content with dolls."

"There are some toys for a young boy, too." She raised her eyes to meet his. "My brother was four when he died."

He leaned one hand on a mullion in the large window. "I did not realize you had a brother. What a tragedy for your family!"

"If he had survived, he would have lived in unbearable agony from his injuries. He had so many broken bones and such damage inside him after being thrown from the runaway pony cart. I was sad, but I have never forgotten it was a blessing for him to be released from that."

"I don't know if I could be as accepting of God's will." He gazed out at the windswept garden. "I found it almost impossible to see grown men cut down in battle and continue to have faith that God had them in His hands. To lose a child…" He shook his head, and several black strands fell forward into his eyes. He swept them aside, revealing more of the scar that reached almost to the top of his skull.

Sophia shifted her gaze to her own fingers. She clasped them in front of her to keep from combing them up through his hair. Was she mad? The scar might still hurt. After suffering such a wound, he was lucky to be alive.

"I cannot bear to think of losing Gemma or Michael," he went on.

Sophia did not hesitate this time. She put her fingers on his arm to offer him comfort. He looked from her hand to her eyes. She wondered what he hoped to see, because he said nothing.

His fingers rose slowly toward her face. She imagined her cheek against his palm. His hands belonged to a man accustomed to a hard life of riding hard and fighting hard and struggling to stay alive. What would his touch feel like against her cheek? She slanted toward him, eager to discover the answer.

"There you are, Winthrop," called Mr. Bradby from beyond the longcase clock.

Sophia straightened, edging away from Lord Northbridge, who snatched his fingers back to his side.

"You are a sight for sore eyes and sorer ears," Mr. Bradby continued as his long legs made short work of the corridor. "Instead of Herriott being grateful that his bread is buttered on both sides, he has been lamenting that his life has become a hodgepodge of misfortune. I don't know what is horrible about inheriting this astounding estate and a peerage. True, he will probably have to leg-shackle himself to the old lord's long shanks daughter, but if it were me..."

Sophia's face burned with embarrassment as Mr. Bradby noticed, belatedly, that she sat on the other side of the clock. Mr. Bradby's mouth closed, then opened and closed again without a sound like a fish yanked out of water.

Lord Northbridge's eyes narrowed as he turned to Mr. Bradby's, whose face had turned a sickly gray. Mr. Bradby stepped back and raised his hands as if in surrender.

She did not wait to hear what the earl might say to the other man. She rose and edged past both men before the hot tears pricking her eyes escaped to flow down her cheeks. It was appalling enough that she was expected to do her duty and marry Cousin Edmund without question. To hear her cousin's opinion of her bandied about casually by Mr. Bradby… It was humiliating.

She rushed away before she said something she feared she would not regret until she offended her cousin to the point he sent her family to the battered dower cottage. Up until that moment she had not realized how utterly her life was no longer her own.

Chapter Three

Voices rose up the stairs as Sophia came down them. She hoped that tonight would not be as much of a mess as the day had been.

She wore one of her favorite gowns. The pale lilac cambric with darker stripes was appropriate for both receiving guests and half mourning. White chenille decorated the cuffs of the short sleeves and the three flounces at the gown's hem. On each step the ornate ribbed design on her stockings could be seen above her white kid slippers. She dared to believe she was prepared for the evening.

That belief vanished when she heard a familiar male voice say, "It is a pleasure to meet you, my lord. This is my sister Vera."

Mr. Fenwick! What was the vicar doing here *tonight*? Oh, heavens, had Cousin Edmund invited him to make plans for marrying her?

She looked over the banister to discover the Fenwicks stood with her sister and Lord Northbridge in the foyer. Neither Cousin Edmund nor Mr. Bradby was in sight.

The urge to run up the stairs and lock herself in her

room was thwarted when her eyes met her sister's. Catherine had a paisley shawl wrapped over the shoulders of her gown whose glorious rich yellow was perfect for her pale complexion and dark eyes. She was as unlike Sophia as two sisters could be. Sophia was tall, and Catherine was petite. Sophia was a blonde like their father while Catherine's curls were as black as Mama's…and Lord Northbridge's.

A surge of warmth rose, unbidden, through her. By the window this afternoon she had been drawn to him as to no other man. To fancy her cousin would have been convenient, but she did not want to have such feelings for the earl. He would soon leave Meriweather Hall to resume his life, a fact she should never forget.

Catherine came up the stairs, drawing the eyes of everyone in the foyer after her. She smiled as she took Sophia's hand and said, "What a party we shall be tonight! When I invited the Fenwicks to join us, I never had any idea our numbers would grow so." Under her breath she added, "I am sorry. With the uproar today, I forgot I had invited them after church on Sunday."

"Did you inform Mrs. Porter?" asked Sophia as quietly, not wanting to chide her sister who took every opportunity to invite Vera, her dearest bosom bow, to Meriweather Hall.

Catherine blanched. Sophia knew her sister had not remembered to tell the cook that the Fenwicks would be joining them tonight. Catherine, who was four years younger than Sophia, had no head when it came to details.

"I will tend to it," Sophia said. With a smile she hoped did not look forced, she raised her voice and added, "The more the merrier."

When she saw Lord Northbridge's eyes narrow at

her banal answer, she wondered if there was a way to
keep her gaze from shifting toward his often. She pretended she had not noticed him looking at her and hurried down the stairs to greet their pastor and his sister.
There was no question that the Fenwicks were closely
related. Both Mr. Fenwick and his sister Vera were of
average height and with open faces that invited one to
stop and talk. Mr. Fenwick's dark hair was thinning
on top, but Vera's was a lush mass of curls pulled back
with silver combs. She was dressed in her best gown,
a pristine white with pale pink ribbons decorating the
modest bodice. Did she hope to make a positive impres-
sion on one of Meriweather Hall's guests?

Sophia scolded herself as Vera laughed at some sally
her brother must have said. There was nothing calcu-
lating about Vera Fenwick. She was a sweet soul and
served the church and its parishioners as wholeheart-
edly as her brother. Why was Sophia looking for hidden motives where she knew there were none? Simply
because she had been overset by her cousin and his un-
settling friends was no excuse for being ill-mannered
herself, even in her thoughts.

"Good evening, Mr. Fenwick," Sophia said, offering her hand to the vicar. "And, Vera, you look lovely
tonight."

Vera threw her arms around Sophia and gave her
a quick hug. The motion said more than words could.

When Sophia stepped back, the foyer went uncom-
fortably still. She understood why when she saw Cousin
Edmund and Mr. Bradby stop in midstep as she had
on the stairs. Her cousin's gulp when his eyes focused
on Mr. Fenwick's clerical collar echoed through the
open space.

Mr. Bradby gave him a clap on the shoulder and kept

coming down the steps. The redhead had sought out Sophia earlier to express his apologies. That did not make her any less uncomfortable with him, even though she could not fault the man when he had done no more than speak the truth. But did her cousin believe that she intended to force his hand by inviting the vicar to Meriweather Hall tonight?

"Oh, dear," said Catherine under her breath. She was clasping and unclasping her hands, a sure sign of her anxiety.

Sophia had to do something, so she smiled up at her cousin. She hoped her expression did not look as bizarre as it felt. "Lord Meriweather, do come down and meet our dear pastor and his sister. Mr. Fenwick and Miss Vera Fenwick have long been regulars at our table. If you want to know anything about Sanctuary Bay, he is the man to ask."

"Yes, yes," Cousin Edmund said, continuing toward them. He offered his hand to the vicar. "I look forward to our conversation, Mr. Fenwick."

"As do I, my lord."

From behind her, Sophia heard, "Well done, Miss Meriweather. You seem to have set your cousin somewhat at ease."

She looked back to see Lord Northbridge's faint smile. "High praise coming from you."

"Indeed."

Resisting the urge to laugh, Sophia asked, "Shall we go in to dinner? Cousin Edmund, we are informal here at Meriweather Hall. If you do not mind, I would ask you to follow Catherine while I confirm one matter with Ogden."

Catherine accepted Mr. Fenwick's arm while Cousin Edmund offered his to Miss Fenwick. When Mr. Bradby held out his to Lord Northbridge, everyone laughed, his antics shattering the last of the suffocating tension. Mr. Fenwick continued to chuckle as the guests walked in the direction of the dining room, but it was Lord North-bridge's laugh that echoed lightly within her. It was like his son's, deep and free. Suddenly there was nothing she wanted more than to hear it again.

Was she mad? Mr. Bradby had been unable to look her in the eye when he spoke his apology, and she had no idea what he thought about her and Lord Northbridge talking alone. He could not have seen her hand on the earl's arm or Lord Northbridge's fingers reaching out to her. Even so, she needed to take care that she was never found in such a possibly compromising position again.

Sophia waited until they were out of earshot and then spoke quickly with the butler. She saw questions in his eyes. As much as she appreciated his concern about how she was dealing with the changes in Meriweather Hall, to speak of such matters would be inappropriate.

"Ogden, please let Mrs. Porter know that the Fenwicks have joined us for dinner."

He nodded. "I will alert the footmen who are serving, too."

"Thank you." She was glad she could depend on the household staff to make food prepared for five serve seven without any of the guests suspecting they were being offered more vegetables with their meat than had originally been planned. The soup course would pose no problem because Mrs. Porter always made extra, and the meringue for their dessert could be cut into smaller slices.

Sophia hurried after the others to the opulent dining room. Thick rafters wove across the ceiling, and magnificent paintings of bucolic scenes were laced among them. The murals on the walls were of the moors, not far to the west. Ruined buildings and tiny villages were painted among the wild, rolling hills. Two chandeliers hung above the black walnut table that would seat twenty. Rainbows danced on the walls as the crystal prisms caught the candlelight.

Everything was perfect, except…

Sophia realized everyone else had taken their seats. Cousin Edmund sat at the head of the table, a place that was rightly his as the latest in a long line of barons. Her sister was to the left of their cousin and next to Mr. Fenwick. On Lord Northbridge's right, Mr. Bradby talked with Vera.

A groan rushed up from deep within Sophia when she realized the only empty place was between her cousin and Lord Northbridge. There were other vacant chairs farther along the table, but to choose one of those would be a blatant insult to both men. It was very cozy…and a reminder that she should be making every effort to become better acquainted with her cousin.

The men rose when Sophia neared the table, and she gestured for them to retake their seats. As she sat between Lord Northbridge and her cousin, she waited for someone to speak, but the conversation that had been animated when she entered the room seemed dead. Footmen served the white consommé with quiet efficiency. They stepped away from the table, and the room became silent again.

Catherine shot Sophia a desperate look, and Sophia asked, "Mr. Fenwick, would you say grace?"

"Of course." He bowed his head over his folded hands, and they all did the same. "Lord, we give thanks for this company and this food. We ask for Your grace upon both. Amen."

After they repeated his amen, everyone started to speak at once, clearly worried that the silence would return and smother them.

Lord Northbridge picked up his soup spoon and began a conversation with Mr. Fenwick. Initially Sophia thought he was using the vicar in an effort to avoid her. After what had happened by the window, he probably thought saying nothing to her was the wisest course. He might be right. As a once-married man, he would know more about such matters than she did.

"I am pleased Meriweather Hall has such a skilled cook," Cousin Edmund said.

"Mrs. Porter never disappoints," Sophia replied, turning to speak with her cousin.

He said nothing more, giving her short answers when she asked his opinion of the house and his journey north. She wondered if he was as nervous as she was. And it was not solely because she sat next to a stranger she was expected to marry. It would have been simpler if the earl had not sat beside her. Was Lord Northbridge making as much of an effort as she was to keep their elbows from brushing? She had not realized he was left-handed, which made the chances of them bumping into each other even more likely. A sense she could not name made her aware of his every motion as if it were hers. She wanted to savor it, but she needed to take care. An earl could have his pick of any young lady in the *ton*. He might find her amusing for a short time and quickly forget her as her erstwhile beau Lord Owensly had during her Season in London. She did not want to risk such shame and hurt again.

Lord Northbridge spoke her name, and she stiffened until she realized he had said, "Mr. Fenwick, Miss Meriweather said you are an expert on the history of Sanctuary Bay and its coastline. Can you tell us how it got its intriguing name?"

Mr. Fenwick set his spoon next to his emptied soup dish. "There are many opinions about that. The most popular is that it was named because the residents hid on the cliffs to evade Viking raiders. That is probably not true. The Viking longboats could easily have navigated into our small harbor as they did in many others along the shore."

"It sounds as if you favor a different tale," Lord Northbridge said, then took a sip of his soup.

"I would not say that, but there is another suggestion of how the town was named." The vicar smiled at Sophia. "It is the theory your father developed, Miss Meriweather. Why don't you explain it to the gentlemen?" He gave a throaty chuckle. "As I disagree with some facets of it and am uneasy with others, I prefer not to repeat it."

Lord Northbridge and his friends looked at Sophia. Honest curiosity gleamed in the eyes of Cousin Edmund and Mr. Bradby, but she read more than curiosity in the earl's. To avoid his gaze until she was more composed, for the first time she avoided them. She looked down at her bowl and realized she had not taken a single bite.

The clatter of wooden heels sounded as a boy rushed into the dining room. Sophia recognized him as Ben, an apprentice at the village baker's shop. He skidded to a stop beside Mr. Fenwick's chair as a maid came into the room in pursuit of the boy. She flushed as she hurried at a more studied pace toward the table.

Ben ignored the glare the maid fired at him. Instead he spoke to Sophia, but kept glancing at the vicar. "Miss

Meriweather, I am sorry to interrupt." He turned to Mr. Fenwick. "'Tis Mr. Joiner. He has taken a bad turn, and the family asks for you to come as soon as possible."

The vicar got up, placing his napkin on his chair. "Thank you, Ben. Will you have the horse hitched to my cart?"

"I stopped by the stable, and one of the lads said he would see to it, Mr. Fenwick. I will go and help him." He raced out of the dining room with the maid following hastily with a guilty glance at the butler. It was well-known that Ogden insisted that only footmen be in the dining room to assist him during meals.

Mr. Fenwick said, "I beg your pardon for taking my leave abruptly."

Sophia stood, and the other men did, too. "Please don't let us delay you with goodbyes, Mr. Fenwick, when you are needed elsewhere now."

Vera set herself on her feet, as well. "Thank you for the invitation, Catherine. I will see you and Sophia again soon, I hope. My lords, Mr. Bradby, it has been a pleasure to make your acquaintance. Do stop by the parsonage when you visit the village." She took her shawl from her brother and draped it over her shoulders as she hurried with him out of the dining room.

Looking across the table, Sophia saw her sister's dismay at the idea of the two of them being alone with the new Lord Meriweather and his friends. Sophia knew it could be worse. She and Cousin Edmund could be dining alone as he prepared to propose.

Neither Sophia nor Catherine had needed to fret, because Cousin Edmund seemed to have found his tongue, and he prattled like a chatter-box. He directed the conversation toward his friends, never to her.

Sophia saw her sister begin to relax and smile when

Mr. Bradby told amusing, but silly stories. The red-head's grin got wider each time Catherine reacted to one of his jests. Sophia was glad she had accepted his apology because he was making every effort to make the evening convivial for Catherine.

She wished she could let her guard down, too, because Mr. Bradby, aside from his unconsidered words upstairs, was both endearing and skilled with gaggery. However, the very idea of unbending when Cousin Edmund sat on one side of her and Lord Northbridge on the other was unfathomable.

Instead she watched the interaction between the three men. Even though the earl did not speak as often as the others, each time he did, the other two were quick to defer to his sentiments. It was clear they held him in the highest esteem. At the same time, Lord Northbridge was enjoying their company. When Cousin Edmund mentioned something about the war, the earl glanced at her sister and said, "Herriott, the ladies."

His words confirmed Sophia's suspicions that the three men had fought together against Napoleon. That would explain both the earl's scar and his friends' respect. She could easily picture Lord Northbridge giving calm orders in the midst of gunfire. Had he honed his ability to control his emotions under such stress?

When the last course, a sweet and light meringue, was crumbs on their plates, Sophia said, "Please allow us to withdraw so you gentlemen may enjoy your port." She started to push back her chair to rise.

The men surged to their feet, and both Lord Northbridge and her cousin reached to help draw out her chair. The earl pulled back his hand as if the wood had suddenly burst into flame. He bowed his head slightly to her cousin who assisted her to stand, and her cousin's eyes narrowed.

Confused, Sophia wondered what unspoken message had passed between them. She thanked her cousin, then turned to leave the table. A firm chest covered by an embroidered waistcoat halted her. Oh, bother, she should have gone in the other direction, but Cousin Edmund had been standing too close on that side.

She raised her eyes to Lord Northbridge's, and her breath caught over her heart, which seemed to have forgotten how to beat. His eyes were no longer hooded, and she saw the powerful emotions warring within them. She should look away, but she was held by the shadows of sorrow in his eyes. He must continue to grieve for his wife, even after more than three years. Many questions begged to be asked. Many words of comfort she wanted to offer, to speak of how deeply she understood his loss.

But she was unable to speak because she could not breathe. If she drew in another breath, his powerful essence would come with it. They could not have stood unmoving for more than a moment; yet it seemed like one life she had known had ended and a new one had started. A life in which he played a role. Which role she did not dare to guess, but that brief second of connection eased the icy cocoon that had surrounded her heart for longer than she wanted to admit.

Sophia stepped away. She had to fight her feet, which wanted to take her back to Lord Northbridge. Instead she walked slowly to where her sister waited at the end of the table. Together they left the room. She saw curiosity on her sister's face, but how could Sophia explain that she was captivated by the good friend of the man she was expected to marry?

* * *

"When I saw the vicar in the foyer, I thought I was done for, about to be caught in the parson's mousetrap." Herriott shuddered as he grimaced.

"Did you really believe that Fenwick was here because Miss Meriweather intended to force you into popping the question the very first night you arrive?" Bradby put down his glass and folded his arms on the table and chuckled. "Stop acting like a scared rabbit, and put yourself in the lady's place. She knows nothing of you, save that you are a distant relative."

"Listen to him, Herriott," Charles said, stretching out his legs beneath the table. "Why would she command you to make an offer? From what I have seen of Miss Meriweather, she would never do something skimble-skamble."

Herriott leaned forward. "What do *you* think of her?"

Bradby cleared his throat and shifted uneasily, a sure sign that Charles must not hesitate on his answer. He would not lie, but how could he say that Herriott's future wife invaded too many of his thoughts? He had never met a woman who exhibited a grace that suggested she moved to music the rest of them could not hear.

"It matters less what I think of her than what you do," Charles replied, hoping Herriott did not see his answer as an evasion.

Across the table, Bradby smiled tautly. Charles had given him the rough side of his tongue after Miss Meriweather had fled, and Bradby had taken the dressing-down he was due.

"You are no longer in garrison," Charles had snapped. "You are in the company of ladies, not soldiers. You can no longer speak churlishly and expect nothing to come of it."

Bradby had apologized, then made a joke, as he did whenever he was under stress. Had he always done that? Charles could not recall, but he seemed to be jesting more and more of late.

Just as Herriott seemed unable to make a decision of any sort. As the baron of this estate he would be forced to do so, but, for now, his indecision might be a boon for both Herriott and Miss Meriweather.

"I know what is expected of us," Herriott said, breaking into Charles's thoughts, "but I would like to become better acquainted with my cousin before I ask her to be my wife."

"I am sure she shares your opinion."

As Bradby chuckled, looking relieved, Herriott reached out to clap Charles on the shoulder. "I am glad you two agreed to come here with me. I should have guessed I would be in need of your counsel at some point. Promise me one thing. If Miss Meriweather— or anyone—mentions the words *banns* or *wedding,* you will change the subject immediately."

Charles laughed. "As I said, I don't think you need worry."

"Better forearmed than unprepared, as you said often enough before we faced the French."

"Fortunately tonight, the only enemy we face is your baseless apprehension."

This time Herriott laughed along with them.

An hour later, Charles stood and bid his friends a good night. Before the war, he had enjoyed sitting for much longer after dinner, conversing with friends. An odd restlessness had taken over since his return to England. Should he check on the children? There was no need, because Mrs. Smith, a matronly woman and the wife of the head groom, had been sent by Lady Meriweather to sit with the children.

If the weather was not foul, he would walk off his agitation outside. Maybe something to read. Mr. Fenwick's unfinished story about Sanctuary Bay had been intriguing. The late Lord Meriweather might have a book on the subject.

A quick question to a footman obtained him directions to the lord's book-room. It was on the first floor, but down a corridor he had not noticed previously. The light from the lamps on the walls was enough so he could avoid bumping into a quartet of suits of armor in the hallway. On the morrow, he would bring Michael and Gemma to see the armor. He guessed they would find it fascinating. Or would it frighten them?

Sophia would know.

He stopped as if the thought had been a brick wall in the center of the hall. When had he started thinking of her as *Sophia?* His mouth tightened. No matter how he thought of her, he was not ready to own to *Miss Meriweather* or anyone else that he was unsure how to rear his children.

Charles continued along the dusky corridor and paused in an open doorway where light spilled out into the hall. The dark shelves of the book-room were packed with more volumes than could fit. More were piled on the floor, on the window seat, on any flat surface.

"Come in," said Sophia as if she had emerged from his thoughts. Now that was a most discomforting idea. She stood at a rosewood desk set in front of a double window.

"Now it is my turn to say I hope I am not intruding," he said, wondering if he would be wise to retreat. To be alone with her, far from everyone else in the house, might be stupid. He turned to leave. "I can return another time."

"Of course not. You are not intruding."

"It would appear I am."

"Are you suggesting that I am being less than honest with you, Lord Northbridge?" A smile curved along her lips before rising to twinkle in her eyes.

"I would never suggest anything except that you are being too polite to tell me to take my *congé*. I should have guessed that you had sought a quiet haven here."

She gestured to the open books on the desk. "I was doing a quick review of the estate's accounts, so I can go through them with Cousin Edmund whenever he wishes. I am glad to say I am done and was about to douse the lamp."

"You have many tasks within these walls, don't you?" He entered the room, but kept a pair of upholstered wing chairs between them.

"Soon they shall be Cousin Edmund's." Her teasing smile would have been perfectly at home on Gemma's face. "I will have more time to do things I enjoy."

"And what are those things?"

She ran her fingers along a shelf of books. "Reading and maybe some traveling." Her eyes grew distant. "I have longed to see the amazing cities on the Continent."

Charles's mouth twisted. "I have no wish to return there."

"I have also thought about visiting America."

"I have traveled as much as I wish. I came here as a favor to your cousin. I look forward to spending the rest of my life tending to my estate while I watch my children grow up."

Her expression suggested she was as shocked as if he had suddenly announced rain was falling up. Her fingers tightened on the shelf, but he was unsure which of his comments had upset her. Reminding himself that he had come to the book-room solely to get something to read, he cautioned himself not to question too closely her reaction to anything he said or did.

Or his reaction to her.

He could not pull his eyes from her half profile as she gazed at the bookshelf. He had been wrong to call her remarkable. Magnificent was a better word.

"Read any book you would like," Sophia said.

"Thank you." The two words gave him time to escape his enticing thoughts of dancing with her to the sumptuous notes of a waltz, but the fantasy returned as he watched her weave through the stacks of books with the ease of practice.

She stopped by a section of shelves at the rear of the room. "This is where Papa kept his favorite books. He loved historical treatises and overly melodramatic novels." She turned to face him, her expression once again that of a gracious hostess. "If either interests you, you will find them here."

"Is there a history of Sanctuary Bay on that shelf?"

Sophia shook her head as she went to the desk and sat. "There is no such book, as my father lamented far too often. He always spoke of writing a history of the bay, but he never did."

He rested his arms on the back of the wing chair. "Mr. Fenwick mentioned that the late baron had been doing some research in that direction and that you had further information."

Her stiff pose softened. "Papa and I spent many evenings trying to trace the bay's name to its origins. It was quite fascinating to discover that the bay might have been a sanctuary for miscreants."

"Ah, now that is far more intriguing." His smile broadened. "What sort of criminals sought a hiding place among the cliffs long ago?"

"Pirates."

"Definitely more interesting." Coming around the chair, he sat in it, pulling it closer to her. "Tell me more."

She did, warming to the story she and her father had pieced together out of legend and dusty tomes. Charles listened intently while she explained how, several centuries before, the English pirates had preyed on trade ships going to and from the Low Countries and north toward Germany and Norway.

"They could very easily slip in and out of the bay, which has deep water," she said, her hands moving as if they were ships on the sea. "Once they reached their target, they were swifter and with nothing to lose, so they often convinced the captains to hand over their cargo without a single shot fired."

"And hied to Sanctuary Bay. But that cannot be the end of the tale. The ships' captains must have set chase." He wanted to keep her telling the story, because he was fascinated by how her expression emphasized each facet of it. Without the grief that too often shadowed her face, she was even more beguiling.

He started to reach out his hand to put it over hers. He drew it back quickly. Hadn't Bradby's interruption this afternoon taught him anything? He could not risk her reputation by giving in to the yearning to touch her.

"The ships did come to Sanctuary Bay, but the crews never found any signs of their stolen cargos in the village."

"Tell me, where in this house did they hide their loot?"

"There is supposedly a deep cellar, more like a cave

actually, beneath, but we have never found any sign of it." Her laugh caressed him like a spring breeze. "How did you guess? Nobody outside the village ever knew of it."

"Mr. Fenwick's reluctance to speak of your father's theory was a good clue."

"There are rumors that my ancestors played a large part in the crimes."

"That did not disturb your father?"

"Quite to the contrary. He thought it great fun to have pirates in our family line, but he was also glad that we live in a far more civilized time."

Charles sighed deeply. "I would not say we are more civilized. We simply prey on each other in different ways now."

"I read the dispatches in the newspaper about the battles against the French," she said in little more than a whisper. "I cannot imagine how much more horrendous it must have been on the battlefield."

"No, you cannot. Not unless you were there."

"I would be glad to listen if you wish to speak of it. Mr. Fenwick has often reminded us that a problem shared is a lessened burden."

He recoiled, shocked by her words. "Why would I wish to relive that?"

"I have no idea, but—"

"Miss Meriweather, I do not wish to speak it." He clenched his teeth as he felt the all-too-familiar surge of heated anger rising from his gut. He struggled to dampen it, but his temper seemed to have a will of its own, wanting to lash out in every direction.

Sophia stared at him in shock. The so-very-brief connection between them was now completely broken. He told himself that it was for the best. She should be getting better acquainted with her cousin, not with him. That thought stabbed him. What did it matter? If she knew the truth about him, she would run in the opposite direction.

He stood when she rose and gestured at the bookshelves.

Her voice was polite and nothing more. "Please feel free to read any book that appeals to you." She faltered, then said, "Some of the volumes are old and fragile. If you wish to read in your room tonight—"

"Michael and Gemma have been taught to respect other people's possessions," he replied crisply at the implied insult. Telling himself that she had not meant her words that way, he tried to push his anger deep within him again. It was like trying to squeeze a cannon into a snuffbox.

"As I said, I am done here." She did not look at him. "You are welcome to stay. I hope you feel free to run tame through the house."

"You have made us feel comfortable in your home." He raised a hand to halt her answer when her gaze slid toward him. "I know it is Herriott's estate, but it is *your* home. I daresay I would not show such equanimity if a stranger came to Northbridge Castle and laid claim to it."

Her eyes narrowed. "We have had time to adjust because we have been awaiting Cousin Edmund's arrival for more than ten months."

"But to hand over your home without a protest…"

"We are fortunate he is a kind gentleman, who already is making efforts to put us at ease."

He found her trite answer vexing. Before he could halt himself, he fired back, "Really? Are you as at ease with the idea of wedding your family to his?"

She flinched at the word *wedding.* "That is too intimate a question," she said in a frigid tone, "but you would be wise to remember that I shall do what I must for my family. And I ask you, my lord, would you *wed* your family to another if it was for the benefit of your children?" She pushed past him to go to the door.

His fingers closed into fists. How dare she use such an officious tone that suggested she was a better person, more willing to sacrifice than he was! She sounded like Lydia. His late wife had delighted in looking down her nose at him whenever she had had the chance. Now Miss Meriweather was doing exactly the same. Had she no idea how much he was fighting to control his temper that she seemed determined to incite with her verbal attack? Cold fury pumped through him. If she wanted a battle, he would oblige.

"Odd," he said to her back. "I may not know you well, Miss Meriweather, but I have learned to trust my first impressions."

She spun to face him. "Which means?"

"I don't see you as a woman willing to settle for a neat solution."

"A neat solution?" Tears glistened in her eyes. "Is that what you are looking for in your life and your children's lives? A nice, neat, boring solution? May I suggest, Lord Northbridge, that you deal with your family's problems and allow me to deal with mine?"

She was gone before he could reply, but not before he saw tears bubbling out of her eyes.

He gripped his hands on the chair so tightly that his knuckles turned white. Was using cutting words to find a woman's most vulnerable spot the only thing he had learned during his marriage? He thought of Bradby's

teasing about the fairy tale of "Beauty and the Beast."
Was his friend closer to the truth than he guessed?

He slammed his left fist into the oak door. It crashed
against the wall as pain surged up his arm. Cradling his
hand, he edged away from the door that was now stained
with the blood from his scraped knuckles.

Charles turned away from the door. He hated how
his temper had become a vicious monster, ready to shed
any hint of humanity and leap into battle at the least
provocation. He did not want to lose himself again and
again to his temper, but he feared he no longer knew
how to prevent it.

Chapter Four

He had not asked her to marry him.

Not yet.

Sophia glanced at her cousin Edmund who had shielded his eyes as he looked out over the sea where the water broke far out from shore. His greatcoat flapped in the strong wind off the water. Did he notice how she held her breath each time he opened his mouth to speak? *Dear Lord,* she prayed, *help him understand that there is no hurry for us to do our duty.*

They had walked down the steep hill to the headland at the south end of Sanctuary Bay because Edmund wanted to explore the estate beyond the gardens. The storm clouds were gone, but the powerful wind remained, driving the salty scent up onto the raw cliffs. Tall clumps of grass stretched over so far the tips almost touched the ground. No trees or even tall stacks of stone offered shelter from the wind.

"This is my favorite vantage point," Sophia said, clamping her hand to her bonnet as a gust of wind tried to yank it away. From this spot the village of Sanctuary Bay was almost hidden from their view in its narrow slit between the cliffs. Only a few roofs were visible, though the beach was broad with the low tide. Between the village and where she and Edmund stood, the entire curve of the sheer rock walls could be seen rising along the shingle shore.

"Stunning," Edmund shouted over the wind. He moved closer to the edge of the cliff.

"Take care!" she called after him. "The rocks are not always stable in this area."

He edged two steps back. "Then I shall wait until we get to a more secure area before I give in to temptation to peer over the rim."

"There are several places where paths lead down the beach, but even with those, we always need to be careful of rocks coming loose."

"I see there is much to learn about Sanctuary Bay and Meriweather Hall. Shall we continue?" He offered his arm as he had earlier when they emerged from the garden to walk along the cliffs.

Then, Sophia had pretended not to notice. It had been simple because they had been pushing past the trees and shrubs growing at the edge of the garden. Now, when they stood in the open, she had no excuse not to take his proffered arm.

She put her hand on his sleeve. Oh, dear! Her fingers were trembling so hard that he could not fail to notice. She hoped he did not think she was frightened to be alone with him. Not that they were truly alone, because a footman stood several yards away as a discreet chaperone. She must make sure he did not get the idea that she found him distasteful. Quite to the contrary! If she was not fearful that the next word out of his mouth would be a marriage proposal, she would enjoy his company. His sense of humor was not as broad as

Mr. Bradby's, and he possessed an intelligence that rivaled Lord Northbridge's.

No! This was no time to be thinking of the annoying earl. She must find a way to prevent any further discussions like the one in her father's book-room. Sleeping last night had been impossible. She regretted letting him goad her into speaking coldly to a guest. But she did not regret the moments when his gaze held hers too long, even though she should not be thinking of that.

"Avoiding the very edge of the cliffs is always wise," Sophia said, knowing she must say something so her cousin did not suspect her thoughts were on his friend. "It is the first lesson my sister and I learned when we got old enough to explore on our own."

"Now you are passing it along to me as the new Lord Meriweather."

She forced a smile. "Consider it simply one of the Meriweather estate traditions."

"One I will take to heart. After all, I can't depend on Northbridge to save me this time." Color flashed up his face, and he looked quickly away.

He had said something he had not intended. Sophia should change the subject and put him at ease once more. But her curiosity had been whetted. The earl had saved her cousin's life. During the war? It must have been. What had happened? Was that when the earl had received the wound that had left a scar on his face? She wanted to ask, but she would be wiser simply to say nothing.

"Please, I implore you," Cousin Edmund said, "forget that I said that, Sophia."

"It is forgotten," she said, though she wondered if she could ever do as she stated.

He gave a relieved sigh. "Thank you. Northbridge

prefers to let what took place during the war remain unspoken. On that, I agree with him." He cleared his throat and looked past her toward the village. "Do tell me, Sophia, about the rumors I hear that pirates once held sway in Sanctuary Bay."

Sophia grasped on to the new topic with eagerness. To discuss Lord Northbridge, even obliquely, made her uncomfortable. She wanted to keep the discussion with her cousin light, and he seemed to be making every effort to do the same.

When she retold the story she had related to the earl last night, Edmund asked insightful questions about the pirates' vessels and how they disposed of their ill-gotten goods.

"You look astonished," he said.

"I am. Most people focus on the adventures upon the seas rather than what the pirates had to do once they were ashore in order to profit from their crimes."

Edmund smiled, and her heart caught when she saw a shadow of her father's features on his face. It was the first time she had noticed a family resemblance. "I must admit to what is scandalous for a peer, even a new one. Before I bought my commission, I was involved in importing fine woods and other materials for the houses my company built or rebuilt in London and in the countryside. Anyone in the import business loses sleep over a ship being sunk or pirated."

"You may not want to mention your past business worries in such terms when you visit the village."

"Because the piracy continues?"

"Not the piracy. Papa and I were never able to find actual proof that it ever occurred." She smiled as she held her bonnet to her head as the wind tried to pull it off again. "I am sorry to tell you that we cannot say the same about smuggling."

Her cousin snorted so loudly that the footman turned to stare at them in curiosity. "If there are men in any port along the British shore who have not taken advantage of a customs officer's lack of attention, I have not heard of them." He glanced at the sea. "I think I shall enjoy my visits here."

Sophia paused, astonished, as they rounded the end of the headland and turned up the hill toward the house. Its chimneys could be seen over the trees that protected it from the worst of the sea storms. So many times she had taken in this view, but for the first time, she felt like a stranger who had washed up on the shore.

"You are not planning on making Meriweather Hall your home?" she asked.

"For part of the year. I worked too hard building my business to sell it simply because I was made a peer." He looked back at her. "That probably sounds silly to you."

"No, not at all." Her admiration for her cousin rose because he was willing to step outside the expectations of the *ton* to hold on to his dreams.

"Thank you." For the first time, his smile seemed genuine. "I am glad you understand. I assure you that I will not neglect Meriweather Hall."

"I never even thought that."

He began walking with her toward the house. "But I cannot ignore my company either. I must oversee it until I can find a manager I have faith in."

"You must have had someone to stand in your stead while you were on the Continent."

He rubbed his hands together, then rammed them into the large pockets of his greatcoat. "I did, but the fellow has told me that he no longer wants the responsibility. It was one thing, he has told me, to carry the load of another man's business during the war. It is quite a different situation now."

"None of your other employees will do?"

"I have several good men in mind, but I must make a decision on that." He sighed as if he faced a very distasteful task. "I will also be obligated to go up to London for the parliamentary season, of course."

"Of course." She must have failed to keep her bitterness out of her voice because her cousin looked puzzled and as uncertain as she had felt during most of their walk.

"I would have guessed that you and your sister would enjoy visiting London during the height of the social Season."

"I am sure Catherine would." Seeing his eyes narrow, she hurried to add, "I attended part of one Season with my father a few years ago."

Did Edmund believe she was fishing for a proposal by speaking of her sister being fired-off? She must be more cautious with every word.

"Part of one Season?" he asked.

"Yes."

He hesitated, and she knew she had aroused his curiosity. She should have known better than to speak of going to London for a partial Season. A young, unbetrothed woman in her first Season would leave Town early only for embarrassing reasons—a lack of funds, a ruined reputation, or because she was cast aside by a fiancé.

"My London house is available to you and your sister and mother whenever you wish to participate in the Season again," he said.

"That is very kind of you."

"It seems only fair as you have welcomed me here."

"I am glad that you are making yourself at home at Meriweather Hall. I hope you will always feel that way." Heat slapped her face when his took on an odd shade of gray.

She had not intended for her words to mean anything more than the trite phrase she would have spoken to any guest. His reaction warned that he had read a different meaning into them. Would she have to be on guard each time she spoke for fear that he would construe her words as a request for him to propose marriage?

A motion along the headland drew Sophia's attention away from her cousin's ashen face. Even from a distance she could not mistake Lord Northbridge's assertive stride. His children walked in front of him, as if he herded them down the narrow path. Michael stopped to examine something on the ground. The earl spoke, his words lost to the wind, and the little boy stiffened, straightened and kept walking.

"It appears we are not the only ones eager to enjoy the air." Relief gushed through Edmund's words.

Sophia resisted the temptation to grasp her cousin by both arms and tell him that she wished they would speak plainly instead of skirting the truth. She was in no more hurry to marry him than he appeared to be to ask her. She would be happy not to marry him if the dower cottage were in good enough repair for her and her mother and sister to retire there.

But she could not say any of that when he was being kind and offering his Town home for their use. He must know that they could not be a part of the Season without making an investment in clothing and entertaining costs.

Hope suddenly rushed through her. If Edmund was

willing to pay for a Season for his two cousins, a dear investment of hundreds of pounds for clothing alone, maybe he would allow them to use that money instead to fix up the cottage. The small inheritance she had from her father would not be hers for another year...or until she married.

But she would not need to marry if she could take care of fixing up the cottage before she moved in with her mother and sister. Her hope was followed quickly by uncertainty. How could she ask her cousin to agree to such a plan without insulting him? Handling this would require God's help in finding the right words.

Father, show me the way.

Maybe the cottage would not need expensive work. She had not visited it for many years. Last time the odors of damp had made her sneeze, and the skitter of rodents had sent her and Catherine fleeing. She should have gone after Papa died, so she would know what needed to be done to make the house comfortable. She vowed to visit the little cottage farther inland the very first chance she had.

In fact she would be happy to go right now...and avoid Lord Northbridge. She could not, not after what she had said to him last night.

Sophia made sure she was smiling while Lord Northbridge and his children continued toward them. Her expression faltered when the earl's step stuttered, and she realized he had just noticed her beside his friend. Did he wish to pretend last evening had not happened...as the men seemed determined to forget the war? He might, but she needed to apologize for her heated words.

"Good afternoon, Northbridge," her cousin called. "Make sure you hold tightly to your children in these winds. You may need calling-bands to keep them from being blown away."

Gemma scowled at Edmund's suggestion that she was still young enough to wear cloth strings that her father could hold like a dog's leash. The little girl's expression changed into a grin when Sophia bent to give her and her brother a hug.

Squatting so she was on a level with the children, Sophia asked, "Are you having fun seeing the sea?"

Michael's glum demeanor dropped away, and he bounced up and down like a marionette. "So big! Looks like the sea by Grandmother's house."

"That is because it is the same one." Gemma rolled her eyes.

"Are you sure?" he asked, looking from his sister to Sophia. "Can't be. Right, Sophia?"

"*Miss* Sophia," his father corrected quietly.

Michael ignored him. "It cannot be the same sea. We rode days and days."

"Yes, 'tis the same one," Gemma retorted.

His face tightened, and Sophia was astonished how his eyes sparked as his father's had in the book-room. "Not true!"

Sophia took Michael's hand and then Gemma's. Looking from one to the other, she said, "Michael, your sister is being honest with you. The sea goes around England."

"Really?"

"Yes." Sophia nodded as the anger eased from his face. "And do you know what is even more amazing than that? Your father and his friends have gone across the sea."

Both children spun away from Sophia and faced their father.

Excitement brightened their eyes, startling Charles. He could not recall a single time they had regarded him without suspicion or anger. This was a welcome change. A very welcome change. Wanting to thank Sophia, he kept his focus on his children.

"Is that true?" asked Gemma, mistrust creeping into her voice.

"Yes." He pointed toward the eastern horizon. "Over there is Europe, just past the point where the sky and the sea meet. There are cities and fields and…" He faltered, not willing to speak in the children's hearing of what he had seen there.

"And," Sophia said quickly to fill the silence, "perhaps a boy and girl like you standing on that shore and wondering about us. Wouldn't it be grand to travel across someday and visit them?"

Charles listened as his children grew more excited while they spoke with Sophia. They vied with each other for her attention. Envy taunted him, because he could not help wondering if he would ever be as natural with his children as she was. No walls stood between her and Gemma and Michael.

Herriott arched a brow, and Charles shrugged at his friend's unspoken question. He had no idea how she brought about the change in his children.

Moving to stand next to his friend, Charles said beneath the children's babbling to Sophia, "I hope we are not interrupting anything important."

"No! Of course not!" Herriott said so quickly that Charles fought back a laugh. "Just chitchat. She seems far more interested in what the children have to say."

"And they in what she says." He watched as Michael bent and picked up a stone, which he held up to Sophia. "Once they took note of her, they made a beeline here."

Michael's shout rose over Herriott's answer. "Want to see the sea. Want to touch the water."

Sophia stood and asked the children to wait for her. As she walked to where Charles stood, he found himself wondering if she was being propelled by a gentle breeze. Every motion was as fluid and graceful as if her feet had wings.

Beside him, Herriott mumbled something under his breath. Charles could not discern what his friend had said, but he hoped his own thoughts had not been vivid on his face. He had no place admiring the woman who was meant for Herriott.

"My lord," she asked, her voice like a song in his ears, "would you be willing to let me take the children down to the shore? There is a path down to the beach that is not too steep. Even Michael could manage it, though holding the children's hands would be the best idea." She faltered, then said, "The choice is yours. I did not tell them what I planned to ask you."

"I see no reason not to let them get closer to the water," he replied, "as long as this path is as gently sloped as you say."

She drew herself up to her full height, and he was amazed anew how pleasant he found having her eyes close to his own. Even when they snapped with green fire as they did now.

"I would never put your children in danger." Her voice was as cool as a winter morning.

"I know that. If my words suggested otherwise, it was never my intention." He folded his arms over the front of his greatcoat. "I have become accustomed to being blunt in the company of men. I see I need to watch more words with more care in a lady's company."

"Oh, no!" Her icy facade fell away as she looked

from him to Herriott and back. "Please do not fret about each word you speak. If we feel we must do that, our conversations will consist of pleasant nothings."

Charles was taken aback at her fervor, and he wondered what she and Herriott had discussed. Not that it was any of his bread and butter, but he clearly had touched a nerve.

When Sophia returned to the children to tell them what had been decided, Herriott said, "I am wearing my new boots, which I have no interest in ruining along the shore. I trust you will escort my cousin to the house."

"Certainly."

"Good." Herriott turned on his heel to leave, but stopped when Charles spoke.

"Are you all right? If we truly were intruding…"

"It is nothing, Northbridge, but concern for my boots and some work I delayed doing earlier today." His tone was bleak.

Charles nodded, though he guessed his friend was still wrestling with how he would balance a business enterprise in London and an estate in North Yorkshire. Herriott seemed utterly overmastered by the obligations that had become his. Charles hoped Herriott would find a way to handle both with the ease he once had shown in business.

So much had been easier before they went to war…

Shaking the dreary thoughts from his mind, Charles went to where Sophia waited patiently and his children far less so. He quickly explained that Herriott had excused himself. Sophia had questions in her eyes, but she did not ask them, and he did not offer further explanation.

"Shall we go?" she asked in the mirthful tone she seemed to reserve for the children.

She held out her hand, and both children reached for it. They glowered at each other, but she quickly defused their competitive spirit by saying she would hold Michael's hand going down and Gemma's on the way up. Gemma started to protest, but Sophia halted her with a smile.

"Do let me hold your brother's hand while it is relatively clean," Sophia said. "You know how boys are." Her nose wrinkled as if she had smelled something bad. "Digging in the dirt."

Gemma nodded. "I know! He is always dirty, Sophia."

"*Miss* Sophia," Charles corrected gently.

His daughter scowled, then smiled when Sophia said, "If I hold your hand on the way up the cliff, I shall have an excuse not to hold his dirty fingers then."

"He can hold Father's hand on the way up." Gemma shot him a triumphant glance.

Charles kept a smile from his face. Even though that was not the expression he longed to see on his daughter's face when she looked at him, anything was better than the frowns she usually aimed in his direction.

When Sophia had taken them to where the narrow path led down the cliffs, Charles thought she had been overly optimistic about the children managing on their own. It cut down the cliff at sharp angles. Yet, as they went slowly along the path, he discovered it was actually simpler than it appeared from the top. Boulders edged the path, so there was less chance of someone toppling down to the shore. At only one spot, where the path dropped more steeply down, did Charles have to pick up his wiggling son and carry him. He set Michael down as soon as the grade eased again.

Sophia did not release Michael's hand when they

reached the bottom. She swung their hands between them while they walked to a large boulder that had either fallen or been thrown up on the shore by a storm.

With a shout, Michael broke away from her. His sister took after him as they raced along the shingle beach, running close to the water and then fleeing toward the base of the cliff as the breakers washed over the stones.

Charles opened his mouth to call them, but Sophia said, "They will be fine. The worst that could happen would be a skinned knee."

"It sounds as if you had plenty of those." He spoke without thinking, but now all he could think about were her legs that must be as willowy as her arms.

"Most children do." She strolled along the rounded stones that clicked on each step.

He kept pace with her, his gaze on his children, though he would have enjoyed taking in the lovely sight of her beside him. Gemma picked up a stone and threw it into the water. Michael did the same with a stone too big for him to manage. It fell close to them, splashing them both. They fled from the water, giggling.

"If," Sophia said, "you wish to join in their games, go ahead. There are some quieter pools where you could teach them to play ducks and drakes."

"They could use some help in learning to throw." He smiled when Michael tried again with the same result. "It has been a long time since I tried skipping stones across water. I used to be quite good at it."

"Show them. It is good for a child to discover that his or her father can do astounding things."

His smile fell away. "But some day they must accept the reality."

"Except that you *have* done astounding things," Sophia said.

Charles clasped his hands behind his back so she would not see his fingers quake as if he had palsy. The thought of those wretched days and nights of battle sickened him. At the time he had not had time to think about what might happen. Only react. Now…

"Forgive me," she said into the lengthening silence.

"There is no need to ask my forgiveness for a chance remark." He walked along the water's edge toward where Michael was picking up yet another stone too large for him.

"Not only this one," she said to his back, "but the horrid one I made last night before I left you in Papa's book-room. I regret speaking with such iciness."

"Even when I deserved a dressing-down?" He turned to face her and was treated to her wide-eyed astonishment. It was an appealing sight, for usually she was in control of her emotions.

Her bright green eyes focused on him as she pushed aside golden strands that the wind whipped from her chignon and twirled around her face. He longed to reach out and brush her hair back at the same time he caressed her soft cheek. Would she quiver beneath his touch? He thought of her eyes closing, her thick lashes curving on her face, as he bent to kiss her warm mouth.

He took a step toward her, and her lips parted in an unspoken invitation for him to press his over them. Slowly his hand rose to cup her cheek. He could not halt himself. She might be intended for his friend, but he would go mad if he did not kiss her once…or twice… or…

"Stop it!" came a shout that shattered his fantasy of holding her.

It took Charles a moment to realize that neither the warning voice in his head nor Sophia had called out that order. Gemma's anger rang along the shore, and he turned to see Michael intentionally tossing a stone where it would send water flying into his sister.

He strode along the strand to where Michael was reaching for another stone. As his son hauled back his arm to throw it, Sophia ran past him. She tossed a stone into the water right in front of Michael, and water soaked the front of his son's coat.

A wail rose from Michael as he spat out the salty water. Gemma laughed. Sophia whispered something in his son's ear and then motioned his daughter closer. They grinned and turned toward him, then his children looked at each other uneasily.

"Go ahead," Sophia ordered as she pointed at Charles. "Splash him!"

The children stared at her as if she had taken a knock in the cradle. With a laugh, she scooped up a handful of water and tossed it in Charles's direction. It spotted the front of his coat.

"Like that," she said with a laugh.

The children splashed water at Charles. The water fell short. They ran forward and tried again. Giggling, they splattered through the shallow water at the edge of the sea. They yelled in excitement when some of the water reached him.

"Splash them," Sophia said, as she came to stand out of range beyond him.

Charles shook his head. "You saw Michael when he got water in his mouth. He was upset."

"Surprised rather than upset because *then* he tossed water at his sister and laughed when it hit her bonnet." Her voice softened. "My lord, they are your children. They want to play with you. Play with them."

Something pierced the pain that had scarred his

heart. She was right. They were his children, and he wanted them to be eager to spend time with him.

Bending, he ignored the cold water soaking his sleeve as he swept a handful toward them. He made sure it hit them on the legs, not in the face. He held his breath as he waited for their reaction.

Instead of the giggles he had hoped for, the children froze, stunned that he had thrown water at them. Then their gazes slid past him, and slow smiles brightened their faces. He turned to see what motion Sophia had made. Water struck him directly in the face.

He sputtered and sent a handful in her direction. She leaped out of the way, and the children crowed in delight.

Spinning, he splashed more water toward his children. Michael laughed and pointed at Gemma who had not moved aside quickly enough. Soon they were laughing and covered with wet spots. Sophia called for a halt when Michael almost slipped on the stones. The children started to protest, but she reminded them how nice a warm tea would taste after playing in the chilly water. They scampered up the sheer path, begging on every step for another chance to play on the shore.

"Soon," Charles affirmed. "But only if you promise not to come here on your own."

He was astonished when they agreed before they ran toward the garden, both talking nonstop. He followed at a more sedate pace with Sophia. For a moment he considered offering his arm, but he doubted he would be satisfied with that chaste touch when he could not stop thinking about kissing her.

"They had fun," she said, her gaze on the children.

"Thanks to you."

She shook her head. "No, my lord. It was thanks to

you. You agreed to let them go down onto the beach, and they were happy to have the chance to play with you." She paused to take a deep breath, then said, "I hope you will accept our offer to open the nursery for the children. They enjoy playing together, and there are plenty of toys in the nursery for them to use. I know you want to spend time with them, but they need to have time to be children."

Charles realized that she was right. He had never seen his children so filled with joy as when splashing in the water. It would not do for Sophia's concern about Gemma and Michael to be greater than his own.

"Very well," he said. "Let's see how they do in the nursery."

When she smiled at him, he suspected he would agree to almost anything she wanted for the chance to see her smile again. That realization shook him to his core. He had made one huge mistake when he had believed Lydia's pretty smiles. He could not be foolish again.

Chapter Five

Why had he agreed to such a want-witted thing? Charles asked himself that question over and over as he had listened, while he had tucked the children in last night, to their prattling about what they might find in the nursery. Through breakfast and during their short walk in the garden while servants packed their clothing, Gemma and Michael discussed what toys were waiting there. It was clear that they were eager to escape from the close quarters of his rooms.

Or maybe they wanted to get away from him.

They had been happy until he had announced it was time for prayers and bed last evening. When they had protested that they should stay up a little longer, he had insisted that they obey. They had whined until he had ordered them to bed. This morning they had treated him with the chill they had before. He'd hoped yesterday that he had found the way to make up for the time they had lost, but they seemed only interested in finding ways to avoid him.

Now he had given them the perfect way.

Forcing a cheerful smile, Charles asked, "Shall we go to see the nursery?"

"Yes, sir," Gemma answered. The little girl he had seen laughing and dancing by the sea was gone.

He had no idea how to bring her back or to elicit the mischievous glint from his son's eyes, so he opened the door and ushered them into the house. He made a few attempts to get them talking, but it was futile, so they walked in silence up the main staircase and along the corridor.

As they turned a corner to reach the stairs that led to the nursery floor, Charles sensed rather than saw someone coming toward him. He stepped back quickly before he could run into the young woman rushing in the opposite direction. She was, he realized, Sophia's sister, Catherine. Last evening she had sent her regrets that she would be unable to join them for dinner. No reason had been given, but Charles was pleased that she looked well.

"Miss Catherine, good morning," he said as he motioned for the children to halt alongside him.

At first glance the two sisters could not look less alike. Yet their eyes had the same intensity, and their mouths conveyed an identical kindness.

If that were so, then why did he think of kissing Sophia's warm lips but felt no such yearning when he encountered Miss Catherine? The only longing he experienced now was the hope that he could put Sophia's younger sister at ease.

"Good morning, my lord," she said, apparently fascinated by a button in the middle of his waistcoat. "Good morning, children. Are you on your way to call on Mother?"

Gemma shook her head, but Michael piped up, "Going to see Sophia and the toys!"

"Michael, you must address her as *Miss* Sophia," Charles said.

Miss Catherine's gaze flicked up toward his. "Which toys?"

"Your sister has kindly offered the nursery," he replied, "for the children's use during our stay. Michael and Gemma are eager to see the toys there."

The young woman smiled as she looked at the children. "You will be pleased by the toys up in the nursery, but don't ride the rocking horse until you have Sophia tell you what he might do." With a nod in his direction, she added, "If you will excuse me..."

Charles stepped aside as she rushed past him. When Gemma asked him about the rocking horse, he could only shrug. Both children looked disappointed that he could not ease their curiosity, and they almost ran toward the stairs. His request that they slow to keep from running into a member of the household fell on deaf ears as they scampered up the steps.

By the time they reached the top of the last stairwell, even Michael had slowed to a walk. The upper floor was plain compared to the lower ones. Beige paint covered the walls, and there were no paintings or fancy woodwork. The frames around the closed doors were simple and painted what might once have been white. On the floor the wide oak boards were darkly stained. No rugs or tile added interest because it was the domain of children and servants.

That changed when a doorway opened, and Sophia gestured for them to come into a small chamber where two small desks sat in front of a larger one. Charles paid no attention to any other details as he drank in the sight of Sophia. She was a vision in a simple, pale green gown that accented her expressive eyes. She smiled at Charles and the children, and for a moment, he greedily wished all her smiles were for him.

"Ah, right on time," she said. "I believe we have everything ready. What do you think, children?"

"Where is the rocking horse?" asked Michael, his eyes wide.

Sophia's smile broadened. "You have heard about Robbie, have you?" She held out her hands, and the children eagerly grasped them. "We keep him in a special place."

Charles followed when she led the children through another door and to an alcove set between the schoolroom and the next chamber. A trio of stained glass windows displayed three fanciful scenes of the sea, the village and the moors farther inland. The rocking horse itself did not look different from the one he had as a child. Made of wood, it had a dark horsehair mane and tail. The saddle was painted garish reds and golds.

"This is Robbie," she said as she picked up the leather reins connected to the horse's head by brass rings. "He is a very special rocking horse."

"How?" demanded Michael.

Charles started to caution his son not to interrupt, but Sophia shook her head slightly. Leaning toward his son, she said, "When you ride him and look hard enough at one of the windows, you can pretend you are galloping across the moors or up the shore to the village."

"Or across the sea?" he asked.

"That is silly," Gemma said. "Horses cannot run across the sea."

He spun to face her. "No? What about seahorses?"

Sophia put her hand over her mouth, but not before

Charles saw her grin. He swallowed his own laugh and stepped in to halt the squabble before it became heated. Promising the children that they would each have many opportunities to ride the horse, he followed them and Sophia into the main room of the nursery.

It was painted a vibrant yellow. White shelves, pushed against the long wall, gleamed in the sunshine pouring through four windows marching along the opposite wall. Toys and books were neatly stacked on the shelves.

In the center of the room, a small table was surrounded by four tiny chairs. The carpet underneath might once have been used in the more public areas, but had been relegated to the nursery once its pattern faded.

Gemma and Michael slowly turned around to take in the whole room.

"Can we play with these toys?" Gemma asked.

"Certainly." Sophia laughed warmly. "What good are toys if they are not being played with?"

The children needed no further invitation. Both ran to the shelves.

Sophia turned her smile on him, and Charles wished she would run to him as eagerly as the children had rushed to the toys. He would hold her as gently as Gemma did with a doll she had found. He would examine her face and run his fingers along her cheek, brushing back her spun-gold tresses, as he lost himself in her wondrous eyes.

That image vanished when Sophia went to help Michael lift down a wooden box. She knelt on the rug beside him and opened it. His son reached in and pulled out a simply carved alphabet block.

A sharp pain thudded in Charles's heart when he saw the color on the block was fresh and vibrant. He could not help recalling Sophia's sorrow when she'd mentioned how her brother had died as a child. If she still grieved, he saw no sign of it as she dug more deeply into the box and lifted out a wooden dog. She set it on the rug, then placed another beside it.

Michael rose to his knees and began searching in the box. Excitement rang through his voice as he called to his sister. Gemma came over to help him search for the matching animals of a Noah's ark set. They began lining the pairs up on the floor.

"That is an elephant," Sophia said when Michael closely examined a gray animal. "The female. The male has tusks." She pantomimed how the ivory tusks would stick out on both sides of its trunk.

His son laughed, and his daughter did, too, when she held up a long-necked creature that he knew was meant to be a giraffe. As Sophia patiently named each animal and told the children about where it lived, a deep longing almost choked Charles. Anyone walking into the nursery would assume that Sophia was the children's mother and he was a stranger.

Standing, Sophia said, "You are welcome to play with anything you like."

Michael jumped to his feet and flung his arms around her legs. "Really?" he asked, tipping back his head to look up at her.

"Yes."

"Do we have to take them outdoors?"

Puzzlement creased her brow. "Why do you ask that?"

Gemma answered as she cradled a doll in her arms, rocking it gently. "Grandmother preferred for us to sit quietly or play out in the garden."

Sophia's mouth grew round in a gasp of astonishment, and Charles resisted the need to defend himself. While he had been on the Continent, he had had no influence on how the children were reared. He was not surprised that his mother-in-law had insisted on such rules, for she had no more maternal instincts than Lydia had. His prayers that Lydia would be a loving mother to Gemma and their unborn son had been for naught.

The children squealed with excitement as they explored the collection of toys. Sophia halted Lord Northbridge from quieting them.

"This is one of the reasons the nursery is isolated up here," she said as she edged aside before Gemma, with Michael in pursuit, could run into her. They collapsed in laughter on the floor.

He nodded, but remained somber. She wished he would smile, because the expression brought forth an inner light. Grief filled his dark eyes. When he smiled, they twinkled, and she saw a hint of the man he could be if he dismantled the wall he kept between him and his children.

Gemma shrieked as her brother knocked over a stack of blocks into her lap. Both children jumped to their feet and began chasing each other again.

"Maybe my mother-in-law had a good reason," Lord Northbridge said wryly, "to ask them to play out of doors."

Sophia chuckled. "I think I have the perfect thing to persuade them to play more sedately." She turned to the shelves to take down a box from an upper one.

As she stretched up, one of the children bumped into her. She did not see which. She wobbled and grasped in vain for the shelf. Her hand found nothing, and she stumbled backward.

Her elbow was caught by strong fingers. A powerful frisson skittered up her arm, a heated sensation that tingled even more strongly when she raised her eyes to meet Lord Northbridge's. All sound, even the children's eager shouts, faded until it was only her and him. As he steadied her, his other hand settled at the back of her waist. His strength surrounded her, and, for the first time in longer than she could remember, she felt exactly the right size. A single motion would slant her up against his chest, her mouth just below his. How would his expressive lips feel on hers?

"Are you all right?" he asked.

Was his tone breathless, or was it how she heard him past her thundering pulse? Every breath she took was flavored with the scent of fresh air and salt, telling her that he must have walked outside this morning.

"Yes." She tried to keep her words from quavering, but she failed when she added, "I am fine."

"I would agree." His voice dropped to a husky whisper that sent a new wave of sweet sensation sweeping over her.

She closed her eyes to savor how his fingers glided along her cheek to brush her chin. His touch was as light as wisps of cloud, but wondrously warm. She leaned into it and opened her eyes to gaze up into his. For once they were not hooded and drew her toward him.

"Sophia!"

The urgent voice barely cut through her gentle haze.

"Sophia!"

A hand tugged at her skirt, and Sophia tore her gaze from Lord Northbridge's. As she looked down to see Michael holding her skirt in his small hand, she took a ragged breath. When had she last drawn a breath? Had she forgotten to while lost in the earl's eyes?

"What is it, son?" Lord Northbridge's voice had an unsteady edge to it.

Sophia stepped away, overtaken by her reaction to him. Had she lost her mind? Not only was it assumed she would marry another man, but Lord Northbridge remained in mourning for his late wife. She should help him become closer with his children, not closer to her.

"Can we play draughts?" Michael asked, pointing to an upper shelf. "I see a board right up there."

"Of course." She congratulated herself for how serene her answer sounded. "I will bring it over to the table, and we will set it up there."

Michael ran away, calling to his sister to come and play the game with him.

Sophia rose on tiptoe to take down the red-and-black checkered board and the round draughts the children soon would be skipping across it. Her hand bumped into Lord Northbridge's as he reached for the board, too.

"I can get it," she said.

"I know you can, but allow me to do so in an effort to atone for my son's intrusion."

"There is nothing to atone for."

"For him or for me?" His low voice was almost as warm as his touch.

"Neither of you."

"I am glad to hear that." He raised his hand again toward the shelf. "If you will allow me..."

Sophia stepped aside to let the earl take down the board and box of draughts. Unlike Lord Owensly who had ended their brief courtship when he could no longer abide his friends teasing him about her height, Lord Northbridge acted as if it were nothing extraordinary. His acceptance touched her more than she expected. He had chided Mr. Bradby when his friend spoke out of turn, but defending a lady was a gentleman's duty. This was something more.

A soft rapping came from an inner door to their left as Lord Northbridge carried the board and box to the table. A young woman peeked around the door like a shy deer. Her fawn-colored hair was pulled back in a tight bun. Beneath her apron, her simple gown was only a shade lighter than her hair. She was short, not even five feet tall, but her smile was warm as she watched the children playing on the floor.

Sophia waited until the young woman came closer to where the children were lifting the wooden disks out of the box. They paused, and Sophia said, "Gemma, Michael, this is Nurse Underwood."

Michael stumbled on trying to repeat the name.

"Why don't you," the young woman asked, "call me Alice? That is easier to say."

"Alice," Michael said and grinned.

When the nurserymaid knelt beside the children, Sophia motioned for Lord Northbridge to walk to the other side of the nursery with her.

Charles did not hesitate. Even though he was curious if the children knew the game and who had taught it to them and if they would invite him to play one of them after their first game, he had questions about the nurserymaid. He had assumed Sophia would introduce her to him before the children.

Yet all he wanted to do was admire Sophia's beauty. She acted as if she were totally unaware of its effect on a man. Unlike Lydia, she did not flirt or tease so that every man in a room watched her. It was unnecessary, because Sophia drew every man's eye without any effort. Maybe on first look her height caught the eye. On a second look—and each one after that—his own gaze was held by her fetching loveliness.

"Yes?" he asked as Gemma shouted with triumph behind him.

"She jumped two of Michael's men," Sophia said when Michael let out a howl of dismay.

He started to go to the table, but she halted him by saying, "Alice Underwood can deal with it."

Sure enough, the nurserymaid quickly soothed Michael at the same time she reminded Gemma that winning graciously was important.

"I chose her," Sophia went on, "because her mother worked in the nursery when Catherine and I were children."

"She is very young."

Sophia gave him a wry smile. "She is my age."

"As I said…" He looked again across the wide room to where his children were giggling at some comment Alice had made. "She does appear to have a skill at amusing them as you do."

"Probably because we grew up together. *My* Nurse Underwood urged us to use our imaginations in our games. That is what I have been doing with Gemma and Michael." She smiled at him. "You might want to give it a try, my lord."

He started to reply, then looked down when a small hand tugged on his coat. He hoped Michael did not see his astonishment. It was the first time that his son had approached him without being asked.

"Father…" The little boy halted.

"What is it, son?" Charles asked.

The boy shuffled his feet.

For the first time Charles noticed Michael's chin was square like his own, and his hair tended to tumble forward into his eyes, as Charles's did. His son's long lashes and slender nose were a legacy from Lydia. Did Michael have her dimples, too? He was appalled that he could not answer that simple question about his own child.

"What is it, son?" he repeated.

"Come with me." He grasped one of Charles's hands. "Help with soldiers."

He looked over his son's head to see lead soldiers strewn across the floor. His stomach twisted, for he wanted nothing more to do with soldiers, toy or otherwise.

"You know about soldiers," Michael insisted when Charles did not answer. "Help with soldiers."

"I would be happy to, son." When the little boy grinned, Charles returned it.

Thank You, Lord, he prayed, *for opening my son's heart to me.*

They walked across the nursery, and Charles glanced over his shoulder to see Sophia smiling, as well.

His happiness faded when Gemma turned her back on him. His son might have reached out to him, but his daughter would not be as easy to win over.

Chapter Six

Sophia smiled as she walked along the hallway. The morning had gone far better than she had dared to hope. *Thank You for persuading Lord Northbridge to heed my request to bring the children to the nursery. And thank You, as well, for having him see what it means for his children to be children.*

She was so happy she wanted to throw out her arms and spin about as if she were no older than Gemma. Joyous tears filled her eyes as she thought of how Michael had come up to his father and invited him to play with the soldiers. Lord Northbridge had had a moment of discomfort. Why? Because he was uncertain how to share his son's make-believe adventures? She doubted Michael had noticed. If only Gemma had not remained standoffish...

One small step forward is wonderful, Sophia reminded herself. More were sure to follow.

She closed her eyes and whirled around. A huge mistake, because, the moment she shut her eyes, Lord Northbridge's handsome face filled her mind. The memory of the powerful sensation that had raced along her at his touch when she stood within the arc of his arm halted her in midstep.

Warning herself not to be foolish, Sophia hurried along the corridor to her sister's room. She had promised to spend some time with Catherine once the children were settled in the nursery.

"Miss Meriweather?"

At the call Sophia settled her face into its usual composure, then turned to face Beverly Jassie, the head housemaid. Beverly never had a red hair out of place, a wrinkle in her gown or was seen without a smile… until now. A frown tilted down her lips, and a deep furrow created a shadow between her brows.

"Is something amiss?" Sophia asked, even though Beverly's expression made the answer quite obvious.

"We cannot wait any longer, Miss Meriweather. We need someone to decide if the Michaelmas rent day will be held here in the great hall or at the justice of the peace's house. The staff needs to know which."

"Lord Meriweather is the one to ask."

Beverly sighed sharply. "And I have, Miss Meriweather. More than once. He keeps telling me that he will let me know as soon as he has made a decision."

"I will speak with him on the matter."

"Thank you!" The maid's stormy expression eased into her usual smile. "I did not want to bother you, but…"

Sophia nodded. The announcement for the quarter rent day's location needed to be made during church, so that the word spread throughout the parish. Thanking the maid, Sophia continued on her way and was stopped twice more with similar complaints. Her cousin was not making the necessary decisions to keep the estate running. None of the problems was any more complex than where to hold the quarter rent day. If he could not make such commonplace and simple decisions, how would he deal with the big problems that every estate faced?

Deciding to talk with her cousin during dinner, she continued along the hallway to her sister's rooms. They were around the corner from her own in the family's wing.

She knocked on the door and opened it when she heard a call for her to enter. Her sister's room was a confection of white and pink, which suited petite Catherine completely. She saw her sister sitting on her favorite settee near the large arched window beyond her bed. Catherine was lowering a book to her lap.

Sophia sank into a chair near the settee and draped her arms over the side. "I am fadded out. I love playing with Gemma and Michael, but they require constant attention, especially Michael. He is curious and mischievous, which makes being with him fun, but he does not stand still for a second."

"Really? They seemed quite subdued when I saw them with Lord Northbridge earlier."

With a sigh, Sophia leaned her head against the chair and stared up at the bedroom's coffered ceiling. "I wish I could say what you saw was an aberration. However, far too often, the children and Lord Northbridge seem equally uncomfortable in each other's company."

"But he is their father!"

Sophia glanced at her sister. "And that is what makes the situation sad. Today, he and Michael enjoyed playing together. I can tell that he wishes he could be closer to Gemma, too, but she keeps him distant."

"Is he always so…?"

"You do not have to choose your words carefully with me." Sophia sighed, wondering how she could get everyone in Meriweather Hall to stop worrying about each thing they said.

Catherine smiled. "Very well." She became serious again. "Is the earl always so intimidating? I could not help but notice that he seemed to be looking down his nose at me."

Sophia laughed. "That is because you are short, Cat."

Her sister wagged a finger at her. "I thought we agreed to leave that name behind in our childhood."

"I miss it. When I saw Gemma and Michael playing hide-and-seek today, I thought about when we did the same. Do you remember the time when we were playing and accidentally locked Nurse Underwood in a storage closet?"

Catherine clapped her hands in sudden glee. "I had forgotten that! She was livid with us, even though she remained calm while we tried to unlock the door."

"And she never told either Papa or Mother."

"No, but she made us learn how to lock and unlock every door in the house." Catherine laughed as she relaxed on the settee. "I think I still could open most of them blindfolded." She moved the book to a nearby table. "You did not answer my question. Is Lord Northbridge always intimidating?"

"No, not always." Sophia stretched out and patted her sister's hand. "When we were with the children on the beach, he was laughing and splashing with them." She did not add that he had done so at her insistence.

Catherine wrapped her arms around herself. "I keep thinking that if *he* was our cousin and you decided not to accept his offer of marriage, then I would be obligated." She shuddered.

"You are being silly." Sophia stood and sat beside

her sister. She slipped her arm around her sister's shoulders and gave a quick squeeze. "Edmund is our cousin."

"And you will marry him?"

"He has not asked me to do other than take tea with him each day." She ran her fingers along the upholstery. "Maybe we should consider a move to the dower cottage."

Catherine leaned forward, lowering her voice. "Have you been there? Is it a place we can live?"

"I have not been there. Not yet, but Cousin Edmund may be willing to pay for fixing it, so we can live there. After all, he offered to pay for a Season for you in London."

"Me? A Season? Truly?"

Sophia took in the sight of her sister's beaming smile. Even though Sophia had no interest in being a subject of ridicule in London again, Catherine would never have to worry about that. It was easy to think of her surrounded by admirers, each vying for the opportunity to stand up with her for the next dance.

"Yes. He spoke to me about it when we went for a walk along the headland."

Clapping her hands with excitement, Catherine said, "I cannot believe this! It is a dream come true. A Season in Town!"

"We shall go together then." She would find another way to make the dower cottage habitable.

"Maybe our cousin will not want that." Catherine's smile fell away. "Oh, my! If he asks you to marry—"

"He has not."

"He will. He watches you intently whenever he thinks nobody is watching him."

"Really?" She bit back the rest of her words. It was unseemly to discuss their cousin in such a manner.

"I wish he had never come here."

"Catherine!"

"I am sorry," Catherine said, looking up at Sophia. Her eyes were filled with the tears that seemed to come too easily since their father's passing.

"What do you have to be sorry for, dear one? You spoke from your heart." Sophia searched for the right words. "I should not have acted shocked."

"Even though you were."

"Yes."

Catherine glanced out the window that was rippled with rain. "I don't want a Season if your happiness is the price."

"Let's not jump to conclusions. Cousin Edmund offered the Season with no conditions."

"I cannot go to Town knowing you are unhappy here. Will you excuse me from dinner again tonight? I don't know if I can look at our cousin without weeping. His very presence is a constant reminder that Papa is gone along with every bit of our joy."

"You can look at him without weeping. You are a Meriweather, and we do what we must."

"But I don't have your steadfast heart or your unfailing faith." Catherine shuddered and drew away. "I am angry that God took Papa and left us in this appalling situation."

"God sees more than we can. He is there even when we feel most alone." Sophia sighed silently. How many times had she and Catherine had this conversation? She empathized with Catherine's pain, for she felt it herself, but she had found comfort in knowing that her father was in heaven, enjoying the reward of living a good life.

She hoped her words would ease her sister's heart but Catherine moaned, "I hate this. If Papa were here…"

"But he is with God, Catherine. We cannot be self-ish and wish him back when he suffered so."

"He would not wish for us to suffer either." She clasped and unclasped her hands as if unsure what else to do with them. "Forgive me, Sophia. Maybe if I had your faith, but I don't. Not any longer. Do you know that I prayed that our cousin would stay away forever, and we could continue on as we have?"

"I know." Sophia put her hands around her sister's. She half thought of suggesting that Catherine close them in prayer, but scolding her sister might serve only to drive Catherine further from God.

"And what do I get for the answer to my prayer? *He* is here."

Frustration curled Sophia's hands in her lap. Before her sister had surrendered to despair, Catherine had been like a skylark, filled with song that she had to share with the world. Each person she'd met in the small village of Sanctuary Bay had been left smiling after having spoken with her. Sophia wished she knew how to revive that joy in her sister, but had no idea.

Sophia said, "Yes, Cousin Edmund is here, and Papa would expect us to be gracious."

Catherine took a deep breath, then let it sift out past her clenched teeth. "We must not do anything that reflects poorly on Papa's memory."

"I agree." Sophia relaxed, because the tempest within Catherine had quieted once more. It would return, even though her sister recognized the futility of railing against circumstances they could not change. "Please reconsider not coming down to dinner. I would appreciate your company while supping with the gentlemen."

"Oh, my heavens!" Her sister's face turned pale, then

reddened. "When I declined to come downstairs, I never thought of what that would mean for you. I am sorry."

"You need to stop saying that. If sisters apologized for each time we step on the other's toes, we'd say nothing but I am sorry all day long."

They laughed together, and Sophia was pleased when the conversation turned away from Cousin Edmund and his friends. She was amazed how soon a knock came at the door along with an announcement that the midday meal was about to be served in their mother's room. The hour had passed in a heartbeat.

It was time to join Cousin Edmund for tea. Sophia sent a message with the maid that she would be there soon, then stood. As she turned to go to the door, her sister called her name. Sophia looked over her shoulder to see her sister's face was again taut.

"Will you wed our cousin if he asks, Sophia?" she asked.

Sophia flinched, but replied as she had to herself each time the question came into her mind. "Yes. It is my duty."

Catherine opened her mouth to reply, but Sophia hurried out the door. There was nothing else to say.

Sophia paced in the foyer, glancing up the stairs. Where was Catherine? They were going to be late for the Sunday service.

Again.

Each time Reverend Fenwick had forgiven them, but Sophia had run out of excuses and had no interest in devising another.

Grasping a handful of her white skirt, Sophia hurried up the stairs. She strode in a red haze of frustration to her sister's door. Why was Cat making everything more difficult? Wasn't it enough that Sophia had to have tea with Cousin Edmund in silence each afternoon? No matter what topic Sophia brought up, her cousin gave her a terse answer, then nothing more. The hour for tea seemed like an eternity, and she could not figure out how to persuade him to have a conversation with her. She was unsure if he was shy or despised her company or had nothing to say on any subject she raised.

At her sister's door, she rapped loudly. No one answered.

"Catherine!" she called. "Open the door."

Long seconds passed, her sharp heartbeat marking off each one, before the door swung back a few inches. It was enough for her to see the tears staining her sister's cheeks. Gray arcs revealed that her sister had not slept. Sophia's fury dissipated instantly because her sister's grief was so deep.

Just like her own.

Sophia took a shuddering breath, then asked, "Are you ready?"

"Will you ask Vera to call tomorrow?" Catherine asked in an uneven whisper. "Tell her that I am not feeling well today."

"Why don't you come to church and tell her yourself? Why do you want to worry your bosom bow?"

"No, I cannot go."

"And I cannot lie for you."

"It is the truth. I feel horrible, and I don't want to be ill at church. I…" She stared past Sophia, her eyes circles of dismay.

"Good morning," came Lord Northbridge's deep voice from behind Sophia.

Her heartbeat escalated like a rising storm wind as his warm breath brushed her nape beneath her straw bonnet. He must be standing right behind her. If she leaned against the hard wall of his chest, would he put his arms around her and keep her close?

Her sister's door slamming brought Sophia out of her daydream. She blinked, trying to focus on something other than being in the earl's arms. She heard a gasp and realized that the children were peering around him.

"Good morning." Her attempt at a cheerful tone fell flat, and the two children regarded her with growing concern.

"Why don't you go downstairs," the earl asked his children, "and tell the coachee we are ready to go?"

"Can I sit with him?" asked the irrepressible Michael.

"Maybe on the way back. It depends on how you behave at church."

His son nodded seriously, then, grabbing his sister's hand, ran for the stairs. Their steps racing down resonated along the corridor.

Lord Northbridge cleared his throat, then said, "I did not intend to distress your sister with a simple greeting." He stared at the door.

"*You* did nothing to disconcert her." Sophia sighed as she walked with the earl toward the stairs. "I did."

"You? By insisting that she come with us to church?" He put his hand on the banister, and she noticed his broad palm covered its breadth. "I know she is uncomfortable in our company. If you would prefer, Bradby and I can attend services elsewhere. Herriott may be willing to do so, too, though I know he hopes to speak to Reverend Fenwick today."

Sophia went down the stairs. "It is nothing you did, my lord. She has been like this since our father became ill. Her faith has been shaken."

"She no longer believes?" He matched her step for

step as if they had descended the staircase many times before.

"Deep in her heart, she does. Or so I tell myself. She prayed hard for Papa to get well and then he died. She believes now that her prayers went unanswered."

"But the answers are not always what we hope." His gaze turned inward, and she guessed he was thinking of the men who had died on the battlefields where he'd fought.

"I tried to tell her that," Sophia said, "but she has changed, no longer attending the vicar's services with joy. Now she goes only with a sense of obligation and because she does not want to do anything to upset Mama more. And when she sets her mind on something, Cat will not have it changed."

"Cat?" asked Mr. Bradby as he joined them at the bottom of the stairs. "Am I to believe that fair Catherine has such a mundane nickname?" He chuckled. "I daresay it is fitting, for she is as cute as a kitten."

Sophia held up her hands as alarm surged through her. "Please do not repeat that name in her hearing. She asked us not to use it any longer, but occasionally I forget."

Charles aimed a furious glare at his friend. Why was Bradby making a jest now when Sophia was so upset that even his friend could not fail to see? Draping an arm around Bradby's shoulders, he said, "My good friend *John-a-Nokes,*" he said, emphasizing the name that Bradby despised, "will honor your request, I am sure."

Bradby muttered something under his breath that Charles did not ask him to repeat, because he suspected it would not be fit for Sophia's ears. As his friend went out the door, he sighed. The morning was bright and sunny; yet everyone was in a dark mood.

"Do not worry," Charles said. "Bradby is a decent man in spite of his hoaxing. If he forgets, Herriott and I will remind him of a gentleman's responsibility to grant a lady her wish."

"Thank you." She smiled weakly at him. "I hope it does not come to that."

"I doubt it will." He motioned for her to precede him out the door and toward the carriage that waited for them.

She did not move. "What did you call Mr. Bradby?"

"It is a play on Jonathan, his given name." He set his hat in place as they stepped outside. "John-a-Nokes simply means anyone. He got the moniker when he always was the last one out of bed each morning and seldom made roll call on time. Your cousin actually picked it."

Sophia chuckled as she lifted an excited Michael into the carriage as Herriott greeted Charles. Bradby had the decency to look chagrined. Charles watched while Herriott handed Sophia into the carriage, and he wished his hand was beneath hers. Those slender fingers emphasized her words when she spoke and were loving when she offered her hand to Gemma or Michael. He was startled to realize he envied both his friend *and* his children.

He stepped forward to help Gemma, but she scampered into the carriage, sat next to Sophia, and began chattering nonstop. He had been snubbed by his own daughter. She glanced at him as he closed the carriage door. Her smile was cool and victorious.

Who had taught Gemma such tricks? Her mother or her grandmother or both? He should have sold his commission and returned as soon as he had received word of Lydia's death. Maybe he should never have left in the first place. He had not expected one casualty of war would be his daughter's love and respect.

Charles drew in his horse in front of the stone church with its thick, square tower. It sat at the very edge of the Meriweather lands. It was not as old as the manor house, but, according to Herriott, there had been a church on that spot for centuries. The gravestones in the churchyard tilted away from the sea winds as did the single tree in the lee of the structure.

He dismounted and took Michael's hand as soon as his son bounced out of the carriage. A single glance at the coachee was enough to remind the little boy that he must behave if he wished to ride on the box to Meriweather Hall.

They entered the porch, and Charles kept the church's door open for the others. The interior of the building was simple with two rows of stone columns on either side of the pews that were surrounded by wood panels that stood almost four feet tall. The narrow aisles along the sides and between the pews were littered with memorial stones. Several had blank indentations where brasses once had been set.

Even though the sides of the pews were so tall that they eclipsed several adult parishioners, Charles sensed every eye focused on their odd parade. Except for Sophia, the rest were strangers to the parish. Heads vanished behind the walls separating the pews, then popped up again to observe the newcomers. Whispers echoed oddly up to the rafters.

Sophia led the way to the first pew, on the right side. She glanced at Herriott and nodded. Opening the door to what must be the Meriweather family pew because it had a coat of arms painted on it, Herriott motioned for Sophia to precede him. There was not enough room for all of them, and Charles turned to find another empty pew.

Michael dashed in to sit beside Sophia. His sister followed. When Herriott motioned for Charles to join them, he hesitated. Herriott went across the aisle to sit with Bradby. More whispers rustled through the church.

What a muddle! Herriott should be in the Meriweather pew, not Charles.

"It will be fine," Sophia said softly. "Sit."

Charles did, then shifted when Michael crawled over him to be closest to the door. Suddenly it seemed as if the four of them were cut off from the rest of the world. Sophia did not look in his direction, but he knew she was as aware as he was of how visible they were. If he reached out and took her hand, would she pull it away?

He had no chance to find out because Miss Fenwick stopped to greet them. Puzzlement wrinkled her brow when she asked about Catherine and Sophia quickly answered that they should speak of that after the service. Miss Fenwick nodded before taking a place in a pew in front of where Herriott and Bradby sat. If she was startled at the seating arrangements, he saw no signs. He hoped the vicar's sister's reaction would set the tone for the rest of the parishioners.

A door opened near the pulpit, and Mr. Fenwick stepped up to the altar. He welcomed them before offering up an opening prayer. As his smooth, deep voice flowed over their bowed heads, Charles tried to put aside other thoughts to listen. It was almost impossible when Sophia's lavender scent flavored every breath. If he moved his arm an inch, his elbow would touch hers.

Had Mr. Fenwick chosen the verses for his sermon

especially for the new baron and his fellow soldiers? He read from Psalm 140. "I said unto the Lord, Thou art my God: hear the voice of my supplications, O Lord. O God the Lord, the strength of my salvation, thou hast covered my head in the day of battle."

Charles listened as the vicar spoke of the battles for good that everyone must fight each day. Mr. Fenwick intended his message for all the parishioners, but the vicar's gaze often met Charles's during the sermon. The man spoke well and with great insight.

"Let us sing," Mr. Fenwick said before announcing the number of the hymn that would signal the end of the service.

Charles reached for a hymnal and his fingers brushed Sophia's. Warmth coursed up his arm, even as Gemma held another open hymnal in front of her. Sophia hesitated, giving Michael enough time to slip in front of them to grab the other side of Gemma's hymnal. His daughter scowled, but said nothing as the singing began.

Sophia's voice was a rich alto, and he had to force himself to concentrate on the words for the three verses instead of losing himself in that sweet sound. Too soon the hymn was over. The benediction quickly followed, and he had no excuse but to help his son open the pew door. Once more the rest of the world could intrude, and it did as they were swept up with the stream of other parishioners walking toward the door where Mr. Fenwick waited to greet them.

Outside the church, Charles did not want to let Sophia slip away from him. He nodded absently when Michael asked about riding on the box. As Gemma ran after her brother toward the carriage, Charles said, "That was an excellent service."

"Mr. Fenwick is an inspired speaker," Sophia replied. "I could tell you thought so, as well."

"I did. And what a pleasure it was not to have to strain my neck to an odd angle when sharing a hymnal with a lovely young lady!"

"You are too kind, my lord." A flattering blush rose up her face, and he wondered why she reacted so to any compliment.

"I have seldom been accused of being too kind."

She smiled and shook her head. "Arguing is out of place in the churchyard, but I must mention that I could name several people who would announce that statement to be untrue. Cousin Edmund thinks very highly of you as, I believe, Mr. Bradby does."

"They are my friends. They have to like me. I—"

A woman screamed. He whirled. Just in time to see the Meriweather carriage careen down the road with the coachee in pursuit. If he was not on the box, who was driving the carriage?

He got his answer when Sophia ran after it shouting, "Michael!"

Chapter Seven

Sophia would never be able to catch the runaway carriage, but her legs pumped as fast as she could run. Was Gemma in the carriage, too? She watched in horror as the carriage bounced off the road and toward the cliffs. It swayed wildly, then the wheels found the road again.

A horse sped past her. Lord Northbridge! He was bent low over the saddle and urging the horse to its top speed. She jumped to the side of the road as two more horses galloped after the carriage. Dust blinded her, but she knew Mr. Bradby and her cousin were riding after the earl. Even knowing that they had a chance to reach the carriage while she did not, she kept running until she reached a knoll where she had a view of the road to Meriweather Hall.

Shielding her eyes against the glare off the sea, she watched Lord Northbridge draw even with the carriage. He glanced at the box, shouted something, then sent his horse forward to match the frantic pace of the carriage horses. He waved his arm high in the air, and Cousin Edmund sent his own horse around to the other side of the carriage. Once their horses were running nose and nose with the carriage horses, Lord Northbridge reached out and grasped the harness. He tugged on it as he sent his mount at an angle away from the carriage horse. Cousin Edmund used his horse to herd the other horse to turn, as well. They brought the runaways to a stop.

Sophia gathered her skirt up and rushed to where Mr. Bradby waited in the saddle. When he offered to let her ride, she shook her head and kept running. It would take longer for her to mount than to reach the carriage on foot.

Lord Northbridge was handing his son down to Cousin Edmund as Sophia skidded to a stop by the carriage. She put her hand to her side as she panted from the race.

"Michael is unhurt," her cousin said before she could ask. "He never got a grip on the reins before the horses sped off."

"Gemma?" she asked.

The two men exchanged a horrified glance. She tore open the carriage door. Huddled on the floor, Gemma was crying hysterically.

Sophia called her name. The little girl flung herself into Sophia's arms so hard that they almost collapsed to the ground. Setting Gemma on her feet, Sophia knelt and hugged the little girl. She whispered over and over that Gemma was safe, that Michael was safe, that everything was all right. The child clung to her as Sophia thanked God that neither child had been injured.

A large hand cupped Gemma's head, and Sophia raised her eyes to meet the fear in Lord Northbridge's. He silently asked a question that she understood. She smiled to let him know that Gemma was uninjured. His own face was grim as he walked to where her cousin still held Michael.

Sophia wanted to call him back, tell him to offer his daughter comfort. Such a kindness might bridge the chasm between them. With a pulse of empathy, she knew the earl had not offered even to hug his daughter because he believed he would be rebuffed.

Lord, You know what resides in our hearts. Please help this family find a way to open theirs to each other.

Wiping away Gemma's tears, Sophia calmed the child. She heard other voices coming closer, and she guessed the rest of the churchgoers had arrived to find out if everything was well. She paid them no attention as she focused on Gemma.

The little girl's sobs became gentle hiccups. Taking her hand, Sophia sat by the road and waved away Vera Fenwick. Her friend nodded, then kept others away so Sophia and Gemma could talk.

"It was scary," Gemma said.

"It must have been."

"I should have known that Michael would do something beefheaded after he boasted that he could drive the carriage better than the coachman."

"That is what little boys do," Sophia said, smoothing back Gemma's hair from her damp face. "If Michael had stopped to think, he would know a little boy cannot control two large horses."

"Uncle Walter did."

Sophia heard wistfulness in Gemma's voice, so she asked. "Who is Uncle Walter?"

"Our uncle," Gemma replied in a tone that suggested she questioned Sophia's sanity.

"I see."

She doubted the little girl heard her trite answer, because Gemma hurried on, "Uncle Walter always promised he would let Michael hold the reins, but he never did. Then he would laugh and brag about how he could drive a coach and four when he was younger than me. He said Michael was a baby for not driving."

Outraged that a man would say such a thing, Sophia said, "That is silly. No child can drive a coach and four. He would have been pulled right out of the box." She shivered as she thanked God again for keeping Michael from having had a good hold on the reins.

Gemma folded her arms over her chest and frowned. "Are you calling Uncle Walter a liar or me?"

"Neither." How alike Lord Northbridge and his daughter were! Both bristled when they felt under attack.

Before she could say more, she heard the earl's raised voice. It was razor sharp as he demanded, "Why would you do something foolhardy?"

Sophia drew in a sharp breath when Michael shrank into himself, too frightened of his father's rage to answer. Lord Northbridge had every reason to be upset, but such a tone would sever their fragile relationship.

Coming to her feet, Sophia took Gemma's hand. She led the little girl over to where Mr. Bradby and her cousin looked uneasily in the earl's direction. Putting Gemma's hand in her cousin's, she squatted next to Michael. She did not look at his father, who had gone silent, as she whispered for the child to go to his sister.

"I thought," Lord Northbridge said in the same whetted tone, "that you wished me to handle my family problems while you deal with yours. This is my problem. Not yours."

"You may want to listen to what I have to say before you continue to berate your son publicly." She glanced over her shoulder at the crowd that surrounded the children who stood on either side of her cousin.

He nodded as his jaw worked with his strong emotions.

She led the way to the other side of the carriage where they could talk without being overheard. Quickly she explained what Gemma had told her.

"Uncle Walter?" A puzzled expression crossed his face, then his mouth tightened as he paced in front of her. Anger and frustration billowed off him like a mist. "She must have meant Lydia's step-cousin. He has less wit than these horses."

"But the children would not realize that, so you cannot fault them for believing that Michael could drive the carriage."

He stopped and faced her. "Why are you defending them when they could have killed themselves?"

"I am not defending them."

"Then what do you call it?"

Sophia took a deep breath, then said, "I don't know. I simply am trying to get you to understand the truth behind a poor decision."

"I understand it, but how will they learn to make good decisions if they are not taught?"

"Children listen better when you treat them as children and not as miniature adults. Or worse as soldiers you are commanding!"

"Is that so?"

"Yes. Give them a chance to explain rather than jumping to conclusions. Then they will listen to your guidance instead of rebelling against it."

His shoulders dropped slightly, and the tension in his face eased. "It is worth a try. Heaven knows, nothing else seems to be working with Gemma."

Sorrow ached within her heart for this proud man

who had succeeded in remaining alive during the war, but had failed with his daughter.

"Get to know them better," she urged. "The day should be pleasant tomorrow. You can go to the village and let them explore the streets and the shops." Knowing she was being bold, she put her hand on his arm.

He looked at it, then met her gaze again. "Will you come with us?"

"They need to learn more about you, not me."

"But *I* need to learn more about you."

Her breath caught over her rapidly beating heart as he slid his hand over hers on his sleeve. With him standing so near, she recalled his comment about sharing a hymnal with a woman close to his own height. He had not been derisive. Instead he had been admiring, and his compliment had eased, ever so slightly, the memory of the taunts she had endured in London.

"Say you will come with us," he said. "I am not too proud to know that if I am ever to win over Gemma, I will need your help." A smile touched his lips. "A good military officer knows how to make the best use of his resources, and I am beginning to see that you are my best chance to convince my daughter I am not the ogre she seems to think I am. Say you will help me."

She could not conceive of any answer she could give him other than yes, so she did.

Charles lifted his children out of the carriage as Herriott assisted Sophia on the other side. It was as it should be, but Charles wished that he could be the one handing her out so her eyes would sparkle directly into his in the moment before she stepped to the ground. When Gemma and Michael ran to her, he followed at a more sedate pace.

The wind whipped between the narrow stone houses clumped at the very edge of the cliff. It tried to steal Sophia's bonnet and twisted her gown around her. And it stole the sound of her laugh as she bent to say something to the children. Their answering giggles reached his ears as the fickle gusts died for a moment.

As he approached, she was saying to his friends, "You will understand why we have to leave the carriage here once you step around these houses. The street is steep and winding, and it is difficult for horses both going up and down."

She put her hand on the arm her cousin offered, but her eyes scanned the area along the top of the cliff. When they settled on him, she smiled and motioned for him to join them.

His stomach lurched as the warmth in her scintillating eyes almost staggered him. If he had any sense, he would jump in the carriage and speed away. He must not let her think that he was looking for a mother for his children, though he could not envision anyone else who would be as loving and patient with them as she was.

But Lydia had appeared that way with children, too… at first.

Charles tightened his fists until his nails cut into his palms. The memory of Lydia was not going to ruin another day. She had looked forward to putting him out of her life, so it was stupid that she kept invading his.

Setting a smile firmly in place, he strode over to where the others waited. He was surprised when Bradby clapped him on the back; then he saw understanding in his friend's eyes. Charles wondered how many ways he had betrayed his attraction for Sophia. If Herriott had noted it, he showed no sign. For that, Charles was grateful.

"You were not exaggerating the difficulty a carriage would have here," Charles said as they stepped around the cottages at the top of the cliff.

The curving street dropped sharply toward the sea, but that did not slow villagers who went up and down on their errands with an ease that suggested they walked on a level surface. Cottages on either side pressed close to each other as if to keep from tumbling into the sea. A few narrow alleys were visible. Overhead, gulls screeched in their circular flight that took them far out over the water.

"Quite to the contrary, Miss Meriweather," Bradby said, "you may have been understating how steep the village streets are." He chuckled. "I daresay a wise man would admire the view from here."

"Is that so?" Sophia took her hand off Herriott's arm and held out her hands to the children. The three started down the hill.

Charles's friends exchanged an uneasy glance.

"Shall we allow ourselves to be outdone by a woman and children?" asked Bradby. "Think what that would do to our reputations."

"Nothing could tarnish yours further." Herriott ducked as Bradby pretended to swing a fist at him.

"They will be at the bottom before you begin," Charles said.

Herriott gave an emoted wince, then laughed.

Motioning for the others to follow, Charles descended the precipitous street in Sophia's wake. He was glad to discover that, though it dropped quickly, the street eased into a more gradual slope than it appeared from the top. The houses edging the street added to the illusion of a sheer drop. The front steps concealed how the foundations had been built at an angle so the buildings were perpendicular to the sea and yet firmly anchored.

He left his friends behind as they descended with more caution. He heard Sophia and the children before he caught sight of them. As he came around the edge of a cottage that stuck out into the street, he saw Michael pointing at a window that displayed a bright red-and-yellow kite for sale next to the rows of fruit and vegetables.

"What is it?" Michael asked.

"A kite," Sophia answered.

"What does it do?"

"You fly it."

"Like a bird?"

Sophia smiled at Charles as he drew even with them, then turned to his son. "A kite floats on the wind," she said.

"When a string is tied to it," Charles added, "you can run along the beach and the kite will follow high in the sky."

Michael whirled to look up at him. "Can we buy it?"

"We can make our own," Sophia said. "Then we can take it flying, as long as your father agrees."

"It sounds like a wonderful plan."

Michael jumped up and down in his excitement, and Gemma began chattering about what color she wanted her kite to be as she led her brother down the hill.

"We had best keep up with them," Sophia said. "If they get out of our sight, they probably will end up helping the fishermen unload their boats and gut their fish."

Charles laughed, a real laugh, not one of the polite ones that had become his habit. "Michael might. However, I doubt Gemma would want to be around such a smelly mess." He offered his arm, and she placed her fingers on his coat sleeve.

He would gladly have stood there close to her until he had memorized every aspect of her lovely face that was partly shadowed by the rim of her straw bonnet. The pink flowers sewn to the decorative ribbon matched the enticing shade on her cheeks. That color deepened when she realized he was admiring her, and she quickly lowered her eyes. She might have lifted her hand away, but he put his gloved one over hers. Her lips parted with that soundless offer for him to sample them.

When a man hurried up the street, Charles had to step back to allow the man to pass. He drew Sophia's hand into his arm again. "Allow me to assist you down the hill."

"Will you wish me to do the same for you on the way back up?" she asked lightly.

The children skipped ahead of them, slowing only when she urged them to look into a nearby shop's window.

"Do you think I will need towing up the hill?" Charles bit back his amazement at how readily the children heeded her. They resisted every request he made to them, even reasonable ones.

"That is yet to be seen. The streets of Sanctuary Bay have tested stamina since they were built."

"Which I assume was the builders' intent, if your father was correct about angry ships' captains chasing after pirates who had stolen their cargoes."

"Pirates?" asked Bradby from behind them. "Do not worry, Miss Meriweather. We will protect you." He turned to Herriott and said, "You go first."

"So I can be cannon fodder for pirates?" Herriott retorted.

"You are the smallest target of the three of us," Charles said.

"All the more reason for John-a-Nokes to go first. He will deflect the ball with his boasting." He winked at Bradby and walked around him to lead the way.

Sophia listened to the friends tease each other. For a moment she had a glimpse of what they must have been like before the war. Charming and witty and carefree and as eager for adventure as Michael.

She smiled while she bid a good morning to the baker's wife and looked around the small village. The three men needed a place to escape their memories of the war. Maybe Sanctuary Bay could be that haven for them.

A door opened on one of the cottages. Cousin Edmund backpedaled to avoid it. Vera Fenwick rushed down the steps as he wobbled and quickly grasped the iron ring on the side of the building to keep from skidding on the stones.

"Oh, Lord Meriweather, forgive me," Vera said, straightening her bonnet over her dark curls. "I was not watching where I was going."

Once steady on his feet, Edmund apologized to the vicar's sister. "I should have been keeping a closer eye on where I was bound rather than enjoying the view."

"We have become accustomed to it." Vera's smile lit her round face.

"So you forget what effect it has on outsiders?" he asked.

Vera's smile tightened. Cousin Edmund's question was innocent, but some in the village would not consider it so.

"As Lord Meriweather, you are already a part of Sanctuary Bay," Vera quickly replied. Her voice was not overly loud, but would reach nearby ears. "What do you think of the village, my lord?"

When Cousin Edmund began to chatter with her friend, Sophia listened in astonishment. How did Vera accomplish the task that seemed impossible for Sophia—keeping Edmund talking so that silence did not smother every conversation?

"See the sea," Michael said, tugging on her hand.

Excusing herself while Vera spoke with Cousin Edmund and Mr. Bradby, she took the two children's hands and warned them to watch where they stepped. The street was only wide enough for the three of them, so Charles walked ahead of them.

He stopped by a large wooden drum beside an open door. Overhead a sign was painted with a replica of the bright red drum and the words The Drummer's Gift.

"That drum was used if a press-gang showed up in the village." Sophia chuckled as Gemma and Michael tapped the top. "The women beat it to warn the men to hide. No man has been impressed in Sanctuary Bay since Trafalgar, though several volunteered."

"Where did they get such a fancy drum? It does not look English."

"My grandfather supposedly found it back on his travels. It could be from Africa or the East. When the need arose, it was given to the villagers for their use instead of gathering dust in Meriweather Hall."

"A brilliant solution."

They reached the bottom of the hill where stones had been sunk into the sand to give the fishermen a place to clean their catch and repair their boats and nets. The flat-bottomed boats with their high bows waited on the beach because the tide had pulled the water far away from the shore.

She led the children across a trickle of water that ran down the stones. She pointed out the fishing boats that were called cobles.

"Like the stones?" asked Gemma. "Why would you name a boat after something that would sink?"

"The stones are spelled with two *b*'s, the boats with one." She laughed at the children's bafflement. "I don't know why they are called cobles, but they are built to handle the rough seas here."

"Can we ride in one?" asked Michael.

"Not now, but I'm sure no one will mind if you stand in one." Telling them to take off their shoes and stockings, she bent to help Michael.

"Where does this water come from?" Lord Northbridge asked.

"Years ago, a beck—"

"A what?"

"A beck is what we call a stream here in North Yorkshire. The beck flowed down the hill close to the village. It was channeled through a tunnel to let more houses be built above it. Now the beck emerges out of that gap in the stones at the base of the street." She pointed at the spot where water bubbled out.

"A tunnel?" His eyes narrowed. "A handy tool for smugglers. Do you know where its entrance is?"

She jumped to her feet and grasped his arm as he reached to sweep aside some of the fishing nets that had been hung to dry against a wall of the lowest house. "Don't be foolish, my lord!" She kept her voice low. "Searching for it could be dangerous."

His eyes narrowed. "The smugglers are your own neighbors, but you fear them?"

"Not for myself, but you and your children are out-

siders." She clamped her lips closed. Cousin Edmund
had an excuse for using that word. She did not.

"I thought you said the people here were friendly."

"They are." She held up her hands as if she could
gather his growing vexation and contain it. "But you,
my lord, have served the king. That makes you suspect
in some eyes because they cannot be sure your only reason for coming here is helping your friend get settled."

"If you think we should huddle in fear in Meriweather Hall, then you are mistaken!" His voice rose
on each word.

"My lord, please. Not so loud." She glanced up the
street to see the others coming toward them. Why
couldn't he see that she was trying to protect him and
the children? "If you are seen as a threat…"

"I *am* a threat to anyone who imperils my children."
He did not lower his voice, and his friends were not the
only ones to halt on the street to stare. "Everyone would
be wise to remember that."

She groped for something to say, but no words came
as he went to the startled children. He scooped up his
son and grasped Gemma by the hand. Ignoring their
protests, he pushed past his friends and strode up the
hill.

His friends hurried to her, asking what had happened. She shrugged as she went to gather up the children's shoes and stockings. Holding them close to her
chest, she watched Lord Northbridge and the children
disappear up the curving street.

Would he go to Meriweather Hall, or would he return
to his own estate? Sadness swept over her at the thought
of never seeing him or the children again.

Chapter Eight

Boots came toward the book-room. Sophia looked up from the estate's account books when the sound ceased right outside the door moments before a knock was set on it. She rose, then winced when a knot in her lower back reminded her how many hours she had sat at the desk. When Cousin Edmund told her that he could not take tea with her that afternoon, she took advantage of the time to go through the accounts that had been ignored since his arrival last week.

"You may come in," she said when the knock came a second time, almost drowned out by the wind-splattered rain against the window.

"Maybe you should ask who stands on the other side of the door first."

At Lord Northbridge's answer, her heart did somersaults. She had spent many sleepless hours last night praying that she would find a good excuse not to be in the earl's company any more than absolutely necessary during the remainder of his visit to Meriweather Hall. She would be wise to remember how his quick temper flared at the least provocation. On the other hand he was a loyal friend to his tie-mates, and he longed to be a good father to his children.

"Come in, my lord," Sophia called when she realized she could leave him loitering in the corridor no longer.

She tried not to stare when the earl did as she bade. As always he was fashionably and well dressed. Buckskin breeches were the perfect complement for his navy coat and rust-colored waistcoat. She noticed that in the brief moment before her gaze was caught and held by his compelling, dark eyes. Every inch of her pleaded for her to close the distance between them until she was within his arms again.

He seemed as frozen as she was. She was unsure how long they would have stood thus if maids' voices had not drifted into the room.

"I thought you had gone riding with my cousin," Sophia said into the silence as the maids' voices receded.

The earl left the door open as he walked toward the desk. "He wanted to go to the village to check on something that intrigued him. Not the smugglers, I assure you, because he heard your warning loud and clear, but he wished to go on his own."

"Alone? Why?"

"He did not say." He rubbed his fingers along his chin. "And that is odd, because Herriott is seldom circumspect."

"But he has changed." She did not make it a question as she sat in one of the overstuffed chairs.

His dark brows rose as he chose the one facing her. "How did you know?"

"I hear the stories you and the others tell, and you have mentioned that Cousin Edmund made quick and good decisions on the battlefield."

He stretched his arm along the chair. "And now he cannot make a single one."

"So the household staff has told me." She gestured toward the account books. "I do what I can, but there are certain matters that only the baron can answer."

"I shall speak with him, if you wish."

Sophia almost said yes, because that would allow her to avoid another uncomfortable conversation, if one could call long and awkward silences a conversation, with her cousin. With a faint smile, she said, "Thank you, but it is a duty I must perform."

"And you always do your duty."

"If I can."

"I see."

She did not, but the wisest course would be to hear what the earl had come to say and then excuse herself to continue her work. She was about to say that, then realized that she might be able to solve two problems at once if Lord Northbridge spent more time with her cousin and she spent less with both men.

"On second thought," she said, "I could use your help with my cousin's adjustment to his life here. Will you do me a favor?"

"If I can."

"Cousin Edmund must have many questions, but he hesitates to ask me. I am sure he will be more willing to take advice from a friend than from…" Her smile vanished as she swallowed so roughly she feared he could hear her gulp. She gamely went on, "From a woman he scarcely knows."

"It is the very least I can do to repay you for helping with my children."

"I was not looking to even the scales. Spending time with you and the children is my pleasure."

"Mine, as well."

Sophia stiffened to keep herself from softening at his compliment. His smile dared her to believe his simple words intended to mean far more.

Hastily she stood, forcing him to, as well. In her most matter-of-fact tone, she asked, "How may I help you today, my lord?"

"You might consider granting me two requests."

"If I can," she answered as he had.

"First, will you call me Charles? The children address you, in spite of efforts to remind them of their manners, as Sophia, and I must own that I think of you frequently that way. Spare me the embarrassment of being informal when you continue to address me formally."

She was flustered anew. Not by his request, but that he admitted to thinking of her often. *Don't be mawkish,* she warned herself. Why wouldn't he think of her often? The children talked about her constantly, or so Alice had told her when Sophia visited the nursery. *But what if you remain in his thoughts for another reason?* She ignored that small voice from deep in her heart.

"I would be honored to address you as Charles," she said, relieved when her voice sounded unruffled. "What is the second matter?"

"I was hoping you might accept my apology." He folded his arms on the chair. His pose looked nonchalant, but the strong set of his jaw said otherwise. "I came to apologize. I was wrong to be upset with you when your words were aimed at the children's welfare."

"Tales of smugglers sound romantic and dashing, but the truth is that the smugglers tenaciously guard what they believe are their rights. About thirty years ago, a ship of smugglers rammed an excise cutter and sent it scurrying up the coast."

"They are bold."

"Yes." She gazed out at the sea that was the same gray as the sky. "As the village is not part of this estate, the baron has no jurisdiction over its activities. Mr. Fenwick, like his predecessors, has tried to persuade them to deal with legal cargoes, but his efforts have been to no avail. Others who have tried to halt them have learned that the smugglers will threaten their homes and families."

He took a deep breath and let it sift out between his clenched teeth. "It was chuckleheaded of me to believe that winning one war would mean that others were over."

"But *this* is not your war."

"It is if it imperils my children."

Sophia gazed at him, enthralled by his fervor. She could see him on the battlefield, leading the charge against the French. Being labeled a hero was not a cloak he wore easily, but it was one he could not throw off, because it was a part of him.

"Do not become involved in it. Promise me that," she said.

"I cannot promise that. As I said, if my children—"

"Your children will be safe." She flung out her hands. "Smugglers do not come here as long as the lord of Meriweather Hall does not try to stop them along the shore."

"I am not the lord of Meriweather Hall."

"No, but your friend is."

He stared her for another long moment before saying, "The status quo is vital. Is that what you mean?"

"Yes, especially when my cousin has trouble making

the simplest decision about the estate. Any hesitation on his part if he comes face-to-face with the smugglers' leader could be disastrous."

"Do you know who leads them?"

"No." Her frustration focused on that single word. "I thought I might be on the path to the answer before Papa insisted on me going to London. By the time I returned, the clue I had been following led nowhere."

"The smugglers used the time while you were gone wisely."

"More wisely than I spent my time in London." Sophia wanted to pull the words back into her mouth, but it was too late.

Charles's stance grew less tense as a smile eased across his lips. "I doubt you have ever done anything truly foolish."

"In that, you are mistaken." She looked back out at the sea so she did not have to look at him as she owned to her greatest shame. "I dared to believe that the gentleman calling on me was sincere in his attentions."

"And he wasn't?" The gentleness in his voice threatened to undo her completely.

"Maybe at the beginning, but then he chose to listen to his friends' comments about my height in comparison with his and sought the company of another woman."

Perhaps the stories of her humiliation had faded in the *ton's* minds, but it never had in her own. *Duchess of limbs*, *herring-gutted, long shanks, gawkey* and *beanpole* were only some of the words she had heard. She had swallowed her hurt because she had believed one man outside her family had not cared that she was taller than most of the others in a room. Then Lord Owensly had told her that he could not escort her to Almack's as planned because, he said stumbling over his words, he could abide the teasing of his friends no longer.

Sophia forced her clenched hands to open. She wished she knew how to make that hurt go away. Losing herself in work always helped. She hoped it would now.

"I am sorry," Charles said, "that you were betrayed, too, by what your heart believed to be true."

"Too?" She faced him, astonished he would speak of something so personal. "Who betrayed you, Charles?"

"Does it matter?"

Yes, she wanted to shout, but she waited for him to continue.

"It's in the past," he said when she remained silent, "and I do not intend to let my past taint my future with my children. We all make mistakes, Sophia, but if we learn not to be so foolish again, then the cost of the lesson may not seem as high."

"Then learn to heed what I tell you about the smugglers."

"I will try."

"Thank you, my lord, for understanding," she said. "Your apology is accepted, of course."

"Of course." He made those two words sound silly. "Is that all there is to it? I apologize, and you accept?"

She stared at him, puzzled. "What else would you have me do?"

"Be annoyed with me. Fly up to the boughs and scold me for speaking sharply to you time after time. You are too forgiving."

Tilting her head, she regarded him coolly. "I have been taught that our Lord says when one is asked for forgiveness, one should offer it. Especially when the transgression is by a guest in one's home."

He grimaced, then pushed away from the chair. It

rocked, and she put out a hand to steady it. He did the same. She jerked her fingers back before they could brush his. His lips tightened at what he must see as an affront.

But, when he spoke, she realized she had read his reaction incorrectly.

"We are too much the same," he said in barely more than a whisper. He cupped her chin and tilted her face toward his. "Hurt too deeply to see anything but potential pain in every word and action, Sophia."

When he spoke her name with such warmth, her knees threatened to melt beneath her. Her fingers settled on his sleeve. The thick wool could not conceal the firm muscle beneath it. What would he do if she slid her hand up his arm and draped it over his shoulder? Or if she traced his scar? Would his breath become uneven?

"I am sorry you have been hurt," he murmured.

"You are kind to say that." *More than kind,* that voice added from her heart.

"I hope you can find a way to get past that pain so you no longer are frightened of whatever scares you."

You scare me. You and the way I feel when you are near. Oh, how she longed to say those words.

When he picked her hand off his sleeve, he raised it to his lips for the chastest salute. His gaze held hers over the top of her hand, and she saw the longing that resonated through her as if she were a tuning fork set atremble by his touch.

"Who hurt you, Charles?" she asked.

Pain flickered across his face before he gently released her hand. "Thank you for accepting my apology...again." He turned on his heel and walked out, leaving her more confused and curious than ever.

* * *

The great house seemed too small after Charles left Sophia to stare after him in the book-room. He had wandered through Meriweather Hall for the past two hours in an effort to avoid everyone. How had he allowed their conversation to take such a turn? He had more than allowed it. He had instigated the topic of the pain they both tried to hide with less and less success.

He should have ignored her sorrow. That was impossible, because he did not want to see her unhappy. But he could have spoken of *her* pain without acknowledging his own.

In the past week, he had learned that Sophia Meriweather refused to let any puzzle go unsolved. Now he had given her another. He did not want her to discover that his wife had never loved him. To learn that Lydia had married him solely to obtain his title and its prestige…that she intended to leave him as soon as she gave him an heir.

What a laughingstock he would be! The great war hero who was abandoned by his wife. Other men lived separately from their wives, but none of them had boasted about how much his wife adored him. Nor had any of them spoken often of how much he loved his wife and how their marriage was perfect. Nobody must learn the truth. He had lost much, and he would not have his children hurt by his own blindness where Lydia had been concerned.

He continued to prowl through the house, turning down one corridor when he heard someone in another. He paused when he passed a French window at the rear of the manor. Herriott was pacing on a stone terrace, looking like a captive tiger trying to escape its cage.

Charles walked outside, and Herriott glanced over

his shoulder. The man's face was as strained as the moment before the call to battle was sounded. By all that's blue, he did not want to think of *that*. Not after the near debacle with Sophia.

"Ah, Northbridge!" his friend called, motioning to him. "I trust *you* are having a pleasant afternoon."

"Your comment suggests you are not," Charles said to evade speaking the truth.

"It was not unpleasant." He rubbed his hands together as if trying to work feeling into them. "Lady Meriweather asked me to have tea with her this afternoon."

Charles raised his brows, but said nothing.

"Dash it, Northbridge! Do you think the baroness expected me to state my intentions toward her daughter right then and there?"

"Hold hard! Take a breath." Charles swallowed his laugh.

Poor Herriott was more out of countenance than ever. His friend had overreacted to everything and everyone since word had arrived that he now was Lord Meriweather.

"What do *you* think?" Herriott asked.

"About what?"

"The timing of when I must ask for Sophia's hand."

Charles tried to ignore the pinch in his gut. It felt far too much like envy, a feeling he had endured too often of late, but why should he be jealous of his friend's situation? He had made a muddle of his own marriage, letting himself be betrayed by an illusion he'd wanted desperately to believe was real.

"The only answer I can give is that you will know when the time is right." Another answer that avoided honesty.

"When I know it is the right time?" Herriott kept rubbing his palms together. "I have never considered allowing myself to be leg-shackled to a woman simply as a duty. That has been one of the few luxuries allowed the merchant class that is denied the peerage."

"But now you are a peer with an estate that needs an heir. If you have no intentions of marrying Miss Meriweather, the sooner you let her and her family know that, the better it will be."

"I have never shirked from doing my duty."

Charles nodded. Sophia was equally determined to do her duty to her family, even if she were unhappy for the rest of her life. But would Herriott make her unhappy? Could it be that Charles hoped so because he wanted her himself? He must be touched in the head.

"Then I see no problem." He hoped that was not a lie. When his friend remained silent, he added, "If you want my advice—"

"I do!" Color rose up Herriott's face when he realized what he had shouted.

"Then I say we should get away from here for the rest of the afternoon and allow you some perspective. What say you? Shall we find Bradby and ride neck-or-nothing along the shore?"

"An excellent idea!"

Charles went to change into riding clothes and greatcoat while Herriott arranged for horses and sent a message to Bradby to join them.

Horses were waiting by the time Charles reached the stable. Bradby and Herriott appeared moments later. As soon as they were in the saddle, Charles led the way north along the shore road. It was how they had ridden on the Continent, so they fell into that pattern, even though Herriott should have been in front on his estate.

Overhead, gulls rode the sea winds, shrieking at anything that moved. The sea crashed on the cliffs and sent up a fresh scent that overpowered the odors of rot where leaves had fallen off the trees.

The sense of freedom was heady as they rode past the village at a safe pace. Shouts came from the bottom of the cliff as the cobles were readied to be launched into the tide.

Once beyond the village, Charles sent his horse to a rapid pace along the shore road. He did not look out at the sea, not wanting to discover if the small boats were heading out to gather fish or to smuggle tea and brandy. He wanted to put every worry behind him as the wind blew the horse's mane into his face while he leaned low in the saddle.

Too soon, he drew in with regret. The ride had been invigorating, but he would not ruin his horse when it was impossible to flee the thoughts that plagued him. He realized how far he had outdistanced his friends when he had to wait almost a minute for the other riders to reach where he kept the horse to a sedate walk through the shadows of the trees lining the road.

They rode in companionable silence, but Charles saw his friends reach for their weapons when a rabbit burst out of a hedgerow. He had fought not to do the same. Bradby and Herriott both looked chagrined at the instinctive motion, and he sighed. How long would memories of the war and the training that had kept them alive remain with them?

When Herriott motioned toward a copse, Charles turned his horse in that direction. He had seen the flasks on Herriott's saddle, and he hoped his friend had brought enough to quench their thirst.

Charles dismounted and led his horse into the shade

where Herriott continued their conversation as if there had been no break.

"I truly could use your advice, Northbridge," his friend said.

"Not mine?" asked Bradby as he swung down from his horse.

"*You* have not wooed and won," Herriott replied. "Northbridge is the only one among us who has run the whole race and triumphed with the prize of a woman's heart."

Bradby's nose wrinkled. "Must you turn poet when you think about courting? Save your pretty words for your lady fair."

Charles tied his horse's reins to a nearby bush and let his friends enjoy their squabble. When they first had begun to serve together, he had participated in their battles of words, always eager to be declared the champion. That was before he had discovered that too many victories would soon be proved hollow.

"What say you, Northbridge?"

He faced his friends, hoping his expression revealed nothing of the pain that rode him like a hag upon a nightmare. "I have to say that I stopped listening to your bibble-babble."

His friends laughed, and Charles relaxed. The dangerous moment—the one when he might be forced to own that his marriage was not what he had once boasted it was—had passed.

Bradby winked. "Herriott was lamenting his misfortune in failing to win the heart of lovely Lady Eloisa."

"Eloisa? Lady Eloisa Parkington?" asked Charles.

Herriott's color deepened, and Bradby nodded.

Charles shook his head. "Why would you be muttonheaded enough to be sweet on Lady Eloisa? She made it clear from her coming-out that she would settle for no less than a duke with an annual income higher than the three of ours combined."

"I was foolish to think a childhood friendship could grow into more." Herriott slapped the rock he leaned against. "That is ancient history, part of another life." He stared out at the sea. "The life we had before…" He did not continue.

There was no need. Charles wondered if Bradby heard Herriott's unspoken words in his own mind, as Charles did. *Before we went to war.* Their lives had been altered so much by what they had experienced that what had happened before their first battle seemed to belong to someone else's life.

"Before you gave up hope of a dukedom?" asked Bradby with a guffaw.

Charles ignored his friend's unceasing jokes. When they had been riding north, he had been able to get away from Bradby's jests by joining the children in the carriage. He should have given that some thought before suggesting they ride this afternoon, but he had not guessed when he did that Herriott would ask Bradby to join them. With a start he realized how he had been avoiding Bradby's company more with each passing day. That made no sense, because he had once considered Bradby one of his most boon companions. They had discussed politics, the law and books, and he had admired Bradby for his brilliance.

No longer.

Now Bradby seemed to aspire to the title of court jester instead of returning to his work as a solicitor. Charles could not recall the last time his friend had engaged him in a vehement discussion on some obscure aspect of the law.

Charles touched his cheek. He had thought he was the only one who carried scars of those atrocious battles. Now he was no longer sure.

Herriott opened a flask and handed it to Charles, then reached for another.

"You always think ahead, Herriott," he said.

"I wish I had considered the idea of bringing along sandwiches or even some cakes." Herriott opened another flask. "I should have asked Mrs. Porter, but I know better than to bother a cook in the midst of preparing the evening meal. I poured some lemonade in the flask and got out of her way."

Charles tipped it back to drink and grimaced at the sour lemonade. "Cakes would make this even more grotesque in flavor. Next time taste it before you leave the kitchen and add some sugar if necessary."

"He was too busy," Bradby said as he took the flask, "sweetening up fair Sophia to worry about anything else."

Beside him, Herriott stiffened. "That is not funny," his friend growled before walking away.

"Why did you say something like that?" Charles asked. "Can't you see that Herriott is in no mood for jests?"

Bradby lowered the flask, sudden dismay in his eyes, as if he could not believe that he had spoken so. "I did not mean to jest."

"Think before you blurt out something next time, will you?" Charles capped his flask and shoved it into the pocket of his greatcoat. "Herriott is on edge with the abrupt changes his life has taken. A year ago, he was in trade. Now he has a title, an estate, and the assumption he will marry one of his predecessor's daughters to keep the bloodline unbroken. Have some sympathy for the man!"

"I do."

"Then show it instead of turning everything into some larking comment aimed at making us laugh on cue like a group of traveling players."

"At least I try to help!"

Charles's hands fisted at his sides. "Do you truly consider having us braying like a herd of witless donkeys to be helpful?"

"I am no longer under your command, so I do not have to listen to your bellowing." Bradby spun on his heel and walked in the opposite direction from Herriott's.

Bellowing?

Had he been bellowing?

When he saw Herriott looking at him with uncertainty and disheartenment, Charles knew that he had raised his voice without realizing it. How much of what he had said had reached Herriott's ears? He had his answer when Herriott looked away, fury tightening his jaw.

Thunder! Now he had angered both of his friends. To own the truth, the only friends who put up with his temper…until today.

He turned his back on the sea and the land beyond it. *God, help me control my temper before I drive away even those who understand.*

Chapter Nine

The wood was tangled with vines that had grown thick through the summer. Sunlight filtered through the leaves in shades of gold and orange and red. Birds rose, crying raucous warnings.

Sophia watched a magpie's flight before it was lost amidst the trees. She stood still and took in the beauty of the wood. When had she last come out here to admire God's creation? Sadly she could not answer that. It had been too long.

The past eleven days had been wearying. Her efforts to urge Cousin Edmund to take over more responsibility for the estate had come to naught. Earlier in the week, he and his friends had ridden south to Scarborough, and they had not returned. She had expected the house to feel as it had before their arrival, but the changes had lingered.

Perhaps it was because Gemma and Michael remained at the house. Other than a single question from Michael about where the men had gone, neither child seemed to miss Charles. Sophia spent time with them each day, teaching them games she had assumed every child knew.

But she had come into the wood alone. She did not want one of the children to mention that she had gone to check on the condition of the dower cottage. Having Cousin Edmund take insult at her interest in repairing it might be disastrous.

Ten or more years ago, Papa had talked about using it for married servants, but it was too far from the house when icy winds blew off the sea. So it had sat, waiting for the time when someone would need it.

Now they did. But how could she move from Meriweather Hall? More than a half-dozen servants, including the butler, Ogden, and the housekeeper, Mrs. Williams, had expressed unhappiness about Cousin Edmund's indecisiveness. She had urged them to give him time to adjust to the abrupt changes in his life. They had agreed, though they made it clear they expected him to adapt quickly. For now, they depended on her to help her cousin until he was ready to oversee the estate on his own. She had no idea how long that might be, and she wanted to move out before he came up with the obvious solution that his wife could supervise the staff while he went up to London for his parliamentary obligations.

Trudging on through the thick underbrush, which caught at her boots and her bonnet, Sophia was astonished when she reached what was clearly a path. It was as wide as two men walking abreast, and the dirt underfoot was well trod. Who had come this way often enough that the tangle of vines had been forced back?

Hope rose through her, and she hurried along the path. Maybe someone had checked the dower cottage frequently. Maybe it was in better condition than she guessed.

The trees thinned, and she stepped into a clearing that had a view of the sea. The wood concealed both Meriweather Hall and the village, so it seemed as if the stone cottage were the only building along a deserted shore.

She stared at the dower cottage, elated that it had not fallen into ruins. It was a small building, no more than three rooms down and another two upstairs. The cottage's windows were intact, and the door remained straight. On the roof, the thatch had thinned. Vines had climbed up the stone facade to entwine in the straw, but if those were the only problems, the roof could be easily repaired.

Eager to see inside, Sophia opened the door. She ignored how the hinges creaked. Fish oil would banish that sound.

It took a moment for her eyes to adjust to the dim interior. Looking through the windows, several that were cracked, she was amazed any light got through the dirt caked on the panes. She took a single step, and something crunched beneath her feet. She jumped and stared at dried pods. Mice must have dragged them in. Pawprints of various sizes covered the floor in front of the hearth and led into the open cupboards on the wall to the left. The doors hung at a precarious angle and were gnawed along the edges.

Piles of wood marked where furniture had fallen apart. A table leaned against a wall because one of its legs was missing. The chairs beside it had been upended. Water pooled in low spots on the stone floor by two doors that led to bedchambers on either side of the fireplace. A third door was ajar and revealed steep stairs to the upper floor.

Sophia gasped. Some prints in the ashes did not belong to rodents. They had been made by boots. As she edged closer to the hearth, she saw the prints led to the door on the left.

Going in the bedroom, she opened the shutters over the window. The panes were broken and the floor littered with glass. Otherwise, the room was empty. Not even a bedstead or a pallet. Something had left deep scratches in the floor, and she shuddered. What sort of beast had claws sharp enough to gouge the stones? She squatted to examine them more closely.

"Sophia!"

She whirled at the sound of her name. The motion sent her footing out from beneath her, and she sat heavily on the floor.

"Ouch!" she cried.

A silhouette darkened the doorway, and she looked up to see Charles trying not to smile. His greatcoat was filthy from his travels.

"What are you doing here?" she asked.

He gave in to the grin and held out his hand. "We just returned, and, when you were not there to greet us, I asked a few questions. A footman saw you walking in this direction, so I tracked you here."

"Another skill you learned during the war?" she asked, then wished she had not when his smile disappeared.

"One of the few that still has some use." He grasped her hand and tugged. Once she stood, he released her fingers as if he found the very touch not to his taste.

Sophia blinked back abrupt tears. "I am sorry if my question bothers you."

"I prefer not to speak of the past. It is over and done with." He walked past her and into the main room.

Those tears bubbled out of her eyes. Charles was

fooling himself. The war was not over for him or for Cousin Edmund or Mr. Bradby. They carried it with them every day, a great load of regrets and memories and grief. Even coming to Sanctuary Bay, far from the battlefield, had not let them put down that burden.

Running the toe of her boot across the deepest gouge, she sneezed when dust and the scent of salt rose from it. Winds off the sea must have deposited sea water on the floor. More would come in if she left the shutters open.

Sophia closed them, hooked them into place and then went into the main room where Charles waited beneath a hole in the roof. Sunlight washed down over him, highlighting the strain around his mouth and the gray shadows beneath his eyes.

"You look exhausted," she said.

"We rode straight through the night." He jammed his hands into his pockets. "Your cousin could not make up his mind whether to leave York or wait another day, so, by the time Bradby and I decided, it was late."

"York? I thought you were going to Scarborough."

He gave a mirthless laugh. "We did, but we did not stay long."

"There are coaching inns along the way from York. One of them must have had rooms."

"If your cousin could have decided where to stop…"

Sophia chuckled at his dour tone, and his expression lightened.

"Was this some sort of byre or shepherd's hut?" Charles asked.

She shook her head as she bent to right one of the chairs. "It was built to be the estate's dower house, but it has been sadly abandoned. The sea winds and our cold winters and damp weather have not been forgiving." She looked up to stare at the largest hole in the roof. "I suspected it would be in bad shape, but I did not realize how bad."

Again weak tears burned behind her eyes, and she walked across the leaf-strewn floor to another window. As she opened the shutters, one side crashed to the floor. Fresh air rushed into the cottage, but it could not blow away the remnants of damp.

She dashed away her tears so Charles would not see them. Until she had seen the ruined cottage, she had had no idea how much she hoped there would be a solution other than her marrying her cousin.

Dear Lord, what am I to do now? You can see what lies before me. Help me choose the right path.

She shuddered when she realized that becoming Edmund's wife might be the path she was supposed to take.

Charles's hands curved along her shoulders, and she ached to lean back against his firm strength. Slowly he turned her until she faced him. The features she once had considered austere now urged her to let her fingertips explore every inch. She longed to discover if the whole of his face was as rough as the low nap of whiskers along his jaw. She pushed that stubborn lock of hair from his eyes. Its coarse silk created a wave of delight along her hand and directly into her heart.

"Anything is possible." His voice softened as his fingertips brushed lightly beneath her right eye and then her left. "Even Sophia Meriweather losing hope." He lowered his hand so she could see the damp dust on his fingers.

Heat coursed across her face. "I had no idea that I looked so ghastly." She realized abruptly how alone they were. Leaving straightaway would be the best decision.

He crooked a single finger and put it beneath her chin to tip it up, keeping her from stepping away. Her eyes were captured once again by his intense gaze as he said, "Do you think a bit of dust clinging to your face concerns me right now?"

"I don't know what concerns you right now, Charles," she replied.

"That was an honest answer. I shall be as forthright. What concerns me is you and your reaction to the state of this building." His voice dropped to almost a whisper, the sound like the memory of distant thunder. "*This* is what you believe is your only other choice if you do not marry Herriott, isn't it?"

She nodded, not trusting her voice.

"Do you think he will exile you and your mother and sister if you do not wed him?" The hint of a smile curved his lips.

Sophia pulled back as her eyes widened in shock. "Do you find this amusing?"

"To own the truth, I do." He caught her arm as she turned away. "Because you are worrying needlessly. Herriott is a man of honor. You must have seen that."

"I want to believe he is honorable."

"You can trust me on this, Sophia." His gaze edged along her face in a slow perusal that sent tingles along her skin from head to toe. It settled on her lips.

Did he want to kiss her? Did he want to kiss her as much as she longed for him to?

"He admires you greatly, but…" He raised his hands in a pose of surrender. "Asking you to marry or not asking you requires him to make a decision."

Sadness rushed through Sophia like a renewed freshet. She wished she had known her cousin before the war made him question everything he did.

"I never considered that," she said. "Please do not tell

my cousin that I thought for even a moment he would not do the right thing."

"I will say nothing to him of our conversation here." He swept the room with another glance. "However, he should be made aware of the state of this building. A strong storm might collapse it, and anyone inside could be killed."

"The chances of someone being here are small." She pointed to the footprints by the door. "These could have been made long ago. The ashes are compacted together by the rain that has come in through the chimney and the roof."

"But these aren't." He walked to the hearth. A frown slashed across his mouth. "Look there. These ashes are fluttering in the breeze from the window. Someone had a fire here since the last time it rained."

"It rained the night before last."

"That means someone other than us has been here since then. Someone who had a fire."

Sophia stared at the hearth. How had she failed to notice that? She should not have let her distress at the state of the cottage blind her to everything else.

As if she had asked her question aloud, Charles said, "Taking note of the smallest detail is another skill I cannot rid myself of." He hated every incident that brought the war into his life, and it seemed that any conversation in the past few days had been filled with war.

He had not guessed his journey with Herriott and Bradby would take them south to Scarborough and Bridlington and then west to York. He would have declined the invitation. They spent no more than a few hours in the two seacoast towns before turning inland. In York they had lingered, but nothing they saw or did chased away the memories that haunted them. Charles could have told Herriott before they set off that their quest for forgetfulness was futile.

He ground a cold ember under his boot. During their time away from Sanctuary Bay, he had encountered others who struggled to put the war behind them. Some of them had returned to loving families. Others wandered as he and his friends seemed doomed to do.

Without looking at Sophia, he said, "Many men have returned from the war, and there are not enough jobs. Some have taken to the road to look for work or to find food and shelter. At least one of them may have discovered this cottage. A fire on the hearth would make it warm and allow him to cook any game he poached."

"But why not come to the Hall and ask for food and a place to stay?" she asked. "We have never turned away anyone who needs shelter."

He shrugged, still forcing his eyes away from her. When he had followed her here, he had not guessed she would be alone. He should have returned to Meriweather Hall posthaste. Instead he had joined her in the cottage, longing to ease her distress. Or so he had thought until he touched her. Once he let his hands caress her shoulders, his thoughts had been consumed with the need to kiss her.

"I am sure," he replied, "that there are as many reasons as there are wanderers. Some men are too proud to ask a favor from anyone. Or they may be hoping not to attract any attention." His hands tightened at his sides. Why had he failed to see the obvious? "Or maybe it is not a former soldier. Maybe the local smugglers are using the cottage to stash their booty."

"Don't even suggest that in jest." Color fled from her face.

"I am not Bradby. I don't turn every conversation into a joke."

"But if the smugglers have been using this cottage, that means they are running tame through Meriweather Hall lands." She glanced at the left bedroom. "There are marks on the floor in there. Gouges like something heavy was pushed across it."

"Show me." He went in without waiting to see if she would follow.

She did, easing past him to open the shutters again. The light surrounded her like an aura, setting her hair afire like pure gold. He had to use every ounce of his willpower to look away from that beguiling sight.

He examined the scratches on the floor. They were spaced far enough apart to be made by a crate of smuggled goods. He knelt and ran his finger along one of the deepest depressions. Holding his finger up to his nose, he sniffed.

"Salt," he said.

"I thought it might have been blown here by a storm wind."

Charles stood and wiped his finger on his travel-stained breeches. "That is possible, but it is also possible it fell off smuggled goods."

"I hope you are wrong."

"As I do, but the facts are clear." He leaned one hand on the door molding. "Did you really think that once your father died the thieves would honor any agreement they made with him to stay off these lands?" He waved his other hand toward the sea. "Why would they not make use of a place that is both convenient and easy to guard?"

Her face again became as gray as the ashes on the hearth. "They must be stopped."

"By whom? Are your constable or justice of the peace brave enough to face down the smugglers?"

"If I uncover the identity of the leader—"

"Sophia, you must let Herriott handle this."

"How? He cannot decide whether he wishes fowl or beef for dinner. How will he devise a plan to keep the smugglers off our land?"

Hearing her frustration, he could not offer her some trite words of comfort. "Let me talk to him about this. If you do, he might overreact in his determination to protect you and your mother and sister."

"Play the hero, you mean?"

He fought not to flinch as he nodded. "In so many words, yes. Promise me that you will say nothing to him."

"I promise if you speak to him about it immediately."

"That is a deal, and I will do what I can to help while I am here."

She could not disguise her flinch. "Are you leaving soon?"

"My own estate has been neglected too long. I had planned to be gone for no more than two fortnights. With the time needed to travel here and then south with the children, it has been nearly that long already. I am eager to return to my home. I have traveled too much in the past few years, and, once I am home, I intend to stay there for a long time."

"And never travel again?"

"If I never leave my estates again, I would be a happy man." He watched emotions flicker across her face: shock, sorrow, dismay.

"I see." She turned to latch the shutters again.

"You did not think I would be staying much longer, did you?" He waited until she looked over her shoulder at him. "But I promise you, Sophia, I will do everything I can to persuade your cousin not to continue disregarding his obligations as lord of Meriweather Hall."

"All of them?"

He understood what she meant. Would he urge her cousin to ask her to marry? He almost demanded that she explain why she thought he wanted her to marry another when he dreamed night after night of holding her and kissing her. He halted the words he had no right to speak. He had made a jumble of one marriage by letting his heart mislead him. He would not do that again, not even with Sophia.

Hoping he was not breaking her heart as he was his, he said, "All of them."

Chapter Ten

He had not asked her to marry him.

Not yet.

Maybe because, since Sophia had come into the small parlor to take tea with her cousin, Edmund had not spoken other than to comment on the weather and the delightful flavor of the cakes.

Exactly like each day when they had tea together.

So they sat, while she tried not to show her discomfort and frustration. Had Charles spoken to him yet about fulfilling his obligations as Lord Meriweather and banishing the smugglers from the estate? It had been two days since she and Charles had spoken in the dower cottage. Since then Charles had seldom been in the same room with her. Even when he was, other people were around so she could not ask.

Yesterday, she had had one of the footmen bring her father's old trunk down from the attic. The battered wooden box with its worn leather straps sat in her room, ready to be filled with everything she would need to tour Europe. She had pushed it into a corner, then spent half the night staring in its direction.

She had planned how she would pack it before she slipped out of the house with a much smaller bag and made her way to London. She could book passage to the Continent and arrange for her trunk to follow. Once it arrived, she would visit the places her father had told her about. It would not matter that she was so tall.

And she no longer would be tempted by Charles's touch that urged her to soften within his arms as his lips found hers. The more miles she put between them, surely she would think of him less and less.

She hoped.

Sophia sighed under her breath as she looked across her cup to her mum cousin. As captivating as that fantasy was, she could not leave Meriweather Hall until she was assured that her mother and sister would be able to remain within it.

Lord, please help Charles find the right words when he talks to Cousin Edmund. If that conversation could happen soon, I would be grateful.

Or would she? Would she be accepting of God's will if it was for her to marry her cousin and remain at Meriweather Hall?

Cousin Edmund shifted on his chair.

She had to break the silence. "Oh, I forgot to mention that the Fenwicks will not be joining us this evening."

"Why not?" Edmund sat straighter and looked directly at her. He had not done that since she'd handed him a cup of tea. "Miss Fenwick accepted my invitation when I saw her after we returned from York."

"A pastor's life is filled with many tasks and obligations."

"But that does not mean Miss Fenwick cannot join us." Hope filled his voice.

"I suggested that, and Vera sent back a note that

while she was grateful for the invitation, it is her habit to wait at the parsonage in case her brother needs her to assist him."

"Oh." Her cousin lapsed into silence except for the clink of his spoon against his cup.

"Maybe we can visit them the next time we go into the village," Sophia said to keep the conversation going.

"That sounds like a fine idea. I should have visited the village much more before now, but with the tasks here and so much to decide... Too much to decide..." His face flushed, and he clamped his lips closed.

"Cousin Edmund," she said in the same gentle tone she used with the children, "you need only ask, and Catherine and I will be glad to help in any way we can. Since Papa became ill and Mother spent much of her time with him, we split their duties, so we are more aware of what it takes to run this estate than you may guess. I know I speak for my sister when I say that we are eager to show you around the estate and teach you how we have overseen it. I am sure you have ideas of your own to implement, and I can assure you that neither of us will be hurt by any changes you wish to make."

"That is most kind of you. However, you handle everything with such efficiency and skill that I doubt there will be much I wish to change."

"When you are ready, I will be glad to give you a tour of the estate so you may meet the staff beyond the household one."

"Thank you. I will let you know when it is convenient." He paused in his stirring. "Unless you would rather to let me know when it is convenient for you."

Sophia had sympathy for her cousin who was growing more agitated with every passing second. Did he suspect why she was eager for him to assume full control of the house and lands and the staff? Did he guess that she hoped to grasp her long-delayed dream of traveling?

She offered her cousin more tea. He declined with a curt wave. A groan of frustration bubbled up within her. She could stand no more of the silence. She had tried to be patient, but she could not any longer.

"If the day is pleasant tomorrow," she said, "I would be glad to give you a tour of the tenant farms."

"That sounds fine."

She waited for him to add more. He did not. Was this how their married life would be? A few comments about the business of the estate and then silence. With his friends, he prattled almost as much as Mr. Bradby. With her mother and sister he was reserved, but even then he spoke more freely than he did with her.

"It is necessary," she said, desperate to keep the conversation going, "to decide which buildings will have repairs done before the winter storms set upon us and which can wait another year."

"The buildings are in such a poor state?" He again looked at her, and her sympathy returned. For both of them. It was clear that neither of them was eager to do their duty.

"The sea winds show no mercy to thatch or wood or even stone."

"I have much to learn."

"Papa always said that the most important asset any Lord Meriweather could possess is the ability to admit that he would never know everything necessary to be the perfect baron." She smiled, hoping it did not look as wobbly as it felt. "Because no such man has ever held title to this estate."

Edmund chuckled, and his shoulders eased from their stiff pose. "Then I suspect I shall follow the tradition well, because I am far from perfect."

"Do not worry. You will feel more at ease once you are familiar with the estate."

"Thank you," he said again. Those were the last two words he spoke during the rest of the uncomfortable tea.

Charles put down his soup spoon as he heard Bradby eagerly accept Herriott's invitation to join him and Sophia for a ride around the estate tomorrow. When Miss Catherine chimed in as well, everyone's eyes turned with expectation toward him, including Sophia's. Each time she blinked, her golden lashes brushed her cheeks, and he was reminded of how he had touched her face too briefly at the dower cottage.

He should back out graciously. He had the excuse that he needed to spend time with his children. His short visit to the nursery earlier in the day had been a blatant reminder of how he had let himself be drawn away from them again.

"Shall we walk by the sea tomorrow?" he had asked.

Gemma had replied, "Sophia took us there yesterday."

"We could go to the village again."

His daughter had rolled her eyes. "We went there twice with Sophia while you were away with Lord Meriweather and Mr. Bradby."

"We were pirates," Michael said, looking up from the tower of blocks he was building. He had slashed his arm through them so they toppled atop the soldiers. "Bad, bad pirates."

"*You* were a pirate," Gemma had corrected in her

primmest tone. "*I* was a princess escaping from my tower."

Charles had listened as his children began describing the outings they had with Sophia. It seemed as though even a mere walk along the cliffs or a visit to the sweets shop in the village was turned into an adventure. They repeated the stories she had told them of Vikings and Scottish raiders and Romans.

"You can come with us tomorrow," Michael had offered.

"I thought we would go out by ourselves, so you can show me what you have discovered," he replied.

"I want to go with Sophia," Gemma had insisted.

When Michael agreed, both children had refused to consider going for a walk without Sophia. He had struggled to restrain his temper as they continued to whine that he did not want them to have any fun.

He had pushed himself to his feet and reminded them sternly that, as their father, he made such decisions. That had brought more protests and then tears. Vexed, he had snapped an order to the nurserymaid that the children should be ready to go tomorrow after breakfast.

No one had uttered another word, but his children's resentful glares had followed him out of the nursery. He had not been able to put them out of his mind since.

As Charles looked around the dining room table where the others waited for his answer, he was caught by the sympathy in Sophia's eyes.

She knew.

She knew what had happened in the nursery that morning. It should be no surprise because he guessed Alice had sought her out as soon as he had left the nursery floor.

"You need not come with us," she said with a half smile that chipped away at the ice around his heart.

"That is right," Bradby quickly added. "We can get along fine without a grouchy bear stumbling along with us."

"Perhaps that is true," Charles said, "especially when Herriott and his cousins are going to be saddled with a braying donkey."

Herriott laughed and slapped the table. "Well said, Northbridge."

Miss Catherine chuckled behind her hand. "It is clear that Mr. Bradby is not the only one in a jollifying mood tonight."

When the conversation turned to other subjects as the other courses were served, Charles was relieved. Sophia's glances in his direction during the meal warned him that she had noticed he had failed to give Herriott an answer. Once dessert was finished, she and her sister excused themselves as they always did.

Herriott and Bradby showed no signs of being in a hurry to leave the table. Both of them wished him a good night's sleep when Charles rose to take his leave.

A good night's sleep? He could not recall the last time he had enjoyed that. The faintest sound woke him, setting his heart to pounding like cavalry riding into battle. Another skill from the war that he wished he could unlearn.

His steps were heavy as he climbed the stairs. He considered checking on the children, but it was likely they were asleep by now. Maybe he should come to the evening meal late so he could be there when they went to bed.

He grimaced. Bradby would tease him about being such a hovering father. It would not bother him if it was just Bradby. Others among the *ton* would find his behavior odd, and the gossip might reach his children's ears. They had been hurt enough, and he would not let that happen again.

Show me, he prayed as he opened the door to his bedroom suite. *Show me, Father, how to be a good father. Help me see their needs and let their hearts know that I love them enough that I would gladly lay down my life for theirs.*

He closed the door, his hand tarrying on the latch, as he looked around his empty room. Sophia had been right to suggest having the children use the nursery, but that had dashed his hope of getting to know his children better.

A knock sounded right behind him.

Charles opened the door to find Herriott on the other side.

"Can I come in?" his friend asked.

"It is your house." Charles's attempt to copy Bradby's humor fell flat.

"*That* is one of the things I would like to talk to you about."

Stepping aside, Charles motioned for Herriott to enter. His friend walked in, scanned the room and then chose a chair that had its back to the bay window. Herriott could not have made it clearer if he had shouted that he did not want to look out over the lands he had inherited.

Another knock came at the door seconds after Charles closed it. He opened it again, expecting to see Bradby. Instead a footman carried in a tray with a steaming pot of fragrant coffee and two cups. Whatever Herriott had come to discuss was going to take some time.

Charles followed the footman to where his friend sat. In quick order, the tray was set down and coffee served.

As soon as the door closed behind the footman, Charles sat and asked, "Only two cups?"

"We can speak easier without Bradby."

Charles nodded. Poor Bradby seemed incapable of having a conversation without turning it into a jest.

"Besides," Herriott continued, "he wanted to finish the book he was reading."

"A book on the law?" asked Charles. If his friend had selected such a topic, it could be a good sign that he might be becoming the man he once had been.

Herriott's nose wrinkled. "It was some absurd novel that he found in the book-room. Something about a castle in Austria and a madman whose very presence tainted the family line and the chances of the young prince to marry the heroine. Silly thing."

Charles agreed, but said nothing as he waited for Herriott to get to the point. Taking a sip of his coffee, he set it on the tray and leaned back in his chair.

"Northbridge, I want you to join my cousins and me on the tour of the estate tomorrow," his friend said.

"Why? You don't need me tagging along like the tail on a dog. This is between you and your family."

"I want you there to make sure I don't do something foolish."

"Like?"

"I don't know." Herriott came to his feet. "Maybe I am worried that I will annoy my cousin enough that she will wash her hands of me, although that would make the whole of this far simpler."

Hope erupted out of his heart, but Charles quickly dampened it. Yes, Sophia treated the children with affection and fairness, but he could hire a nurserymaid to give them the same. Yes, she was lovely, and her lips tempted him to taste them, but the cost of trusting a woman again was far too high. He would spend the rest of his life watching over his shoulder for her to betray him.

But Sophia is not Lydia.

He paid no attention to the small voice. He no longer trusted it either.

"Are you leading up to asking me to help you decide whether to marry Sophia?" Charles asked.

"Maybe I should court her as everyone expects," Herriott said, dropping into the chair.

"Maybe you should." He kept emotion from his voice. If Herriott thought to wound him with such a statement, Charles would not let him see how deeply it had pierced him. Instantly he regretted the thought. Herriott was a good friend. "If that is what you want. Remember that marriage can be for a lifetime."

Herriott hung his head in his hands. "I have no idea what I want. It was simple when we were in the army. I wanted to survive another day, another hour, another minute."

"Then decide what you want to do."

"I don't know!" The cry rumbled up from deep within his friend. "I simply don't know. That is why I came to you. I need your help."

Charles put his hand on his friend's shaking shoulder. "I cannot help you with this."

"Why not?" Herriott looked up at him. "You and Lydia were happy. Don't you want the same for me?"

He stiffened. He would not wish what he had shared with Lydia on anyone. "I want you to be happy, but you are the only one who knows what makes you happy."

"I don't know! That is the problem."

Squeezing his friend's shoulder gently, Charles asked, "Have you prayed about this?"

"I have tried."

"Did you receive any answer?"

"Maybe. I am not sure." Herriott's voice grew more miserable with each word. "I believe that the answer is that I must decide for myself."

At last! Herriott was seeing the truth.

"But what do I decide?" his friend asked.

"What does it matter?" Charles pushed himself to his feet. "Decide *something!*" He stamped across the room. If he did not put some space between him and Herriott, he might take his friend by the lapels and shake him until he unearthed the man his friend once had been.

His sharp tone pricked Herriott's pride. "It's not as if I never make a decision."

"Did you decide what coat to wear tonight?"

Herriott gulped, then shook his head. "My valet selected it."

"Did you decide which wine to serve with dinner?"

"The butler made those arrangements. He knows the cellar here far better than I do."

Forcing himself to be calm, because his friend truly needed him, Charles said, "You must start making decisions. You must take over as lord of the manor."

"I want to."

"But…?"

"What if marrying my cousin is the wrong thing?" Herriott stood and walked to the window that offered a view of the sea and the village. He leaned his elbow on its edge. "Sophia is not what I envisioned as my wife."

"Why? She is a lovely woman."

"True, but she is very—"

"Tall?" He snarled out the word. "I thought better

of you. Why are you acting like that fool who stopped calling on her in London because he was too witless to look beyond her height to see the woman she is?"

"Do you mean Lord Owensly?"

Charles almost choked on his outrage. "Is that who led her on? I know the man. He is a bounder, and she is better off not being involved in any way with him. But how could you speak so of your cousin?"

Resting his forehead on his arm stretched across the windowpane, Herriott sighed. "I mean no insult to Cousin Sophia, but I worry about the scandal attached to her after she fled from London. We know that she did nothing wrong, but we also know that people whisper behind their hands."

"I cannot say what you know, but I know that listening to rumors is a waste of time."

"It is simple for you, Northbridge. If you were to marry her, you would know how to handle any hints of past scandal. I am new to the Polite World, and I fear, with such baggage, I will stumble coming out of the gate."

"That sounds as if you have decided not to marry her." Charles again had to submerge his pulse of joy that Sophia would not become his friend's wife.

"Why wouldn't I want to marry her? She is pretty, and she is smart, and she has a warm heart. I doubt any man could see her and not fall in love with her at first sight. Do you know what I mean?"

"Yes, I do." He knew too well.

"But I am now Lord Meriweather, and I cannot shirk my obligations simply because the *ton* may snicker." He pushed away from the window. "I think what I am asking, Northbridge, is for you to help me navigate through the labyrinth ahead of me."

Charles stared at his friend's wan face, and he knew that Herriott had selected his words carefully. How many times had Charles incited his men to be prepared for battle with almost the same phrase? *Navigating the labyrinth of the enemy lines.* It was a warning not to get cut off from the rest of the company as chaos exploded around them.

His throat closed, making it tough to breathe. The horrific sounds of guns firing, cannons spewing destruction and men and horses dying filled his ears. He refused to blink. In that split second when his eyes were closed, images of battle would spew forth, sucking him into that hell.

It is a memory. Just a memory. He kept telling himself that as he struggled to force it into the hidden recesses of his mind.

"Will you?" Herriott asked, his voice the lifeline Charles used to crawl out of that appalling morass.

There was only one answer Charles could give to his friend's question. No matter how much Charles craved the chance to hold Sophia, Herriott felt himself honor-bound to wed her. The memories brought forth a truth he could not forget. Charles owed Herriott more than he could repay in a single lifetime. If his friend wanted his assistance, Charles had the duty of helping him.

"Yes."

Chapter Eleven

Charles woke from a dream that vanished as soon as he opened his eyes. He did not remember the details, only that it had been filled with the horrors he had witnessed during battle. He had thought he had put those terrible nightmares behind him. He had not had one since his arrival at Meriweather Hall.

Now one had stalked him through his sleep, leaving him drenched with sweat.

He tried to relax. What had brought it on? His conversation with Herriott? That must have triggered the dream.

But he had escaped it. All he needed to do was roll over and go to sleep.

He tried to turn over. He could not move. Not to the left. Not to the right. He was pinned down.

By what?

Shifting his arms or legs even an inch was impossible. He was restrained from neck to his toes. Panic crept out of the darkest recesses of his soul.

Where was he?

In France? Maybe the war was still setting the Continent aflame.

Had the French captured him?

His men! Where were they? Had they escaped, or were they prisoners, too?

Sickness boiled up from his gut. Maybe he was not a captive. Maybe he had been shot and was paralyzed. He gagged, struggling not to vomit up his own fear as he thought of Jones. The man, who had served as one of his sergeants, had been shot in the back and afterward could not move anything below his chin.

Charles swallowed hard, fighting the sour taste of bile. He had seen Jones only once after he had been taken from the field on a bloodstained litter. After the battle—Charles could not remember which one—he had found the hospital tent where Jones had been taken.

When he entered the filthy tent, the sharp smell of alcohol and blood burned his nose. The screams of the injured rang in his ears. Medics shouted to each other as they held down a thrashing man and sawed off his arm in an effort to save the soldier's life. Most of those efforts were futile. The men died in agony from blood loss or infection anyhow.

Under his boots, the mud was mixed with blood and gore. Charles paid it no attention. He could not remember the last time his boots had been shined. The leather was creased from hours of holding a position while he fought the enemy.

A hand reached out and grasped his coat. He looked down at a man whose eyes were hidden beneath a cloth tied around his head. His face was half gone, and Charles had to look away. The man tried to talk to him, but no human sounds came out. With a cry of his own, Charles pulled away from the wounded man.

His throat tightened. He could not breathe. He wanted to escape from these nightmare creatures who once had been healthy soldiers, eager to serve their king and keep their country safe from the Corsican monster who ruled France. But he had come to comfort Jones.

Where was he?

He heard his name called.

He turned toward the low cot where Jones lay as still as stone. Only his eyes moved, dull as death. Where was Jones's bluster and his courage that had inspired them?

Charles needed to say something now to inspire his wounded man, but words failed him.

"Sir?" Jones's pain laced through his voice.

"Jones…" *Dear Lord, help me find something to say to ease his pain. Help me help him understand that You are here beside him.*

"I need you to do something for me."

"Certainly." In the wake of each battle, he had many tasks, but they could wait while he helped his sergeant. What could Jones need him to do? A note written home to his family? Someone to sit beside him and brush the flies away from his face? Someone to listen while he talked?

"Kill me."

Again he had no words.

Jones tried to raise his head, but could not. His eyes came alive with an intensity that nearly knocked Charles off his feet.

"Sir," his sergeant said, "kill me. I beg you."

"If there is any hope—"

"There is none." He gasped for breath between each word. "I heard them say that. I will never again be a husband to my wife. I will never be able to hold my children. You understand, don't you?"

Charles nodded. He would never hold his wife again either. Even though she had betrayed him, grief remained in his heart. Grief as he mourned for the life they could have had if she had loved him as he loved her. And his children? To them, he was a stranger. He never had seen his son, and he wondered if his daughter would recognize him. Would his children mourn if he died so far from home?

"I don't want them to see me like this," Jones went on. "Let them remember me as a hero who defended England. Kill me, sir. I beg you."

Steel rasped as Charles had drawn his sword. He raised it. Acceptance and gratitude had bloomed in Jones's eyes. Sweat had poured down into Charles's, and he had closed them while he uttered a prayer of forgiveness to God and to Jones's wife and children.

Voices swarmed around him. Some shouting for him to stop, but he was drowning in Jones's pain and his own. He tried to swing the sword down. He could not. His arms refused to move. What was wrong?

He opened his eyes. He was looking up at Herriott and Bradby who stood over him. *He* was the paralyzed man, and they stood ready to wield their swords. He was begging them to kill him, so he could die as a hero instead of becoming a burden for his children, his children who did not know him. Would anyone love them as they should be loved?

As if in answer to his unspoken question, a cool, soft hand settled on his fevered forehead. Sophia's hand! What was she doing here?

"Help him!" she ordered, looking across him to his friends.

No! He was not ready to die. Not when he needed to see his children…

Confusion halted him. Where was he? Suddenly he could move his arms and legs. He did, fighting wildly to escape the last of his bonds.

"Whoa!" called Herriott. "Stay still! You are going to knock my head off! That thrashing is what got you entangled in the bedclothes to begin with. Relax, man!"

He obeyed, sinking into his sweaty pillow. He turned his head toward Sophia.

She was not there.

Had she ever been?

He was no longer sure what was real and what was part of the nightmare he had brought home with him from France.

Sophia was ready to give up on the tour she had arranged for Cousin Edmund. His thoughts were obviously elsewhere. She wondered what had happened and if his distraction had anything do with why neither Charles nor Mr. Bradby had appeared at breakfast. Both men had sent a terse message that they would not be joining the tour of the estate.

With his mind otherwise occupied, the ride on the unseasonably hot afternoon was proving to be a waste of time. She had given her cousin a list of notes she had written last evening after dinner, but she quickly realized when they made their first stop at the gamekeeper's cottage, that Cousin Edmund had not even glanced at them.

"Mrs. Demaine's husband's family has a tradition of serving as gamekeeper on the estate," Sophia explained as she had in the notes. She smiled at the gawky young man by Mrs. Demaine's side. "This is Alfred. He has provided great service to both his late father and the estate."

The young man put his fingers to forelock as Cousin Edmund nodded in his direction. The conversation petered out from there, and Sophia quickly steered her cousin away from the cottage. The Demaines looked anxious that the new Lord Meriweather had not said a single word to them.

Sophia muffled her annoyance. As the baron, her cousin needed to keep up spirits on the estate and to recognize that each member of the staff played a valuable role.

"Edmund, if you will look at the notes I gave you," she said, glancing back at the thatched cottage, "you will see that my father intended to name Alfred to his late father's post of gamekeeper. However, I did not want to usurp your authority."

He startled her by speaking in a calm voice that did not match the tension across his shoulders. "You brought me out here to meet the lad in hopes that I would give him the position."

"Yes. Please do not think I am trying to manipulate you," she hurried to add. "The Demaines have been on edge awaiting the decision that Alfred would follow in his father's footsteps. You, of course, can select whomever you wish to be your gamekeeper, but I wanted you to see how important it is to this family to have the line be unbroken."

"As it is for the estate's title."

She nodded, even though she wished the conversation had not taken such a turn toward the inevitable match she was expected to make with her cousin.

"Do *you* think the lad worthy of the position?" her cousin asked.

Sophia struggled not to breathe out a huge sigh of relief that Edmund's mind remained on the Demaines and not on an offer of marriage. "I would not have broached the subject of appointing Alfred as the new gamekeeper if I did not think he would be a worthy successor to his father."

"I should have realized that." Edmund released a sigh as big as the one inside her. "May we continue this another day? I owe you an apology for coming to this tour unprepared. Allow me a day or two to read the information you graciously have prepared, and then we will continue."

"As you wish."

He did not answer as he scurried away as if a wolf nipped at his heels.

Sophia walked toward the house more slowly. Her cousin could not make it clearer that he had no interest in her company.

Charles paused as he reached for the pitcher of lemonade to refill his glass. Sophia and her sister came out on the terrace that offered a lovely view of the water garden with its fountains and bushes that were donning their autumnal colors. He could not doubt Sophia really stood there, because his heart beat more rapidly at the sight of her. Dressed in a simple green gown that accented her beauty, she had her amazing hair hidden beneath a straw bonnet.

But had she been by his bedside last night when the night horrors visited him again?

When she turned to speak to her cousin, irrational envy swelled through him. He should be glad Herriott was able to manage a few words in her presence. After all, he had promised to help Herriott make the best of the situation.

The best would be for Sophia to be mine.

He ignored that tiny voice in his head and splashed lemonade into his glass. He forced a smile when Michael held a small tin cup. He filled it as his daughter rushed to stand beside Sophia.

Herriott motioned him over to join him and Sophia. A few feet from them, Bradby was talking to Miss Catherine. As usual Miss Catherine was laughing at whatever silly thing he had said. Sophia's sister had far more patience with Bradby's unending drollery than Charles did.

"Sir Nigel Tresting is a unique person," Sophia was saying when Charles came within earshot. "Many days, you can find him out on the moors, painting landscapes filled with sheep. Other days, he is on the strand where he paints views of the sea. Every wall in his house is covered with his work. He holds a ball for the whole parish each year where he can show off his past year's work before he finds a place to hang it permanently in his house."

"Can we go?" Gemma faced him. "Please?"

He looked over his daughter's head to Sophia who regarded the little girl with open affection. Slowly Sophia's gaze rose toward his, and warmth flowed over him. He kept his own expression from changing, not trusting himself to show any emotion until he discovered if Sophia had truly been by his bed last night and had seen him lost in the weakness that preyed on him, the weakness he hated.

"One must be invited to such an event, Gemma," Charles said.

That was not the answer his daughter wanted to hear. "Sophia said everyone in the parish was invited." Gemma whirled away from him. "Tell him, Sophia!"

"Tell him…?" Sophia prompted quietly.

He started to speak, but she put her hand on his arm to halt him.

Had he forgotten how to breathe? The light touch of her fingertips on his sleeve should not have such an intense effect on him, but it did. "Gemma?" she asked. "Tell him…?"

"Tell him *please!*" Gemma rocked from one foot to the other with impatience.

The smile Sophia gave his daughter faded when she raised her eyes to his. She snatched her hand off his sleeve and clasped her fingers in front of her. He noticed how white her knuckles were.

Had she truly been in his bedchamber while he fought to escape his nightmare? Had she seen him like that? A cold flush of hate flooded him. He did not hate her. He hated his own shameful weakness.

"The invitation was meant for everyone," Sophia said in an overly cheerful voice. She turned to her cousin. "It will be an opportunity for you to meet the gentry and the peers from beyond Sanctuary Bay's parish."

Miss Catherine opened up a folded sheet of paper that must be the invitation. "Sir Nigel is looking forward—very, very, very, very much, if I may quote Sir Nigel—to meeting three war heroes, including the new Lord Meriweather."

"When you express it that way," Mr. Bradby said, "I am sure I speak for my friends when I say that we would like to run as fast as possible in the opposite direction."

"Why am I not surprised that is your answer?" Miss Catherine asked.

Sophia glanced from Bradby to her cousin and back, taking care not to look in Charles's direction. "We should warn you that Sir Nigel will accept no answer other than an acceptance to his annual gala."

"Are you going to attend, Miss Catherine?" Color flashed up Bradby's face and grew even brighter when Sophia's sister smiled at him.

"Of course, Mr. Bradby. Other than last year when Papa was ill, we have attended every harvest gala at Sir Nigel's estate. It is great fun, and I have been looking forward to it all summer. I do hope you plan to attend, as well."

"Most definitely. Everyone will attend, right?" He clapped Herriott on the shoulder. "We promised to see you settled on your new estate, and how better to do that than showing you off to your new neighbors?" He grinned at Charles. "Don't you agree, Northbridge?"

"When is it?" Charles asked.

"In a fortnight. We can stay that long to be feted as heroes, can't we?"

Charles could not think of anything he wanted less, short of returning to battle. He was about to say that, but he made the mistake of looking toward Herriott. His friend had that familiar panicked expression, and Charles remembered his promise last night to help his friend become more comfortable among the *ton*. He could not break that vow so quickly.

As he had last night, he said simply, "Yes."

Chapter Twelve

Childish giggles burst out of the nursery as Charles reached the top of the stairs. That could mean only one thing—Sophia was playing with his children. When the nurse was with them, they laughed, but only Sophia brought forth that lighthearted giggle he had never expected to hear from his daughter again.

"Hee-haw!" Michael shouted. "Hee-haw! That is a donkey!"

A pause, then Gemma made a noise that sounded like a duck with a sore throat. "Am I right, Sophia? Is that a goose?"

"You are right," Sophia answered, the sound of her laughter like a dozen silver bells chiming. "Now guess this one."

Charles, curious what they were doing, went into the nursery, but paused by the inner door. Sophia sat in front of a sunlit window. With the bright blue sky behind her, she could have been posing for a portrait. Her dress was the faint pink of the sky before sunrise, and a ribbon of the same color held back her golden curls.

She held up her slender hands, contorting her fingers and locking them together. On the opposite wall, a horned silhouette appeared.

Gemma and Michael, who were kneeling on the floor, bent their heads together to confer.

"Baa." Charles did his best imitation of a goat's bleating.

Both children jumped to their feet and ran to him. He was startled when Gemma did not pull up short as she usually did. Instead she tugged on his sleeve.

"Come and see what Sophia has taught us," she said.

Sophia stood and regarded him with concern. "How are you today, Charles?"

"I am fine, and I slept fine last night." He regretted his whetted tone. Forcing his voice to lighten, he added, "Thank you for asking, but, as I told your cousin, there is no need for concern."

"I am pleased to hear that." She looked at his children, then back at him, her smile returning. "If you will stay where you are, Charles, you will see better. Come here, children, so you can show him what you have learned." Her smile broadened as she perched on a chair as the children scrambled to stand on either side of her.

He watched while she gently guided the children's hands into the proper configuration, taking extra time to help a very excited Michael keep the pattern steady. The children's faces shone in the sunshine, but it was not just the light. Happiness lit them from within with a brilliance he had not seen since before he left for the war. It came from a simple joy that was beyond price.

"Ready?" Sophia asked.

The children nodded, and she readjusted Michael's hands again before saying, "And let the beauty of the Lord our God be upon us: and establish thou the work of our hands upon us."

The verses from Psalm 90 must have been a signal. Both children raised their hands that they held with their thumbs pressed together. Slowly they opened and closed their hands. On the wall two small silhouettes of butterflies appeared.

Charles applauded. Michael bowed deeply, and Gemma curtseyed before dissolving into giggles.

He looked past them to Sophia. Clapping, he walked toward her. "Another brava is due to the one who created this show."

A lovely blush rushed up her cheeks, and he turned to congratulate his children again before he could no longer fight the temptation to brush his fingers against Sophia's enticing color. As he watched the children display the other shapes they had learned, his eyes kept shifting to watch as Sophia walked around the room, picking up stray toys and putting them on the lower shelves.

When a box fell off and spilled lead soldiers across the floor, he crossed the room to help her gather them. He took the box from her and started to place it on one of the empty shelves.

"No," she said. "That is too high for the children or Alice to reach."

He smiled as she took the box and settled it with care on the next to the bottom shelf. "It is good of you to think of Alice, so she does not need to drag a chair over here each time the children want toys."

"I learned long ago that I must keep in mind that not everyone is as sky-high as I am." She laughed without humor. "Though, if I do forget, someone is likely to let me know."

"Not everyone is as uncharitable as Owensly." When her face paled, he said, "Your cousin mentioned his name. I wasn't digging for the truth behind your back."

She reached for another toy and put it on a low shelf. "I know."

Charles waited for her to add more, but she continued picking up the children's discarded toys, denying him the opportunity to offer her more solace. He glanced across the room when he heard Gemma's and Michael's delighted laughter. They continued to entertain themselves with creating silhouettes of animals on the wall. When Michael had trouble with one shape, his sister helped him without being asked. He watched, fascinated that the children who had seemed distant on the way north now played together with joy.

"I was astonished that they did not know how to make shadow animals." Sophia set several books on the shelves. "I cannot remember when we learned, so I must have been even younger than Michael."

"My wife's family does not believe in a child using his or her imagination." His mouth straightened. "Most likely because none of them had one."

"Oh." She started to add more, then stopped.

"I am stating a fact," Charles said. "I wanted to explain why such a game would seem as foreign to them as driving a coach pulled by fish."

"I would say that you are not lacking in imagination when you make a statement like that." Sophia's smile returned, and he could believe it glowed brightly enough for his children to use for their game.

Or was its warmth solely within him? When he first came to Meriweather Hall, he was wrapped in ice that kept him from feeling too much. His friends had respected that. Sophia had not. She had reached out to him as well as his children, bringing happiness into their lives.

"It would seem you have been a good influence on me as well as on the children," he said.

"I am pleased to think that."

"Me, too." He curled her fingers over his much broader ones.

When he gazed into her soft green eyes, it took all of his strength to keep from sweeping her into his arms. He did not want to talk about the children. He did not want to talk about anything. He wanted to kiss her.

The children ran over to where they stood. Gemma frowned when she glanced at how he held Sophia's hand, but Michael had one thought on his mind.

"See the sea now?" his son asked.

Sophia drew her fingers slowly—and he hoped reluctantly—out of his as she said, "I promised Gemma that we would play the string game."

Michael whirled to his sister. "Don't you want to see the sea?"

Gemma's thoughts were as clear as if she had shouted them when a satisfied smile tilted her lips once Sophia had released his hand. "Yes, and you and I and Sophia can play the string game there."

"The string game?" asked Charles, acting as if he had not noticed Gemma's smile. It reminded him too much of her mother's when she crowed about some victory over him. Gemma had been in the custody of the same woman who had reared Lydia, and he wondered what other unflattering habits she had acquired. The question made him more certain that he had been right when he vowed before God to be the best father possible for his children and rear them himself.

"Cat's cradle," Sophia said, her voice falsely bright. She must have noticed Gemma's reaction, too. "Do you know how to play cat's cradle, Charles?"

He shook his head. "I watched others play it when I was a child, but never played it myself."

"Why don't you join us for our walk along the shore? Gemma and Michael will be thrilled to teach you how to play it." She smiled at the children. "Won't you?"

"Me teach you the string game!" shouted Michael, spinning around in his excitement.

Gemma crossed her arms over her narrow chest and grumbled something under her breath.

"Gemma," Charles said, "if you have something to say, you should say it loudly enough for everyone to hear."

"Maybe everyone else heard," his daughter fired back. "Maybe your ears are stopped up from cannon fire."

Sophia scolded, "Gemma, that is no way to speak to your father. You should apologize."

"I will handle this." Charles felt the familiar tightness of his anger rising. "Gemma, repeat what you said so we can hear."

"I don't remember," Gemma said with a challenging expression that said the opposite.

Beside her, Michael put his thumb in his mouth and edged closer to lean against Sophia's skirt. He gripped a handful of the material, clinging to her as he listened wide-eyed.

"Gemma," Charles said, "I asked you to tell us what you said."

"You really must have gone deaf from the cannons. Grandmother said that happens, and we should not be surprised."

He scowled at the insolence that he never would have accepted from his men. "Gemma…"

"Otherwise," she replied in a superior tone that

brought Lydia to mind, "you would have heard when I said that I don't remember what I said."

"Gemma, I demand—"

Sophia interrupted, "Let's take a deep breath and calm down. Gemma, apologize nicely to your papa."

"Sorry," she said, completely insincere. When Sophia frowned at her, his daughter repeated the words in a nicer tone.

"Better," Sophia said, her hand stroking Michael's hair as he stayed close to her. "Charles?"

"What?" The question came out in a bellow.

Sophia blinked twice, but did not recoil as the children did. "Charles, you should tell your daughter you accept her apology."

Charles almost snarled that Sophia should remember what she told him the night he arrived at Meriweather Hall. *May I suggest, Lord Northbridge, that you deal with your family's problems and allow me to deal with mine?*

Then he saw tears in his son's eyes. In Gemma's, too, he discovered when he looked more closely. Even Sophia's eyes were sad. And disappointed.

In him.

"Gemma, I accept your apology," he said, calm once more, though a storm roiled within him. He had scared his son with his temper. He had backed his rebellious daughter into a corner so she lashed out at him. He had disappointed Sophia. Each of their responses hurt, and, for the first time, he feared he would never persuade his children, especially his daughter, that he truly cared for them.

As Sophia and Charles walked toward the path to the beach, the children raced ahead. She sought the right words to ease Charles's sorrow. "Your daughter really is a caring child."

He snorted a terse laugh as they went past the hedges that divided the garden from the untamed headland. "All she seems to care about is disagreeing with everything I say. She seems ready to do everything she can to raise my ire."

"She does not trust you yet because she does not know you. Give her a chance to get to know you."

"She has had no problem getting to know and trust you."

"I am not her father."

"Obviously." Vexation slipped into his voice again.

Sophia paused. "Charles, the children came here with no expectations of me, so it has been easy for them to trust me."

"They cannot trust me because they believe that I abandoned them." He winced as he spoke, and she guessed he had said more than he intended.

"They don't understand about the obligations that kept you from them. Michael is learning to trust you, because he never had a reason to distrust you."

"But Gemma has memories of when I was there and when I left."

Sophia nodded, blinking back tears. "And she had no idea if you would ever come back. Her mother went away and did not ever return, so why would she expect you to?"

Charles stared at her in silence. Had she said too much, stuck her nose in where it did not belong?

"Sophia!" called Gemma. "Can we go down the cliff?"

She started to turn to answer, but Charles's hand on her elbow halted her. Slowly she looked at him. She had seen his fury. She had seen his sorrow, but she never had seen a candid expression like this one.

"How did you become this wise?" he whispered so low that the sea wind almost blew the words away.

"Experience." Her voice was as hushed as his.

"I don't understand."

"My father died, and he is not coming back. As an adult, I understand he will be there to greet me in heaven, but the small part of me that remains my father's little girl is angry and hurt that he would leave me."

"And you think Gemma feels the same way?"

"Y-y-yes." She bit her lower lip to keep it from quivering more.

"I had no idea."

"When your wife died—"

"That was different."

She wanted to ask him how, but refrained. His eyes had hardened as soon as she mentioned his wife.

"Just as you are different, Sophia," he said.

Her first instinct was to spin on her heel and storm away. He did not need to tell her that she was different. People had been pointing that out since she had sprouted like a bean when she was ten. Why was he being cruel when they had been speaking from the heart?

Before she could ask that, he added, "You are the first person I have met since I returned from France who has not been curious about my scar. Most people stare and many ask how it happened."

"Including your children?"

Again emotion flashed through his eyes, but this time it was sorrow. "I think Michael was half-frightened of me at first, but then I told him how Bradby saved my life when a French soldier took aim at me with his sword. He was so excited to be in the presence of a true hero that he came to accept me."

"Mr. Bradby saved your life?"

Charles sighed. "You know he is not the man he was. A braver man I have never met. When the French ambushed us, he jumped onto a soldier who was about to slice my head off. He deflected the man's blow, leaving me with my head." He smiled sadly. "*That* is the reason I put up with his endless jests."

"They are a small price to pay."

"At times, it feels like the debt is far too heavy."

"Papa!" called Michael from the top of the cliff path.

Charles walked toward where his son and Gemma waited. When Sophia caught up with them, he said, "Thank you."

Sophia did not reply as Charles took Michael's hand and started down the steep path. Picking her own way with care, she was glad to see Gemma standing on the sand.

The breeze was gentle, but swirled around the base of the cliffs. Low waves rolled onto the sand. The soft sound as the water slid in and out of the bay created the perfect undertone for the squawking seabirds.

"What are they doing?" Charles asked, his hand shading his eyes as he looked across the bay toward the village.

Boats were drawn up, and men were stacking rope-draped open boxes on the shore.

Sophia smiled. "Nothing suspicious. Those are the lobstermen who have returned with their catch. Anyone with a more illicit cargo does not come ashore in the daylight."

"What is ill cargo?" asked Michael.

"Not lobsters," Charles answered with a wink at Sophia. "Maybe the cook will surprise us with some for supper."

"See the sea!" Michael jumped up and down.

Holding out her hands, Sophia smiled as Gemma grasped her left one. A larger hand took her right, and she stared down in astonishment to see her fingers enveloped by Charles's. When she raised her eyes, he gave her the smile that thrilled her. She wished he would smile more often because his dark eyes came alight, and that ever-present lock of hair falling over his brow gave him a roguish charm.

"Look how big this stone is!" Gemma ran over to the base of the cliff and slapped a rock twice her height.

Sophia laughed. "If you think that is big, you should see the Bridestones."

"What are the Bridestones?" Gemma asked.

"Large rocks in the strangest shapes. They are on the edge of the moors west of here. Some are taller than you would be if you stood on your father's shoulders. Others are not as tall, but look like beasts out of old stories." She dropped her voice and slanted toward the two children. "One looks like the head of a dragon!"

Michael squealed in delight. "A dragon!"

"A fire-breathing one?" asked Gemma, as excited as her brother.

"I don't think rock dragons breathe anything." Sophia laughed and draped an arm over each child's shoulders. "Maybe you will have a chance to see them while you are here."

Charles smiled. "As I have agreed that we will not leave until after Sir Nigel's ball, it is likely we will have time to pay the Bridestones a visit."

The children cheered.

"And, of course, you will be here tomorrow," Sophia said, "for the clipping of the church."

"What is that?" Gemma asked as she skipped around them. "Do you take off a small piece of the wall?"

She laughed. "No. Clipping is an old word that means hugging."

"You hug the church?" The little girl rolled her eyes. "You are hoaxing us."

"No, it is really a hug, though not like one you would give your brother."

"Ugh!" Her nose wrinkled.

Sophia ruffled Gemma's hair, then said, "It now is the day when we clean up the churchyard before winter. The name came from when there were hedgerows around the church. Those needed clipping each spring and autumn. Now we gather together after the morning service on the Sunday closest to the middle of September. We have a cold nuncheon, then work. Afterward, we have dinner together. At the end of the night the branches and weeds go into a bonfire."

"Can we go? Can we go?" asked Michael, not giving anyone a chance to answer. "Want to clip!"

Sophia put a finger to Michael's lips, and Charles envied his son. How he would like that soft touch against his own lips! "You must let your papa decide," she said with a smile in his direction.

"Papa?" asked Michael.

Charles's heart contracted between one beat and the next as joy soared through him. He had, at last, won the hard-fought battle for his son. For so long the children had refused to call him anything but sir. To hear his son call him Papa was the answer to a prayer. He thanked the Lord.

"It sounds like fun," Charles said, smiling at his children.

When Gemma gave him a grin as broad as her brother's, he wondered if he had ever been happier. He chuckled as Michael grabbed his hand and tugged him around the big rock.

"Play string game," his son announced. He pulled out of his sleeve a length of string that had been knotted together at the ends. He wrapped it around his left hand in a simple pattern, but needed Sophia's help to arrange it on his right hand.

He dropped to the sand and sat cross-legged. With his string-wrapped hands, he motioned for his sister to join him. Gemma mirrored his position before reaching over with two fingers on each hand. She rose to her knees as she manipulated the strings quickly and ended up with them on her hand in a different shape.

With his tongue sticking out between his lips and his eyes intense with concentration, Michael looped one finger into each side of it. He paused and looked at Sophia, who nodded encouragement. A couple of deft motions, and the string was around Michael's hand, but with a different structure.

The children kept moving the string back and forth between their hands. Some of the patterns repeated, but more often a unique one appeared. Finally Michael failed to lift it from Gemma's hands in the proper way, and the string tangled.

As Sophia took the string and unknotted it to shake it out into a straight line again, Michael said, "Papa, try it."

"Can you do it?" Gemma's words were a challenge Charles knew he must take.

"As long as Sophia helps me," he said.

"Me, too!" Michael edged closer to him and began instructing him on what to do.

Charles tried to follow his son's jumbled instructions and was about ready to give up when Sophia knelt by his side. She looped the string around his fingers and then drew his hands apart. He breathed in her sweet lavender scent mixed with the salt blowing through her hair, and his head grew light. Playing the game would be difficult when he was captivated by the beautiful woman beside him.

He forced himself to focus as Gemma deftly lifted the strings from his hands and settled them onto hers. She arched her brows as she held her hands out to him. He recognized the challenging expression that he had used often himself.

Looking down at the string, he had no idea where to start. He said as much, and Sophia laughed.

She rose and took his hands. If she felt how they trembled at her touch, she showed no sign. Instead she said, "Pinch the string on either side." She guided his hands to the proper spot. As soon as he gripped the string properly, she twisted his hands and hers, and he was astounded to discover the string on his fingers in the next pattern.

"See if you can figure out what to do with the next one," Sophia said, "after Gemma takes it from you. Watch what she does. That should give you a hint."

He might have caught the trick to the game if he could have taken his eyes off Sophia. Instead he made a mess of the string. Happily he handed it to his son, who quickly wrapped it around his own hands with Gemma's help. The children passed the string between them rapidly, yelping with excitement each time they created an unusual pattern.

Sophia came to her feet and, slanting against the cliff, watched the children with an indulgent smile. The breeze swirled through her hair beneath her sedate bonnet and twisted her skirt around her slender ankles, offering him a beguiling glimpse.

He put his hand on the cliff near her shoulder. An inch closer and his skin would touch hers. If he laced his fingers through hers, he could gently guide her into his arms. He could place his lips on hers for the kiss that he longed for. His breathing sounded uneven in his ears, and her eyes widened, telling him that she was aware of his thoughts as he was…because his thoughts matched hers.

Her eyes closed, and he leaned in to kiss her. Hearing an exultant laugh from the children, he discovered two sets of young eyes on them.

He drew back with reluctance. The first time when he kissed Sophia would be precious, and he wanted it to be the two of them, sharing what they both yearned for without his children as an audience.

When her eyes opened, surprise filled them before she looked down. Instantly he knew he owed her an explanation, but that, too, must wait until the children were not listening.

As soon as we get to the house, he vowed.

But that was impossible. As soon as they stepped into Meriweather Hall, Herriott met them at the door. His friend monopolized the rest of his day and evening. By the time Charles finally got a moment alone, Sophia had gone to bed. He would speak with her the first thing in the morning. That was a pledge he was determined not to break.

Charles sat up in bed as a shriek echoed through the house. Was it the nightmare back to plague him?

He threw off his covers and jumped out of bed. He took a single step and jammed his toe against a chair. He yelped, knowing he was awake. Grief and sorrow preyed on him in his nightmares, never physical pain.

Another cry sounded. He ran to his door and threw it open. Who was screaming? He rushed to his cupboard and pulled out the gun he had carried with him while riding north. On the road, highwaymen were the threat, but by the sea, it was smugglers. Had one or more invaded Meriweather Hall?

He ran into the corridor and looked both ways. At the next scream he hastened toward the central staircase. His gut cramped. The cries were coming from the direction of the nursery.

As he took the stairs two at a time, candlelight broke the darkness in the hallway below him. A single candle moved rapidly along the corridor above him. He chased after it.

Two other candles lit the nursery, but he followed the single candle into the room where the children slept. On the small cot his son sat up, his eyes wide as he stared sightlessly across the room and screamed.

Charles pushed past Sophia who stood in the doorway. He would apologize after he comforted his son. He knew, all too well, the devastating power of a nightmare.

"Michael," he said gently. "Papa is here."

"No!" Michael screeched. "I want Sophia!"

"Son—"

"I want Sophia! Sophia!" His scream ricocheted through the nursery.

Charles stepped aside so his son could see Sophia. With her hair mussed around her shoulders and her eyes heavy with sleep, she looked more beautiful than ever.

She glanced at Charles, her lips tightening. She said

nothing as she handed him her candle. Michael held out his arms to her, and she sat on the edge of the low bed. His son threw himself against her, wrapping his small arms around her neck. He sobbed as she murmured into his hair and stroked his back. She urged him to tell her what he had dreamed, and they whispered together.

Charles fumed. *He* was Michael's father. *He* should be the one comforting his son, not a woman his son had not even known a month ago. Why had Michael chosen Sophia over his own father?

A hand clasped his shoulder, and Herriott murmured, "Let her calm him."

Charles growled a protest and started to sweep his friend's hand away.

"Give her a chance," Herriott said. "How many times did you tell us that a wise man makes use of the tools at his disposal?"

"Especially," added Bradby, who stood beside Herriott and tried to hastily tuck his shirt into his unbuttoned breeches, "when he is in unfamiliar territory."

Charles had never expected to have his own words repeated in such circumstances. Yet they were right. His son needed Sophia now.

But what would happen next time his son had a nightmare and Sophia was not there?

Earlier, on the beach, Charles had congratulated himself for winning an important battle when his son had called him Papa. Now it appeared he was in danger of losing a very different battle—the one to fulfill the promise he had made to God to keep his children from being hurt again.

But he was not a man accustomed to defeat, and he would not surrender without a fight.

Chapter Thirteen

"This Sunday morning is truly living up to its name," Catherine said as she reached for her gloves and bonnet on her dressing table. "After so many blustery days, it is wonderful to see the sun shining brightly."

Sophia tried to smile, but failed. Everything around her seemed gray. If she had an excuse to stay home, she would. She would sit in Papa's favorite chair in his book-room and try to guess why Charles had pulled away from her on the beach. He had worn such a peculiar expression, and she had seen him glance uneasily at his children.

From the beginning, he had made it clear his children were his first priority. That was how it should be, but she wondered what the children had to do with him kissing her or not.

Maybe the children had nothing to do with it, whispered the small voice of her insecurity. That voice had been silent until Lord Owensly cast her aside publicly. It had followed her home to Meriweather Hall and gradually faded.

Until now.

Charles must have known that she wanted him to kiss her. Though he had mentioned her height, it had been with apparent admiration.

Lord Owensly had been complimentary until he told you that he no longer wanted to be seen with you.

Oh, how she loathed that small voice! Especially when she had no arguments against it.

"I wish Mother was coming with us." Catherine's words drowned out the accusatory ones in Sophia's head. "Both she and Papa always looked forward to the clipping of the church. It will not seem the same without Papa there."

Sophia blinked back tears as she faced Catherine. "It is a beautiful day, and Papa would want us to enjoy it. Every day is a gift from God, and we should rejoice in it."

Catherine wrapped her arms around herself, but bristled. "Why must you sound like the vicar?"

"Mr. Fenwick has helped me understand that I cannot know all the answers." She did not want to argue with her sister, especially when nothing else was right. "I simply must have faith."

"There is nothing simple about that."

"No, there is nothing simple about faith. It is both a gift and a challenge. A gift when everything is going well, a challenge when it is not. But I accept it gladly in both its forms."

Her sister did not reply, which was just as well. Sophia had to keep Catherine from guessing that her cheerfulness was only a mask today.

Sleep had been elusive last night after Michael's nightmare had woken the whole household. Sophia had lingered in the nursery after Michael had gone to sleep. She had reassured Alice that Michael's nightmare was not as a result of something the nursemaid had done or said. The blame was completely Sophia's. The little boy had dreamed of a ferocious dragon chasing him in a runaway carriage, and she was the one who had mentioned the Bridestone that resembled one.

She had assumed Charles would wait outside the nursery, but no one was there when she had emerged. This morning his friends told her that he had eaten a very early breakfast and gone for a ride. He would meet them and the children at church.

At least Lord Owensly had had the decency to end their relationship to her face instead of avoiding her.

Sophia's cheeks hurt from keeping a false smile in place as she walked out of the church. For once she could not recall a single word Mr. Fenwick had preached. Her attention, through the service, had been riveted on where Charles sat in the rearmost pew after arriving a few minutes late. He was the first one out the door at the service's end.

She glanced around the churchyard. If he stood somewhere among the weathered stones or beneath the trees that stretched over the low stone wall and lychgate, she saw no sign of him.

But she kept smiling, because the churchyard was filled with excited children and the parishioners who were eager to enjoy such a beautiful day. Grief further weighed Sophia's heart when she thought of how many years she had spent this day with her parents. Maybe next year her mother would participate again.

Charles and the children will not be here, and you may be married to your cousin. Bother! That small voice was becoming even more annoying with every passing hour. It now prattled almost nonstop as if trying to rival Michael's chatter.

Catherine put her arm around Sophia's waist. "Vera said we could help stack the cuttings so they can dry for tonight's bonfire."

"I thought I would help with the food."

"She already has enough volunteers for that. Cousin Edmund has offered to set up tables, so she is set." She scanned the churchyard.

"Are you looking for someone in particular?"

Catherine's cheeks turned a brighter shade of pink. "Cousin Edmund was wondering where his friends were. I said I would keep an eye out for them."

"There is Mr. Bradby. Over by the back wall." She did not add that it was impossible to miss him in his bright green coat and scarlet waistcoat.

As if she had shouted his name, the tall man strode toward them. He greeted them warmly, then said, "Everyone is bustling about. Will you show me where I can help, Miss Cat—Catherine?"

Sophia's hope that her sister had not guessed he knew her nickname was buoyed when Catherine answered with a broad smile, "Come with me, Mr. Bradby. Cousin Edmund was looking for you, because he has a task that suits you."

"Dare I ask what?"

"You can ask." Catherine dimpled. "However, I cannot answer, because I don't know. He asked me, if I saw you, to tell you and Lord Northbridge to come to the parsonage." She motioned toward the flint house behind the church.

"Northbridge?" He looked around, then at Sophia. "Is he here?"

Sophia shrugged. "I see Gemma and Michael with the other children, so he must be nearby."

"He does lurk around them." Mr. Bradby gave an emoted shudder. "Poor lambs. Guarded by a grumpy old ram."

Catherine chuckled, but Sophia managed no more than her feigned smile.

As her sister and Mr. Bradby walked toward the parsonage, Sophia pondered whether she should ask her cousin more about his tall friend. Her sister seemed quite taken by Mr. Bradby. But Catherine and Mr. Bradby had done little more than chat and laugh together. That was hardly reason to worry that a betrothal was forthcoming.

But you still expect your cousin to ask you to marry, and you and he have talked even less than your sister and Mr. Bradby.

Sophia hoped work would silence that vexing voice, but no matter how many times she gathered up the branches and leaves being cut off the hedges and trees near the church, the voice pursued her. Maybe she should go to the parsonage. Once she was among the other women, conversation might drown out that little voice.

A huge armload of branches walked toward her, so large that she could not see the man carrying them. From behind them, she heard, "I was told to bring these over here. Where do you want them?"

Charles!

Sophia considered scurrying away. He must not have seen her through the branches. She pushed the thought aside and said, "Toss them on top of the others."

He halted in midstep, and some of the branches tumbled to the ground. She said nothing while she picked up the branches and tossed them onto the bonfire stack.

"It is a perfect day for these tasks, isn't it?" he asked as he dropped the rest of the branches on top of the others.

"Yes."

There was silence as he looked everywhere but at her.

She longed to ask him why he had turned away from her yesterday, but feared the answer would be no different from Lord Owensly's rejection. Would it be worse to hear that or to have him keep avoiding her while that dashed little voice taunted her?

"Charles," she said.

"Sophia," he said at the same time.

"You first," they said together.

A fleeting smile raced across his lips, and he offered his arm. She put her fingers on it. Some sensation that had no name rushed through her. The only way she could describe it was that touching him felt right and yet risky, as if she were setting off on a journey she had dreamed of forever but had no idea of the destination.

He led her to a section of the wall where nobody was working. Seating her on it, he clasped his hands behind his back. She recognized the pose as the one he assumed when he had something uncomfortable to say. She prayed she would not cry.

"I have a favor to ask of you," Charles said.

"If I can, I will be glad to comply." Oh, trite words had never tasted so disgusting on her lips.

Suddenly Gemma and Michael ran to them. The children chattered at the same time, and it took several repetitions to understand that they wanted Sophia and their father to come with them. She saw the other children lining up by the church.

"Charles, can this conversation wait until the ceremony is over?" Sophia asked.

He hesitated, then nodded. "If it must."

"C'mon!" shouted Michael. "Want to clip."

Sophia did not wait for Charles to offer his hand to bring her to her feet. She hurried with the children to the end of the line. Telling Gemma to make sure her brother stayed on his feet, Sophia stepped back. She waved to her sister and Cousin Edmund and Mr. Bradby. Vera and Mr. Fenwick were moving along the line, giving last-minute instructions to the children.

The children clasped hands, but there were not quite enough to reach around the church. Shouts went out for family members to step in and complete the circle. When several children called to Sophia, she motioned for her sister, Cousin Edmund and his friends to come with her. Cheers went up as her cousin joined the circle. Herriott flushed, but looked pleased at the enthusiastic welcome for the new Lord Meriweather.

Sophia was unsure if it was by chance or design that she ended up standing between Michael and his father. When Charles took her hand, her resolve to remain cool and aloof melted like butter on a hot pan. He gave it a quick squeeze. Or did he? Maybe he only shifted to take a better hold as the circle contracted, and everyone ran forward toward the church as if to embrace it. They backed away, then repeated the motions twice more. With cheers, the circle broke to surround Mr. Fenwick while he spoke a benediction on the revelers and the church and the parish.

Food was brought out, and the children were allowed to go through the line first. Aromas of freshly cooked chicken and mutton mixed with scents from bowls of vegetables and loaves of steaming bread and a variety of jams and cheeses.

Sophia helped Gemma with her plate while Charles did the same for Michael. As soon as the children were settled on the ground, Charles asked again if he could speak with Sophia.

She nodded. She doubted she could eat because her stomach roiled more with each passing second.

Again he offered his arm. Again, she put her fingers on it, trying not to think that this would be the final time she touched him. Again they walked toward a distant spot along the churchyard wall where nobody was enjoying the feast. Again he sat her on the wall and faced her. Again he clasped his hands behind his back.

She waited.

He cleared his throat, started to speak, then cleared his throat a second time.

"Say what you must," Sophia said, unable to stand the tension any longer.

"All right." His gaze locked with hers. "I don't want you to spend so much time with my children."

She jumped to her feet. "What?" *That* was the last thing she had expected him to say. She had been certain he was going to explain his peculiar actions on the beach. "Have I done something wrong?"

"Quite to the contrary. You have done so much that is clearly right. The children are becoming very attached to you, and that concerns me."

"I never would undermine—"

When his hands took hers between them, everything else she had intended to say fell out of her mind. He stroked her fingers lightly in rhythm with his own words.

"I did not mean to suggest that, Sophia. You have brought smiles to their faces, and they heed you as they heed no one else. But Gemma and Michael have been hurt too many times already in their short lives. First, they lost their mother and then I returned to rip them away from their home." He sighed. "At the time, I only thought of getting them away from the influence of my late wife's family."

"Because they have prejudiced the children against you." She did not make it a question.

"Is it that obvious?"

"Yes, but you should not let that bother you, because you can teach them right from wrong. They are small children who only repeat what they have been taught."

"I regret that they had to listen to such rancor. If I had been there, I might have been able to spare them, but I could not be there and do my duty at the same time. I thought I could make up for the lost time, but I am no longer sure. Not when my son calls out for you after a nightmare."

"Charles, he is a child. You should not let one incident make you think you have failed. Michael calls you Papa now, and it is clear he adores you."

He shook his head and turned away. "But he called for you, and my daughter wants as little to do with me as possible. I need to take my children home where I pray that they can learn to love me as I do them."

Sophia's tears welled at his deep pain. He longed to protect his children from more hurt. Did he suspect that she felt the same about him? The three men seldom even referred to what they had endured on the battlefield, but their silences spoke more eloquently than any words.

She tried to persuade herself that this was for the best. Once she had Cousin Edmund settled in his duties, she would take that grand tour she dreamed of. She had waited so long for a sojourn amidst art and sculpture and beautiful vistas. But recently she had thought little about that journey. Instead her days had been filled with the children and with Charles.

"Are you leaving soon?" she asked.

"I told Herriott that I would stay until after Sir Nigel's assembly. I will not break my word to him, even if it delays us returning home."

His words drove a painful spike through her, but he was being honest. *Would you want him to be any other way?* She wished the little voice would stop.

"You have done the best you could do," Sophia said. "There is nothing else any man can ask of you."

"But God can." He looked away. "I promised Him that if He let me survive, I would be the best possible father any child ever had. He brought me back to them, and now I must do as I vowed."

She put her hand on his cheek and turned his face toward her. His face was rough with low whiskers, and her voice was unsteady when she said, "God knows when we try, and He does not love us less when we fail. As a Father Himself, He knows what an impossible task it is to aspire to His perfection."

"I am relieved that you understand, Sophia."

She wanted to shout that she understood too little. He had said nothing about why he had pulled away from her on the beach. Or was *this* the reason? She was utterly confused.

"I cannot avoid them today," she whispered. "Not unless I leave before the festivities are done."

Charles wanted to take back his request as soon as he heard Sophia's sad words. This had gone wrong. He had hoped to spare his children from grief, and he was creating more for Sophia.

"I never meant to suggest that you avoid them," he said. "Only that you limit the time you spend with them. You have been kind teaching them new games and taking them on adventures by the sea, but I need to do those things with them."

"I will do as you ask."

"Thank you." He had gotten what he wanted, so why did he feel dreadful?

She lowered her eyes that were bright with unshed tears and turned away. "If you will excuse me…" Trembling, she hurried to where her sister talked with Miss Fenwick and two other women.

Charles stamped away in the other direction. He had made a shocking mull of the whole conversation. He had never intended to hurt Sophia, but he knew he had been bamboozling himself when he had thought he could explain without causing her more heartache.

He took no note of where he was walking. If someone spoke to him, he nodded or gave a terse reply. The only conversation he paid attention to was within himself.

Isn't this what I wanted? To keep my children from being hurt again. It should be the only thing that matters. I abandoned them once, and I will not let them feel abandoned again. This is the right choice.

Isn't it?

He gave a wordless growl under his breath. Now he sounded like Herriott, questioning every decision. During battle, there had been no time for second thoughts. Now he had too much time for second thoughts and third and fourth and…

Lord, help me see if I made a mess of the whole of this. I am doing the best I can, but I need Your guidance.

It was a prayer he had repeated many times in the past two years, but never as often as since he had brought the children north.

"Watch where you are walking!" ordered a familiar voice.

Charles stepped aside before he plowed into Bradby who held an armload of branches and twigs even bigger than the one Charles had earlier. His friend's bright clothing glowed in the sunlight. His black boots had lost their usual shine, and his expertly tied cravat was loose.

"Sorry, old cuff," Charles said. "Why are you doing this now? I thought you would be eating."

"I figured I would let the crowd thin." He set the branches on the ground. "Maybe we should move these branches to the top of the cliff. We don't want to burn down the church, because this fire is going to outdo any on Guy Fawkes Night." Bradby put his foot on the pile of branches, ignoring how they cracked beneath his boot. "Why are *you* looking for an excuse to leave the celebration?" His face became serious, reminding Charles of the man he had been when they first met. "Did you have a squabble with Miss Meriweather?"

"No."

"I saw her on my way over here. She looks upset."

"She *is* upset. At me," he quickly added to forestall his friend's next question. "I asked her to spend less time with the children, so I could spend more time with them."

Bradby plucked a long piece of grass and twirled it. "Why not spend time with the children *and* her?"

"It is not that simple."

"No? When you were helping your children with their food, you looked like a happy family."

"She should be spending time with Herriott. Isn't

that the reason we came to Sanctuary Bay? To help him settle in with his new estate and his new bride?"

Bradby looked across the churchyard. "Maybe that is what you and I understood, but I am not sure *he* did." He shook his head with a wry grin. "Herriott seems to be avoiding Miss Meriweather whenever he can. Maybe he doesn't want to be with her while she is with your children, because that might lead the conversation to the topic of *their* children." He put the long piece of grass between his thumbs and blew on it. A sharp whistle cut through the quiet afternoon. Tossing away the grass, he added, "No wonder he is no place to be seen after the charming *tableau* with your children and Miss Meriweather."

"You are reading too much into things."

"Come now, Northbridge. You must have noticed how people have been watching you and the statuesque Sophia. Most of them were smiling."

"If I took note of it, I tried not to think about it."

"That is not like you, Northbridge. When we were on the Continent, you prided yourself on thinking of every possible ramification of any move the French might make."

"The war is over."

"I noticed that." Bradby's smile came and went in the speed of a heartbeat. "I am glad to see that you have figured that out, too."

The familiar anger pressed against his chest, making it hard to breathe. "What is that supposed to mean?"

"You have seen Miss Meriweather as an opponent since she first talked to your children and made them smile. The day we arrived, you declared war." He chuckled. "'The rules of fair play do not apply in love and war,' or so the quote goes."

Charles stared at his friend in astonishment. "Have you lost your mind?"

"No, but I fear you have. You are asking your children to choose between her and you." He gathered up an armful of branches. "Are you sure you are prepared to learn whom they pick?"

"We will be leaving soon, so it will not matter."

"Do you honestly believe that?"

Charles did not. As they walked through the churchyard, he saw Gemma give Sophia an enthusiastic hug before running to join other girls her age. He knew without a doubt that his daughter would gladly go with Sophia and never look back. She truly loved Sophia, and Sophia loved her unconditionally in return.

"I seem to have backed myself into a corner that is nigh to impossible to get out of," Charles said.

"No corner is that impossible to escape."

"Now you sound like a lawyer. Are you going back to practicing the law, solicitor?"

Bradby smiled, but, for once, said nothing.

"What do you suggest?" Charles asked.

"Other than crawling back and begging her to forgive you?"

Charles laughed, surprising himself more than he did Bradby. "All right. I deserved that."

"I would suggest what I have always suggested when you asked my opinion."

"To pray for guidance and listen for God's answer."

Bradby tossed the branches atop the others, then motioned for Charles to follow him to collect more. "I know you are afraid of falling more deeply in love with her."

He considered denying it, then wondered why.

Bradby, in spite of his odd behavior lately, was his good friend. "Have I made myself so obvious to everyone?"

"If you are asking if Herriott knows, I have seen no signs of it." Bradby smiled, his eyes twinkling with abrupt merriment. "To own the truth, Northbridge, I believe he would be more than happy for you to offer for his cousin, so he does not have to decide to do so himself."

"This is no joking matter."

"Matters of the heart seldom are." He became somber again. "Why don't you marry her? You are falling in love with her, and she obviously would make a good mother for your children."

"It is not that simple." He was not about to spill the truth about Lydia's treachery. "I have no wish to remarry. I am only interested in protecting my children from more heartbreak."

His friend considered Charles's words while they carried two more armloads of branches to the stack of wood. As they went to collect more, he said, "Then you should take your leave as soon as possible."

"I promised Herriott that we would stay until after the harvest ball." Charles hefted a large pile. "And I will not break that promise."

"I hope you don't come to regret your decision."

"I won't," Charles said, but why would he expect Bradby to believe his assertion when he did not himself?

Chapter Fourteen

Charles waited in the foyer for Sophia and Gemma. Outside, the carriage was set to take them to Sir Nigel's estate a few miles to the south of Sanctuary Bay. Michael sat on a bench, swinging his feet. His son yawned widely, then tried to conceal it by putting a chubby hand over his mouth. Charles fought a yawn of his own. Last night had been a restless one while horror stalked him through his dreams. After his shouts routed Bradby and Herriott again, his two friends had sat with him and talked about nothing important until the first gray of dawn made it seem safe to seek their beds again.

How many nights had they spent talking in hushed tones while they waited for the morning and the call to battle? He wished he could forget.

Just as he wished he could forget the past fortnight at Meriweather Hall. It had been a study in courtesy. Whenever his path crossed Sophia's, she treated him with the cool graciousness she would any guest. As the days passed, Gemma and Michael started to complain that they missed their outings with Sophia. Those complaints had evolved into whining, and, during the past few days, into weeping. His attempt to protect them had exactly the opposite effect.

He needed to put a halt to the stalemate. The only way he knew how was to follow Bradby's advice. Not about prostrating himself in front of Sophia and begging her forgiveness, even though the thought was tempting. Rather, he prayed for guidance to find the right words as he apologized for ruining the last weeks of their visit to Meriweather Hall.

Even though he had come to that conclusion soon after the clipping of the church, he had not had the opportunity to atone for his silly request. Herriott had insisted the children must see the medieval city of York, and that journey had taken them from Sanctuary Bay and Sophia for almost a week. If his friend thought he was doing Charles a favor, it had been for naught. As they walked through the narrow streets of the oldest part of the city and along the ancient walls, he had been unable to stop thinking how Sophia would have entertained the children and him with stories of the past. Her enthusiasm for everything she saw would have delighted the children…and him.

They had returned only yesterday, and, since then, he had seen Sophia once. She had come to ask if Gemma could get ready for the ball with Sophia and her sister. With his friends nearby, he could not speak of anything else but giving his permission, so the chasm between him and Sophia widened more.

Tonight he would change that. He must. He and the children were leaving within a week, and he did not want to take his departure without healing the wounds he had inflicted on Sophia.

Suddenly Michael crowed, "At last!"

Charles looked up to see Sophia descending the

stairs. Except for a trio of ringlets at her temples, her hair was pulled into a pair of braids that curved into perfect circles at her nape. Pearls were entwined with her braids. No feathers or turban concealed her hair's golden glow.

Like her hair, her white silk gown was elegant. Another string of pearls accented the length of her neck and drew his eyes to her shoulders that were almost bare beneath the wide neckline that dipped in a gentle V in the front. The short sleeves were decorated with a single small ruffle to match the Vandyke along the gown's hem. Gloves rose above her elbows, and a painted fan dropped from a ribbon tied to her left wrist. As she walked down the stairs, tiny pearls glistened beneath her gown. They had been affixed to small bows on her white satin shoes. Over her arm, she carried a fringed white shawl and the silk strings of a reticule.

He stared. He could not help himself, even though he had thought himself unable to be moved by the sight of beauty any longer. He had been sure it was wrung out of him by horror. Yet, as Sophia came down the stairs, one hand holding Gemma's, the other lightly on the bannister, he felt himself come completely alive. Had he been dead until this moment?

"Doesn't your sister look pretty?" Sophia asked Michael as soon as she and Gemma reached the bottom of the stairs.

His son nodded, his eyes wide. He popped his thumb into his mouth again and continued to stare at his sister who wore a pink dress and ribbons of the same color woven through her dark red hair. Her white satin shoes were adorned with tiny pink bows that Sophia must have sewn onto them.

"May I?" asked Charles, offering his left arm to his

daughter who regarded it with uncertainty. He held out the right one to Sophia. When she put her fingers on it and gave Gemma a quick smile, the little girl reached up to take her father's arm.

Sophia's smile lit the foyer, and his heart halted before speeding ahead like clouds scudding before a storm. Her fingertips, light upon his black sleeve, sent heated shivers through him. The words of an apology battered his lips, but he held them back, not wanting to do or say anything to ruin this perfect moment when she stood by his side, gazing up at him with happiness in her vivid green eyes. Even though he guessed her elation had more to do with the children's smiles than his admiration, he was delighted to have her beside him again.

The night was cool, so Charles took a smaller shawl from Sophia and placed it on his daughter's shoulders. He held out his hand for the fringed shawl Sophia was about to fling over her own shoulders.

"May I?" he asked when she paused.

"Certainly. How kind of you!"

He bit back the heated retort burning on his lips. When she had smiled at him, he had dared to believe that the cool courtesy she had shown him for the past fortnight was over. He had been a fool to believe she would forgive him readily.

But he could not stop his flush of pleasure as his fingers brushed Sophia's smooth shoulders. He drew in a deep breath of the lavender that scented her hair and stared at her nape, which was tilted at the perfect angle for his lips to caress it. A quiver raced beneath his fingers. She trembled...or was it him?

Sophia stepped away from him when Michael pointed to the ruffle on her hem and asked a question.

Charles's frantic heartbeat was too loud in his ears for him to hear what his son said.

Stop acting like a youth who is escorting a woman for the first time, he sternly chided himself. It was to no avail, because when Sophia looked at him, his heart pounded harder.

"Where are the others?" she asked as they walked toward his carriage.

Charles was pleased when his voice showed none of his inner turmoil. "They took your carriage because they planned to stop at the Fenwicks' on their way to the ball. Your sister was excited to arrive with her bosom bow."

"I would guess she is not the only excited one among them."

He arched a brow and waited for her to continue, but she turned to warn Michael to stay on the walkway so he did not get dirty. Had she meant the children were excited, or did she speak of her own anticipation of riding with him to Sir Nigel's?

"Dance, dance, dance," chanted Michael as Charles lifted him into the carriage.

Gemma frowned. "I hope he does not repeat that all the way to the ball."

"Or the whole time we are there," Sophia said with a smile.

That brought an answering grin from his daughter as she climbed in and sat beside her brother, and he was amazed at how easily Sophia made the children happy. Then again, he should not be surprised, because he had been much happier himself since she became part of his life.

When he handed her into the carriage, he did not want to release her hand. He yearned for her to turn and tell him that she forgave him and that they could begin anew.

Sophia picked up Michael and put him on the backward facing seat. "Gentlemen, let the ladies ride facing forward."

That brought more giggles from the children, but disappointment flooded Charles's gut, even as he kept his smile in place. He should have known better than to harbor the hope that he could sit beside Sophia while their two young chaperones rode with them.

It was his own doing. His great plan to keep the children from being heartbroken when they left Meriweather Hall had gone wrong. They were as close to Sophia as ever, he had hurt her horribly, and now his heart was doomed to break, as well.

The ballroom was huge and filled to overflowing. Everyone in North Yorkshire must be crammed within its walls. Charles was swept away along with Cousin Edmund to be introduced to their host and to view Sir Nigel's recently finished art. Charles promised to return to Gemma and Michael as quickly as he could, but almost an hour had passed.

With her height, Sophia could get some fresh air in the cramped room, though many breaths she drew in were tainted with odors of sweat and overly strong perfume. The children were not so fortunate. Michael was complaining about the heat. Gemma made a rude comment that had not been—fortunately—overheard by the dowager who inspired it by stepping on Gemma's new slippers, loosening one of the bows.

Sophia took the children to a room that had been set aside for ladies to make minor repairs. One of the household's maids was able to provide her with what she needed to fix the bow on Gemma's shoe. As she bent to her task, the children wandered around the room, peering in drawers and cabinets and pulling faces at themselves in the glass. A woman came into the room, saw the children and made a quick exit.

"Why didn't she come in?" Gemma asked.

"I don't know," Sophia replied, glad that the little girl did not notice how the woman's nose had wrinkled in distaste at the sight of the children. The woman had no idea what she missed by not getting to know Gemma and Michael. Yes, they were rambunctious, but they were warmhearted and curious and intelligent.

Traits they clearly had inherited from their father.

Her hands stilled. She had thought herself prepared to face Charles tonight, but, if the truth be told, she had not been. During the ride to Sir Nigel's estate, she had spent most of her time talking with the children. She had not quibbled when her cousin swept Charles away to join the line of guests walking through the temporary gallery of their host's paintings. Instead she had remained behind with Gemma and Michael.

Putting the mended shoe on Gemma's foot, Sophia forced a smile. She could not remain in the ladies' room. Nor could she hide behind Gemma and Michael while their father was nearby.

Sophia stood and called to the children. They were so intrigued with some ribbons they'd found under a chair that she had to call their names a second time. They left the ribbons and came to take her outstretched hands.

If possible, the ballroom seemed even more crowded when they reentered it. The scores of candles burning in the chandeliers that hung down the middle of the long room brightened the white-and-gold walls, but also made the space stifling. The music had begun, and voices rose over it to be heard.

She found a quiet place for the children to sit so they could watch the dancing. Gemma was fascinated, but Michael began to squirm. Opening her reticule, Sophia drew out a folded page. She bent toward him and read him the short story on the page, then gave him the paper to refold into a variety of shapes. She doubted it would entertain him long. She had also brought a long piece of string for cat's cradle, and she would play that with him if he began to wiggle too much.

She chatted with friends and neighbors who walked past. When the second set began, she smiled when she saw her sister take the floor with one of their neighbors. Vera Fenwick was paired with Mr. Bradby. Cousin Edmund stood up with Sir Nigel's late wife's sister. Sophia scanned every inch of the ballroom, but she did not see Charles. She wondered if he had been cornered by their host who delighted in expounding for hours on the subjects in his paintings.

"Aren't you going to dance, Sophia?" asked Gemma as the dancers began to move with the music.

"A lady must wait to be asked."

"Why has nobody asked you? You are prettier than any other lady here."

Tears threatened to embarrass Sophia, because everyone would assume she wept because none of the men wanted to dance with a woman who towered over them. But these tears filled her eyes because of Gemma's guileless compliment. The children did not deem her odd. They accepted her height as part of who she was. They could not conceive of the fact no man wanted to ask her to stand up with him. To them, she was the woman who loved them exactly as they were, and they returned the favor.

She blinked the tears away as someone stepped between her and her view of the dancers. She looked up to discover the person blocking her view was their host.

Sir Nigel Tresting resembled Father Christmas, because he had white hair, a full belly and was dressed in a forest-green coat and breeches. His waistcoat was a brilliant silver that she would have expected Mr. Bradby to wear.

She came to her feet. "As always, a wonderful assembly, Sir Nigel."

"Ah, Miss Meriweather! Just the person I had hoped to see tonight." Sir Nigel bowed over her hand quickly. Even when he straightened, he was more than a head shorter than she was. "I saw your sister among the dancers, and I had hoped you were in attendance, as well." He chuckled, his belly bouncing. "Who is this handsome young man and charming little lady keeping you company?"

Sophia introduced the children who prettily spoke to their host, though Gemma eyed him with the hint of a frown.

"Is your lovely mother here also?" Sir Nigel asked.

"She has not set aside her mourning."

"I understand." Sorrow looked out of place on his full-cheeked face. "She and your father had one of the true love matches among the *ton*. The loss of your father is one we all suffer, but none as much as Lady Meriweather."

"Thank you for your kind words. I will convey them to her."

"Tell her as well that, if she is agreeable, I will give her a look-in soon." He hooked his thumbs under his lapels. "Other obligations have kept me from calling earlier as I had hoped."

"I will tell her." She smiled, hoping Sir Nigel's visit would be the first of many from their neighbors. Such calls might be the very thing to draw her mother out of her chambers and into the world.

"Perhaps I shall bring her one of my paintings to cheer her."

"That would be lovely," she said, even though she suspected Sir Nigel's work would never be displayed in her mother's elegant rooms. "Did you do landscapes or seascapes this year?"

"Seascapes. Moon-shadowed ones, for the most part." He gave her a roguish grin. "I am sure that does not surprise you, Miss Meriweather."

Before she could blurt that she had no idea what he meant, a footman rushed up and whispered something to Sir Nigel. Her host's face grew taut, so different from his usual good humor. He waved the footman away, took a moment to ask her to excuse him and rushed away at a speed she had not guessed a man of his girth could attain.

"I don't like him," Gemma said loudly enough to cause nearby heads to turn.

Not wanting to scold the child for her unthinking words when many could overhear, Sophia told the children to come with her. She went through the first open doorway she found, making sure both children came with her. She breathed a sigh of relief when she saw the stone terrace was empty. The only light came from the ballroom, because no moon hung among the hundreds of stars. Leading the children to a long, low stone bench, she sat with them.

"I am bored," Gemma said before Sophia could remind her of her manners. "I thought balls were supposed to be wonderful."

"They are," Sophia replied. "If you are there to catch up on gossip or to flirt."

"Flirt?" asked Michael, as always all ears. "What is that? Like flying?" He flapped his arms wildly.

Sophia caught his hands and lowered them to his sides before one struck her or his sister.

Gemma raised her chin and said, "Silly! Flirting is what a lady does when she wants a man to kiss her." She stood and waved an imaginary fan. In a simpering tone, she cooed, "Oooh, my lord, you are such a dear to say that. Let me give you a kiss."

"Who taught you that?" asked Sophia, trying not to laugh at the little girl. Her imitation was close to the actions of some women Sophia had seen in London during her brief Season.

"No one," Gemma said proudly. "I learned by watching Mama. She got lots of kisses from men who came to our house."

Sophia choked back her shocked gasp as Gemma prattled on innocently about her mother's far-from-innocent encounters. Praying that the little girl had misunderstood what she had seen and that Lady Northbridge had been faithful to her husband, Sophia reminded herself of the other times the children had misconstrued what they had witnessed.

Lord, let this be like the other times, she prayed, but she feared it was not.

Charles's own words burst from her memory. *We are too much the same. Hurt too deeply to see anything but potential pain in every word and action, Sophia.* She had asked him who had hurt him, and he had given her no answer.

Had it been his wife? His partner in what his friends believed was a perfect marriage filled with love and devotion?

Sophia hoped her smile did not look as hideous as it felt. "Listen to the music. Didn't we come here to dance?"

The children grasped her hands, and she stood to let them spin around her. She wished she could share their pure joy with the music. They released her hands and hooked arms as they pranced around the terrace, completely immersed in their fun. When the music ended, they dropped to sit, panting. They were on their feet and twirling with the first note of the next set.

Where was Charles? It was unlike him to leave his children for long. Someone other than Sir Nigel must have delayed him from returning. But who?

Her heart leaped when a tall man emerged from one of the doorways and walked toward her. Charles? Had he come to look for his children? Had he come to look for *her?* When the man was a few steps from her, hope withered inside her as she recognized her cousin.

"I thought you might like something to quench your thirst." Cousin Edmund held out a small glass of lemonade and then handed two cups to the children. "Your sister is wondering where you are."

"It was stifling and stuffy in there, so I thought the children would enjoy themselves more out here. Thank you for bringing us something to drink, but do not feel that you have to keep us company." She smiled. "I saw you and Mrs. Goodman cutting papers in that lively dance earlier. Few can keep up with her, but you made a good show."

He glanced at the children, who had gulped down

their lemonade. "They still look thirsty. Don't you think so?"

Sophia guessed he did not want Gemma and Michael to hear what he had to say next. She asked the children if they wanted more lemonade. When they gave an eager yes, Cousin Edmund gave them directions to where they could find it only a few feet from the doorway.

"You will find chairs to sit on that will be more comfortable than this chilly bench," he added.

"Want to dance with Sophia," announced Michael.

"And we will dance more," she assured him. "While you drink your lemonade, I will speak with Lord Meriweather. I will be inside soon to get you, and then we will dance more. Does that sound like fun?"

"Yes!" Michael shouted as he ran after his sister who took his hand before they went into the ballroom.

"Where is Northbridge?" her cousin asked the moment the children stepped inside.

Sophia stood. "I was going to ask you the same thing. I have not seen him since you took him to meet Sir Nigel."

"He had little interest in what our host calls paintings. Nor did I. Most of them looked as if they had been caught in the rain. I assumed Northbridge would look for the children and you as soon as he excused himself."

"We have seen no sign of him."

Cousin Edmund sighed. "Maybe he fell asleep somewhere. He had another bad night." He leaned one hand on the low stone wall and stared out into the darkness. "What are those lights?"

Sophia looked where he pointed, and she saw small pinpoints of light slowly rising and falling far out in the sea. "Fishermen in their cobles."

"Or smugglers?"

She nodded. "That is possible. With the local peerage and gentry being entertained by Sir Nigel, it is the perfect night for them to be about their nefarious business."

"Should we alert the authorities? The constable can be waiting when they return."

"One man against a half dozen or more?" She wrapped her arms around herself to keep out the sudden chill. "Hardly a fair fight, and it is altogether possible that the constable is allied with the smugglers. But enough about smugglers. You said Charles had a bad night, and you look like you got no sleep yourself."

"None of us did." He rubbed his eyes with his knuckles as if he were no older than Michael. "When Charles has one of his nightmares, he can wake the dead with his shouts." His face blanched in the moonlight. "Maybe he is hoping to bring back the dead who fell in battle."

"Nightmares? Like Michael's?"

He drew in a deep breath, then let it sift out through his clenched teeth. "Not exactly."

Sophia put a calming hand on her cousin's arm, which quivered like a sapling in a high wind. He looked down at her hand, then up at her as if he could not believe she would touch him. When she asked him to explain about Charles's nightmares, he nodded.

It was as if she had loosened a dam. He began to relate what Charles endured in his nightmares, talking faster and faster until she struggled to understand him. She listened, shocked that the stern, composed Lord Northbridge shattered inside his dreams. Edmund revealed that it was not the first time Charles had acted so, waking them with his shouts and being found nearly bound to his bed by sheets and blankets from his fighting whatever filled his nightmares. He did not know the exact events in the nightmare, but he had seen the results.

As Cousin Edmund became more agitated, Sophia guided him to the bench. He remained sitting when she perched beside him and gestured for him to continue.

"Thank you for telling me," Sophia said when he was done. She wondered how Charles had managed to hide his horror from everyone but his two closest friends. No wonder he kept a crusty exterior in place. It allowed him to conceal his suffering.

"I thought you should know." He jabbed his toe at the edge of a stone in the terrace. "Since he met you, he has been less volatile."

"Less? Really?"

His smile was weary. "Yes, really. When we first met, he was the most even-tempered man I had ever met. Even if everyone else was discomposed, Northbridge was serene. It was a trait we admired. We asked him how he could remain unperturbed by the chaos around us. He told us that he was blessed by a strong faith and a strong marriage."

"What changed?"

"Each time we faced Napoleon's men," he said, his voice again unsteady, "it was as if the battle went on and on inside of him."

Sophia guessed Charles was not the only one haunted by what had happened. Her cousin's face was drawn, and she saw lines in it that she had never noticed before.

"We first believed," Edmund went on, "that the fury of the fight lingered within him. That is not unusual among the soldiers, and other men were quick to anger in the hours after the fighting ceased. He never got into fisticuffs as some did, and his temper diminished quickly. We were exhausted and drained from the battle, so we gave each other leniency in such matters.

"Then, he took leave to go home for a fortnight. His wife had sent letter after letter pleading with him to come to her, and he did as soon as he could. Something must have happened, because a short time after he returned, his temperament had changed."

"How?" she asked.

He sighed and pushed himself to his feet. "Where before he had been filled with anger after a battle, he became as cross as crabs all the time. He would rip and tear into anyone for the slightest reason. Or no reason." His gaze turned inward.

Sophia guessed he was recalling a specific occasion.

"But," Cousin Edmund said, his good cheer returning, "since we arrived at Meriweather Hall, he has been much more forgiving of us."

"But he cannot forgive himself."

"For not being there when Michael was born and Lydia died." He kneaded his hands together. "He and Lydia seldom quarreled, and they adored each other." He shook his head. "But maybe all was not as it appeared. Obviously some rift had opened between them, a rift he blamed himself for. When she wrote to tell him she was going to have a baby, he seemed to withdraw more and more into himself. Except when his temper exploded out at the slightest provocation."

"You don't know what happened?"

His mouth twisted. "No, but not through lack of trying. Both Bradby and I asked him several times quite bluntly. Each time, he told us quite bluntly to mind our own business."

"Thank you for telling me what you can," she said and put her arms around him for a quick hug.

He looked startled at her action, then smiled. Not the smile of a man who wanted to marry her, but the smile of a man who could become a good friend as well as a beloved cousin. She hoped that was what he would be for many more years to come.

Chapter Fifteen

Charles wished he had not come to Sir Nigel's assembly. First he was dragged away to look at what had to be the worst paintings he had ever seen. The canvases were gritty with sand and salt, and he guessed Gemma would be more skilled with a paintbrush. He had made excuse after excuse to try to leave Sir Nigel to his admiring devotees. Finally when their host was expounding at length to a group of elderly ladies who crowded around him, Charles had slipped away to return to the ballroom.

There a gauntlet of mamas with marriageable daughters awaited him. One, a lady whose name he had forgotten as soon as he heard it, refused to accept no for an answer when she asked him to dance with her daughter, a simpering chit who giggled each time he looked at her. She did not stop tittering through the whole set, and she had clutched on to his hand longer than the dance allowed, nearly ruining the pattern several times. The other dancers had given him cool frowns.

He would have thought his apparent clumsiness a way to escape from the dance floor, but another matchmaking mama latched on to him and introduced him to her daughter. This young woman was charming and did not giggle. Under other circumstances, he would have enjoyed footing it with her.

But he wanted to find Sophia and have the conversation that was far too overdue. He searched the ballroom. No sign of her or the children. Where could they be? By his third circuit of the ballroom and evading a few other women intent on catching his attention, he was thoroughly discouraged. Sophia would not have gone home without leaving a message for him, would she?

Charles stopped a footman and asked if he had seen Sophia. He had not. Charles intercepted another footman and asked the same question. He got the same answer. Finally the fifth footman mentioned seeing Miss Meriweather on the terrace with a man, but not the children.

"Who?" he demanded before he could halt himself. The strength of his jealousy drew Charles up short.

The footman shrugged. "I did not recognize the man. Not too tall, well-dressed. I saw him with you and Sir Nigel earlier."

That description soothed him. The footman must have seen her with Herriott.

Thanking the footman, he hurried toward the door the footman had pointed to as the quickest route to the terrace. He ignored the calls of his name and even the woman who planted herself directly in his path. He swerved around her, greeting her politely and continuing on his way.

Charles emerged from the ballroom and onto the terrace. He halted at the lovely sight of Sophia whirling his children about in a simple country dance. Even Michael had mastered a few steps and kept pace with his sister and Sophia. She spun Gemma around gently, then did the same for Michael. Both children laughed with excitement before they caught sight of him. Michael rushed to fling his arms around Charles's legs, but Gemma remained by Sophia.

Both his daughter and Sophia watched him with wary eyes as he walked toward them, but Sophia said, "You are welcome to join us, Charles."

"That sounds like a wonderful idea." He bowed first to her, then to Gemma. "Ladies, may I have the pleasure?"

"Me, too?" piped up Michael, dipping his head as his father had.

"Certainly you, too," Sophia said before he could reply. "But a gentleman doesn't bow quite like that to another gentleman. Only to a lady."

"And this is how a gentleman greets a special lady," Charles said. Taking her hand, he raised it to his lips. His gaze held hers while he kissed her knuckles. Her eyes softened, and he longed to lose himself within them.

She started to withdraw her hand and turn toward the children, but he flipped her fingers over. Slowly, not relinquishing her gaze, he drew off her glove. Her fingers quivered as he tossed the glove toward the children.

"And this, son," he said, his voice as ragged as her breathing, "is how a gentleman greets a *very* special lady."

He pressed his mouth to her palm. Her quick intake of breath sent shivers along him. Not icy shivers, but heated ones. He drew in the scent of her skin as his mouth roved from her palm to her fingertips. Her other hand curved along his face as he raised his eyes to see the yearning in hers. A yearning only he could satisfy with his lips on hers.

"Let me!" shouted Michael.

For a moment he considered ignoring his son as he had the eager mamas in the ballroom. Then Sophia, with an apologetic glance toward him, held out her other hand to his son. Did she guess how he longed to send the children away so he could be alone with her long enough for one kiss, though he knew he wanted more than a single kiss?

Music rippled outward from the ballroom, and he asked, "Do you waltz, Sophia?"

"I have, but only with my sister." She grinned, setting her eyes to twinkling like the stars overhead. "And I led."

"May I—and I alone—have this next dance, Sophia? You may lead if that makes it easier for you."

"No, I will leave that to you, but remember that is my excuse if I step on your toes."

"That will not happen, for you are always graceful."

Sophia started to give Charles a sassy retort, but she paused when she saw the intensity of his expression. It was almost identical to when they had stood on the beach two weeks ago, and she had believed he would kiss her. If she had the sense God gave a goose, she would turn and run, but she took her glove from Michael and drew it on before she raised her hand to place it in his father's.

The texture of his gloves was far smoother than his palm, but the heat of his skin oozed through his gloves and hers. When he put his hand at the back of her waist, she stepped closer. She settled her other hand on his broad shoulder as she gazed up into his dark eyes. He turned her into the waltz, and her feet followed his as if she had danced with him countless times.

As she had in her dreams.

Twirling in his arms from illumination to shadow and back, she watched light play across the stern angles of his face. He possessed a stark beauty that amazed her, for she never had considered that a man might be beautiful or make her feel beautiful as his eyes held hers. His eyes glittered as they caught the candles' glow and sent that flame spiraling along her. When he drew her even closer, she leaned her head against his broad shoulder. It was, she was thrilled to discover, exactly the perfect height for her.

"I hear," he murmured, "that I am not the first man you have been seen with here on the terrace tonight. Have you changed your mind about your cousin?"

"Yes." When he tensed, she hurried to add, "I have changed my mind after realizing what a good man he is. I think we could be very good friends."

"Nothing more?"

"You know I have a duty to my family." She missed a step, but he drew her into the pattern.

"Forgive me, Sophia," he whispered. "I should not have asked that question."

"You are forgiven, of course."

"Will you forgive me again for what I said to you during the clipping of the church?"

She tilted her head so she could see his face. "You need not apologize. Your request on behalf of the children was reasonable. I do not want them hurt either."

"That is not why I am apologizing." He grimaced when she arched her brows. "All right. It is part of the reason why I need to apologize. In my fervor to keep my children from being hurt, I wounded you. I let you think that I did not want you in their lives. Or in mine."

"And you do?"

"Yes." His lips brushed her forehead.

Suffused with joy, she rested her cheek against him again. Charles and the children would be leaving Meriweather Hall soon, but that could not change her feelings.

She loved him.

So simple, and yet it complicated everything. How could she marry Edmund, if her cousin asked her, when she was in love with his best friend?

"Thank you for keeping them entertained tonight when I could not," Charles said as he, Sophia, and the children were driven toward Meriweather Hall. He sat beside her because the children were curled up on the other seat, sound asleep. In the dim light of a small lantern in the carriage, Gemma snored lightly, and Michael sucked his thumb.

Sophia heard the regret amidst his gratitude. Even though both of them would have preferred spending the night dancing beneath the stars, it had been impossible. Too many people wanted to meet the dashing war heroes, and dozens of toasts had been drunk to their health. Many women wanted to dance with Charles and his friends. Sophia had been consigned to the sidelines along with her sister and Vera. Catherine and the pastor's sister had a few invitations to dance, but they chose to remain with her.

"The children had a wonderful time," she said quietly, so she did not disturb Gemma and Michael.

Charles laughed, the sound low and husky. "So wonderful that, for once, Nurse Alice will not have to coerce them into bed. Maybe I should let you take them dancing every evening."

"I suspect they soon would become bored."

"Dancing with you? I doubt that." He lifted a strand of her hair from her shoulder and slid it behind her ear.

She shivered as his touch set off a firestorm within her. When he reached for another loose tress, she grasped his finger. Her motion shocked her as much as it had him, if she were to judge from how his eyes narrowed slightly. Did he think he could hide his thoughts from her like that? No longer. His touch connected them in a way that words could not express.

Slowly she drew his finger down and enfolded it between her hands. She gazed into his shadowed eyes, wondering if even a lifetime would be enough to explore the secrets within them.

"Sophia…" A yawn interrupted him. "Forgive me. I am not suffering the least bit of ennui, but rather from fatigue. It is exhausting playing the triumphant hero and meeting everyone's expectations."

"Especially when you did not sleep well last night. I am sorry a bugaboo intruded on your sleep."

"Bugaboo?" he asked, drawing her head down to his shoulder.

"It is a silly word that means someone has had a nightmare." Sophia nestled closer to him. "I know there was probably nothing silly about a nightmare."

"No one can control what appears in a dream." Charles started to shrug, then stopped, not wanting to push Sophia away when she was where he longed for her to be.

"Or a nightmare."

"You *were* there."

She drew back, and, in the dim light, her pretty face showed her bafflement. "Where?"

"The first night I had a nightmare at Meriweather Hall, you…" He let his voice trail away, realizing that she would have said something before now if she had come into his room with his friends that night.

"We never heard a thing in the family's wing that night or last night. I am glad that Mr. Bradby did hear you and fetched Cousin Edmund," she said, her smile returning.

Disappointment dropped like a lead weight into his belly. Then he asked himself why he had wanted her to be there, to witness the mewling mess he was when the war burst into his dreams. The answer came quickly. If she had seen that and had not turned away from him, maybe she cared for him. Truly cared for him, not pretending as Lydia had.

He frowned as his fist tightened on the door. "How do you know about my nightmares?"

"Cousin Edmund told me."

He was astounded that Herriott had blown the gaff about Charles's nightmare. He would have guessed Bradby would be the one who could not keep the secret to himself.

"He is a good friend," she added.

"I agree, which is why neither Bradby nor I hesitated when Herriott asked us to come to North Yorkshire." He ran the back of his fingers along her soft cheek. "And I am glad we did."

She leaned away from his touch. "Do not try to distract me," she said, slightly breathless.

Was that what he was doing? He did not want to talk about his nightmares when he had Sophia to himself with only his sleeping children as chaperones.

"Why are you embarrassed by your nightmares?" she asked.

Embarrassed? No, he felt anger, frustration, disappointment, terror.

"I am not embarrassed."

"Really?" she fired back. "I have noticed that, if I ask you something that you would prefer not to answer, you try to distract me. You do the same thing with your children and your friends. It is as if you believe that by you distracting us, we will forget what we have asked." Sadness crept into her voice. "But those who truly care about you don't forget, Charles, because you cannot."

He hung his head. "I wish I could. I had hoped leaving everything familiar to come here would clear my mind."

"Cousin Edmund thinks that it has."

Could she surprise him any further tonight?

She took his hand and folded it between hers again. "What I told Michael holds true for you. If you talk about what you experienced in your nightmare, you will come to see that it is not as frightening as you believed when in its throes."

"It is not the same."

"No? Your son told me that he dreamed in part about being in the out-of-control carriage again, and you dreamed about something out of control during the war. I see no difference."

"That is because you don't know what I dream."

"You could tell me. Your son trusts me enough to tell me. Do you?"

Yes, called out his heart, but that part of him was too trusting. It had trusted Lydia until she had paraded the truth in front of him.

She stroked his hand as she had Michael's back when

a nightmare had woken his son. Gently, offering solace
and a reminder that she was willing to listen. No matter what he had to say.

"Your son," she whispered, "regrets what he did so
much that he dreamed about it. We all have regrets."
Even though he could not see her face well, he heard the
sorrow in her voice. "If you did something…"

"It is nothing I did, but something I was asked to do
and could not do."

She waited, but when he added nothing more, she
asked, "If you had to make the same choice again,
would you?"

"Yes!" His shout routed the children, but they snuggled into the seat and went to sleep when Sophia blew
out the lantern. Lowering his voice, he said, "Not that
it mattered. The man died anyhow."

She gasped.

"I am sorry, Sophia. There are some things not meant
for your gentle ears."

When Sophia sat straighter and put her hands on
either side of his face so he could not look away from
her, Charles was astounded. He could not see her features, but he sensed her tension and her gentle concern
through her fingertips.

"Charles," she whispered, "tell me please about those
battles you still fight in your dreams. I want to understand."

He was certain he could never explain about the
sights and the smells and the appalling sounds of a
battlefield, but once he began talking, he could not halt
himself. Her fingers laced through his, and she became
his only anchor to the present. It was, he realized, the
first time that he had spoken of the cannon blasts and
the gunfire and the smoke and the reek of death with

anyone. Even when he sat with Herriott and Bradby, they spoke of the other aspects of the military life. Bad food, sore feet, stupid and conflicting orders, language problems with troops from the other allied countries.

Until she put her arms around him, he did not realize he was quaking as if with a great fever. She drew his head to the silk shawl covering her shoulder and held him as tenderly as she had his son. He kept talking and talking, and she let him go on. He doubted he could stop. The words of pain and grief and the utter senselessness of one man surviving while another was killed poured from him.

The carriage slowed, and bright light burst into it. Charles raised his head to stare at the front door of Meriweather Hall. In astonishment he realized his daughter had squeezed in on his other side while Michael sat on the floor, clinging to Charles's leg.

Neither of them spoke nor did Sophia who had tears coursing down her cheeks. Her shawl was damp where his face had rested, and he touched his own face to find it wet, too.

A footman opened the carriage door, and Sophia let him hand her out. She guided the children to the ground. She kissed Gemma and Michael on the cheek and wished them a good night's sleep before asking the footman to take them up to the nursery. Only then did she look at Charles.

He got out of the carriage and motioned for the coachee to take it to the stable. He was about to offer his arm to Sophia when she took it with both hands and guided him into the house. She steered him into the formal parlor where they had first met.

Candles lit the middle of the room, but the edges

were in darkness. She took off her shawl and folded it over a chair.

"Can I ring for something for you?" she asked.

"No…thank you." His voice sounded raw and un-steady as it did in his nightmare.

"Is there anything else I can do for you?"

Tell me that you love me. Me, the half-ruined man who is struggling to continue to pretend that nothing has changed.

He shook his head, too drained to speak his thoughts aloud when she might say only that she had her duty to Herriott and her family.

"Well, then, I will wish you a good and peaceful night's sleep," she said, backing toward the door. "Don't forget that we will be leaving shortly after midday for the moors and our visit to the Bridestones."

He nodded.

She turned to leave, then rushed back to him to press her lips against his cheek as she had his children. Be-fore he could draw her into his arms, she was gone, her light steps fading up the stairs.

He came to his feet to go after her, but slowly sat again. He rested his elbows on his knees and stared across the room. She had listened to his babbling and let him fall apart in her embrace. She had cried with him and for him. She had been willing to sit longer with him and listen to whatever else he had to say. She had gazed at him with a longing that told him she wanted him to kiss her soft lips. She had found a special place in his heart, which begged him to tell her that he loved her be-fore she accepted an offer of marriage from her cousin.

But he had sent her away because he had not been

able to disclose the darkest secret that haunted him more than his nightmares. How would he ever be able to trust his heart's desires after Lydia had made a mockery of it?

Chapter Sixteen

The second day of the long ride to the Bridestones at the far eastern end of the moors had begun before dawn. Yesterday, after leaving Meriweather Hall shortly after midday, the travelers had stopped at a country inn with enough rooms for them. Sophia shared a room with her sister and Miss Fenwick. The children had small cots in Charles's room, and Cousin Edmund and Mr. Bradby took the last available room. After a cold supper, Sophia had sought her bed at the same time the children had.

Charles suspected sitting in the carriage and doing nothing but bounce as the wheels found yet another chuckhole was exhausting and boring. By last evening even Miss Catherine and Miss Fenwick had run out of things to talk about, and the children had complained about being shut up in the carriage again this morning.

How much better to ride with his friends! Herriott and Bradby laughed and joked and seemed completely carefree. Charles joined in, glad to leave regret and grief behind at Meriweather Hall.

Thank you, Lord, for this good day. I pray it stays filled with joy.

When the carriage rolled to a stop at the base of a wooded hill early that afternoon, Sophia jumped to the ground on her own. She helped the children down and stepped aside when Herriott offered his hand to her sister and Miss Fenwick.

Charles tied his horse to the rear of the carriage, then stepped aside to let Herriott and Bradby do the same. He came around the carriage to where Sophia stood. She returned his smile as she had often, but there was a connection between them now that he could not ignore. Not that he wanted to.

"Where are these amazing stones?" he asked. "All I see are trees."

"Beyond the wood. This way." She pointed up the hill.

Bradby groaned. "Once we should try going somewhere where we can walk downhill."

"It will be downhill on the way back." Sophia laughed.

"And it was downhill in the village," Herriott added, coming to join them.

Rolling his eyes as if he were no older than Gemma, Bradby said, "But that was so steep going down, it was as difficult as going up. You almost knocked Miss Fenwick off her feet because you were skidding down the street."

Herriott laughed. "I will endeavor, Miss Fenwick, not to stumble over my feet into you on either the way up or the way down."

"You are not the first to run into someone on those steep streets," Miss Fenwick said with a warm smile. "Nor, I assume, will you be the last."

"Can we see the stones?" asked Gemma impatiently.

"Come with me." Sophia led the way into the trees

on a narrow path that was edged on both sides by knee-high grass. She held Gemma's hand, so his daughter walked right behind her.

Charles followed, enjoying the gentle sway of Sophia's skirt. He smiled when Michael grabbed his hand and began babbling about everything that interested him, which was...everything. The others passed him as his son asked why the insects whined and why butterflies chose one flower and not another. Charles gave him what answers he could and enjoyed his son's enthusiasm.

Michael gave an excited shout and pointed at the ground. A pair of slugs oozed away from his feet.

"Ugh!" Gemma cried, when she peered down at the dark brown slugs.

"Can I take them home?" Michael asked at the same moment.

"Let's let them explore while we explore," Charles said.

His son nodded and skipped on ahead. Gemma hurried to catch up with him.

"That was the perfect reply," Sophia said as he strode toward where she stood. The others had continued up the hill along the winding path. "I heard the questions Michael was asking, and you answered each one as if it were the most important question in the world. Children appreciate that."

"I have had a good teacher."

Sophia placed her hand on Charles's proffered arm. She was happy to see his smile and to touch him, even this chastely. After everything he and his friends had suffered, they deserved to be happy. She would have liked to hold on to his arm all the way to the top of the hill, but in a few steps the trail narrowed again between the trees. She promised herself that there would be time later for them to talk privately. She was not sure when, but maybe when they stopped for the night on their return to Meriweather Hall.

"A little farther," Sophia said when Mr. Bradby groused about the steep hill. "It will be worth the walk."

"To see big stones?" His mouth twisted in a crooked smile. "I normally would not cross the street to look at stones."

"These are not normal stones. The ones on this side of the beck are astounding, but the ones on the far side are even more fascinating. Wait until you see them!"

He grumbled something more, but kept walking.

Charles chuckled behind her. "Bradby always likes to have the last word."

"And today those words will be thanking us for bringing him here."

"Don't be certain of that." He laughed again.

She savored that sound before Gemma tugged on her hand. When Sophia inquired what the little girl wanted, Gemma asked, "Can we see your cottage?"

"My cottage? I don't know what you mean, sweetheart," she replied.

"*Your* cottage," Gemma said as if repeating the words would make them clearer. "In the wood."

Charles put his hand on his daughter's shoulder. When she wiggled away from him, the light dimmed in his eyes. Sophia wanted to console him by reminding him that at least Gemma was not spitting some sharp retort at him today.

"I told them about your dower cottage after you and I visited there," he said with an apologetic smile. "Michael wanted to know why my boots were covered with mud and leaves."

"Oh, now I understand," Sophia said in her brightest voice. "My cottage is not here."

"But this is a wood," Gemma insisted.

"Yes, but not the wood where the dower cottage is. That is closer to Meriweather Hall."

"Can we see it?"

Sophia grimaced. "You would not like it. The roof is falling in, and I suspect there are bats in the rafters."

Michael whirled around. "Bats?"

Charles herded his son up the path and laughed. "Now you have done it, Sophia. Anything that is creepy and crawls or slithers or flies intrigues my son." He ruffled his son's hair. "Wait until you see the folly at Northbridge Castle at twilight. There will be enough bats even for you!"

"Look, Papa!" Michael had already forgotten about the bats as he pointed at the grass and something else that interested him.

Grabbing Charles's hand, Michael pulled him up the hill. Gemma raced after them, not wanting to miss anything.

Sophia watched the family together. They had shared so much sadness. It was wonderful to see them happy together. Even Gemma had set aside her contentious tone and was now almost dancing in her eagerness to get Charles's attention, something Sophia had never seen her do before. Sophia had urged Charles to have patience with his daughter, and maybe Gemma was finally willing to forgive him for leaving.

"Thank you, God," she said quietly, even though she wanted to shout her praise from the hilltop.

"You look happy," her sister said as she drew even with Sophia. "I bet I can guess why."

"I am sure anyone could." She glanced around. "Where is Vera?"

"With Cousin Edmund and Mr. Bradby." Her voice dropped to a conspiratorial whisper. "Why didn't you tell me?"

Sophia tore her eyes from where Gemma was picking flowers and handing them to Charles. "About what?"

"You and Cousin Edmund." She slanted toward Sophia, and her voice grew even quieter. "Out on the terrace during Sir Nigel's ball. Mr. Bradby told me that it took all his considerable charm to persuade some of the gabble-mongers that you embracing our cousin was not a guarantee of an impending betrothal."

"What?" Sophia squeaked.

The others looked over their shoulders, and she motioned for them to keep going.

She had not guessed that anyone had seen her hug her cousin. She thought about the ball and how people had glanced at her with smiles after she came into the ballroom with Charles and the children. She had assumed the other guests were pleased at how well behaved the children were upon their return to the party. How naive of her! In the small circle of the *ton* in North Yorkshire, any tidbit of gossip was treasured and swiftly shared.

Did Charles know about that embrace? If so, he had said nothing of it. There had been plenty of opportunity during the evening and in the carriage before they spoke of his nightmares. Then she thought of how he had not asked her to sit with him any longer in the formal parlor. If he had heard the talk…

But he offered you his arm while you were climbing the hill, argued her heart. Common sense reminded her that Charles was a gentleman, and his offer might have been only courtesy.

Sophia paused when Catherine called for her to wait. Lost in her thoughts, she had not noticed that her sister had stopped.

Catherine shook her foot and grimaced. "A stone in my shoe." She leaned against a tree. "I never thought I would say this, Sophia, but I cannot wait for you to marry Cousin Edmund." Catherine took off her boot, tilted it and shook out the pebble. "It was fun to dance at Sir Nigel's and to laugh and to share the latest *on-dits*."

"A wedding is not simply for fun."

"It is when it is someone else's wedding." Catherine laughed as she drew her boot onto her foot.

Sophia looked away. She could not chide Catherine for her words, because they were true.

"You have certainly changed your mind about Cousin Edmund," Sophia said. "You seem to like him better."

"It is not how *I* feel about him. Will you marry Cousin Edmund? Surely you must intend to if you let him embrace you in a public place."

"It was not like that."

"Then what was it? Why did you hug him?"

Lying was abhorrent, but how could Sophia tell her sister the truth? Neither Cousin Edmund nor Charles had asked that she say nothing about Charles's appalling nightmares, but revealing the truth seemed wrong.

"I was grateful that he guessed the children and I were thirsty, and he brought us lemonade." That was a feeble excuse, and she wished she had not said it.

When her sister nodded and smiled, Sophia could not believe that Catherine had swallowed such a tale. Yes, it was true, but it was not the reason she had embraced her cousin.

"But don't you see, Sophia?" Catherine tested her right foot by putting weight on it. Satisfied that there were no other stones in her boot, she added, "Such attentive behavior is the first step toward showing you how he feels."

"Then let us take it one step at a time."

Catherine smiled and looped her arm through Sophia's, so they could walk together. Her sister continued to talk, but Sophia did not hear a single word.

Heavenly Father, she prayed. *You know my heart better than I know it myself. You know Charles's heart and Edmund's, as well. If there is a way for Charles to know the love in my heart, I pray that You let him discover it. If it is meant that I be Edmund's bride, please help me find a way to accept Your will.*

She added the last because she knew how difficult it would be. For the first time that day, she thought of how Charles and the children would be leaving soon. Her life and her heart would be empty. Tears rose in her eyes, and she was glad her bonnet shadowed her face.

Ahead of her, Sophia heard gasps of amazement when the others caught sight of the bizarre rock formations at the top of the hill. She pushed aside her dreary thoughts and followed them out of the wood.

The great chunks of stone stood in an irregular line along the top of the hill. A narrow beck cut through a ravine on the far side of the stones. Across it, like a warped reflection in a glass, more of the gigantic formations stood, each one unique. They appeared pale brown from a distance, but as she walked closer, she saw darker sections where water and dirt had gathered.

The closest Bridestone resembled a spindle standing on its tip, frozen at the exact moment the top fibers were caught by the wind and pulled to the left. So narrow at the bottom, it looked as if it would fall over at any moment.

As Cousin Edmund went forward to examine it, the children raced to the next Bridestone that was more than eight feet tall.

"This one looks like a cake that fell out of the oven," called Gemma, running her hands along the layers of stone compressed one atop another. "There are flowers growing out of its side." She plucked the blossoms before running around the rock.

"More stones!" Michael jumped up and down. He pointed to other strangely shaped rocks along the ridge. "More stones! Go see more stones."

"We will see them all," Charles said. "Together."

"But, Papa—"

"Michael, we will see them all. First the ones on this side of the beck, then the others."

The little boy drew in a deep breath, and Sophia guessed it would come out in a loud protest. His sister spoke before he could.

"But Sophia said the most interesting stones are over there," argued Gemma, emerging from the far side of the rock with a handful of flowers.

"And," Sophia said, "we will visit them together. I will make sure you see the one that looks like the head of a dragon. I know some old stories about these stones. If you would like, I shall tell you those tales as we walk along."

The children exchanged a frustrated glance, then nodded.

"Good." Sophia offered her hands to the children. "Take your time here, gentlemen. Catherine, Vera, you know the path down to the beck. We won't go across it until you get there."

"Dragon! Dragon! Dragon!" chanted Michael.

With a smile, Sophia led them along the faint path

between the great stones. The children explored each rock before running to the next one. She told them how once the hill must have been much higher and the rocks were hidden before water washed the soil away. That did not interest them as much as the odd shapes, so she let them devise their own stories about each one.

The path curved down more sharply toward the beck. They stopped by a huge rock that resembled the collapsed cake stone. Yellow flowers and greenery grew out of any flat surface, and Gemma collected all she could reach to add to her bouquet.

"Let me help you," Charles said as he strode down the path. He picked Gemma up so she could pluck the rest of the flowers.

She giggled when he set her on her feet again. She and her brother hurried to the next Bridestone where the path dipped toward the beck.

"Wait there for us," Sophia said at the same time Charles did.

As Gemma called that they would, Sophia smiled. "They say great minds think alike."

"Certainly those who keep an eye on boisterous children must." He held out his hand.

She wove her fingers through his, then raised her eyes past his stubborn chin, past his expressive mouth, past his strong nose with the slight bump that she had never noticed. Had he broken it as a child or was it another visible war wound like the scar that wound up into his hair? When her gaze met his, everything she intended to ask him—Did he find the Bridestones interesting? Were his friends having fun? Had he heard the rumor about her being in her cousin's arms?—all of it fled from her mind. For once his eyes hid nothing from her. She lost herself in the intense emotions within them.

He held out his other hand. She took it as if she were following the steps of a dance that needed no music. He slowly drew her around the side of the giant stone. In its shadow, out of view of the path, he paused. The others' voices, the whispers of the wind, the birds' songs... they vanished beneath the thudding of her heart as his broad hands cupped her face. Did he breathe her name as his mouth lowered toward hers? She could not be sure, but she was certain how much she longed for him to kiss her.

He paused, so close to her mouth that she could feel the heat of his skin upon her lips. For one heartbeat, a second, then a third, he did not move. When she thought she could not wait a second longer, his lips brushed hers lightly.

She held her breath as delight danced through her. He kissed her again, and she returned it, hoping this sweetness told him what she could not with words. In his arms was where she wanted to be.

He raised his head enough to whisper, "You do know we are being want-witted, don't you?"

"Yes." She doubted she could say more while his finger ambled gently along her cheek.

"I should not—"

"Keep talking!"

His laughter tickled her face in the moment before he drew her back to him. He sprinkled kisses on her cheeks, on her nose, on her eyebrows. Just as his lips found hers again, someone called her name. She paid no attention. Too many times, they had let others intrude, tearing them apart. Not today. Not now. Not when he was kissing her.

"There you are! Didn't you hear us calling? I..." Her sister's voice ended in an embarrassed gulp.

Sophia blinked and saw Catherine peering around the huge stone. Her face was as red as Mr. Bradby's most garish waistcoat. Sophia quickly stepped out of Charles's arms before her sister's eyes could pop out of her skull.

Even so, Catherine recovered from her shock first. "Sophia, oh, thank heavens! Are the children with you?"

"No."

Her sister's face grew wan.

"What is it?" Charles asked, his voice rising with dismay.

Catherine gulped again. "My lord, we don't know where Gemma and Michael are. The children have vanished!"

Chapter Seventeen

Charles's battle skills burst out of memory. Everything around him came into pristine focus. The woods, the stones, the people beside him. How could he use each one to complete his mission? How could each be used to keep him from success?

First he needed information. Miss Catherine had little to tell them. Herriott had noticed the children playing near the beck. When he looked back a few moments later, they were gone. They had assumed the children were with Charles and Sophia, but then realized Charles and Sophia were nowhere to be seen either. That was when his friends had started calling out to them.

He shouted to Herriott and Bradby. They came running down the path with Miss Fenwick following close behind. One glance at him and his friends snapped to attention, ready for his orders.

"Did you call for the children?" Charles did not wait for an answer. He cupped his mouth and shouted the children's names.

He held his breath, hearing the faint echo resound off the other side of the hill.

No answer.

"Where did you see them by the beck?" asked Sophia.

He fought his annoyance. That should have been his first question. Bradby and Herriott looked hastily at each other. Were they beginning to question if he had truly lost his sense of command once he took off his uniform?

A useless thought that he had no time for. All that mattered was that the children were found safe. His gut clenched. He had promised to keep them safe. The moment he'd allowed Sophia to distract him, they had gone missing.

Focus, his military knowledge warned him. *Focus on the goal. Use everything to achieve it.*

"I saw them go down the path," Herriott said. "Or so it looked from where I stood."

"They must still be on this side of the beck." Charles paced until Sophia put her hand on his arm. He wanted to shake it off, but he stopped when she gave a slight shake of her head.

"We cannot assume that," she said.

"*I* know my children!" he shot back.

She yanked her hand away from him as tears blossomed in her eyes. By all that's blue, he did not want to make her cry after she had been soft and warm in his arms.

"Let us help, too," she said.

Awed by the strength of her compassion for him and his children, he choked out, "I must find them. You know that I would die for my children."

Herriott stared at him in disbelief. "That will not be necessary."

"How do you know?" he shouted as he glowered at Herriott. Bradby wisely stayed silent.

But not Sophia. "Berating yourself will not help find the children," she said.

"That is right," Vera added. "They cannot have gone far. We saw them moments ago."

"Little legs can move quickly when something catches a child's eye." Sophia made a quick decision. "We need to break up into teams, so we can cover more ground more quickly."

Again Charles fought vexation as the others nodded to Sophia's suggestion. Why were they fighting him on every point and yet concurring with her? He shoved those questions aside as he had the others. He had no time to examine his feelings. He must find the children.

"Herriott," he said, "you and I are the best trackers. We will head down the hill toward the beck. Bradby, you and Miss Fenwick go back toward the carriage. Look everywhere. They may have wandered off the path and gotten lost."

His friends nodded.

Charles turned to Sophia. "You and your sister need to retrace the path along the top of the hill."

Instead of agreeing, she protested, "No, Charles—"

"We cannot waste time talking. Whatever you have to say can wait." He waved his hand in the air. "Let's go. We will meet here in ten minutes."

"Charles, please, listen to me. I know—"

"Not now, Sophia!" He turned away, but not before he saw her flinch.

He motioned to Herriott to follow and left without saying another word. Why couldn't Sophia follow his orders without question as the others did? The answer almost staggered him. She could not follow his orders because she saw through him straight to his heart. She saw his fear and the guilt that he had let himself be bemused by her kisses when he should have been watching over his children as he had vowed. He could not let himself be distracted again.

Pain burst from his heart, a pain he had not felt since Lydia's betrayal. Only this time he was the traitor. He had accepted Sophia's affection and now was tossing it aside. He hated himself, but he refused to break the oath that he had made. The oath that had kept him alive when he had been as ready to die as the man in his nightmare.

As he hurried down the path, Charles called out his children's names, then paused to listen for a reply. Fury almost blinded him. A branch broke, and he spun to his right.

"Gemma! Michael!" he shouted.

But it was only Bradby and Miss Fenwick walking along the edge of the wood toward the carriage. He frowned. Where were Sophia and her sister? He had told them to search the upper sections of the hill, but he could not see them.

"Northbridge, this may not be the time to speak up." Herriott cleared his throat as they approached a pair of Bridestones, one tall and thin while the other was squat and barely peeking out of the side of the hill. "But after what we interrupted…" He coughed again.

"Spit out what you have to say." He shielded his eyes with his hand so he could get a better view of the twisting path among the odd stone formations. The children could be hiding behind any of them. Even the top-heavy sculptures were wide enough at the base to conceal a small child.

"All right." Herriott walked around the tall rock, then said, "Sometimes sacrifices must be made. Didn't you tell me that?"

Charles waved aside his words. "I don't want to talk about sacrifices now. *Now* is not the time for anything but finding my children."

"You can listen while we search."

"If you insist…"

"I do. You have been lambasting me for being unable to make a decision."

Usually Charles would have apologized to his friend for being unsupportive of Herriott's difficulties during the transition from war to peace. Yet this was not the time. His eye caught a motion, and he whirled around. It was a branch rocking in the breeze.

"I have made a decision," Herriott said.

"Good for you."

"No." Herriott stopped and faced him. "Good for *you*."

"What are you babbling about?"

"I have seen how you look at my cousin and how she looks at you. It is clear that you have feelings for each other."

"Can't this wait, Herriott?"

"No, it cannot." His friend jumped onto the shorter stone and glanced at its far side. "Solid rock. No place for them here."

"Come on. There are several more before we get to the bottom of the ravine."

Herriott grabbed his sleeve. "I need you to listen to me."

"Not now." He tried to jerk his arm free, but heard threads rip on his coat. Not that he cared about the state of his coat when his children were missing. But he needed Herriott's help. His friend was a skilled tracker. He and Bradby used to joke that Herriott could trace a flea across a long-haired dog.

His friend did not heed him. "I want you to know that if you wish to woo my cousin, I will not stand in your way."

Even as his heart leaped with elation, Charles paid it no mind. What sort of father was happy when his children were missing? Not the kind he had vowed to be.

"I suspect that Sophia would be very eager to marry you," Herriott continued. "What woman would settle for being a mere baroness when she could be a countess?"

He stared at his friend, then pushed away from the rock he had been examining. He reeled blindly down the hill, desperate to get away from Herriott's question.

Herriott shouted, "Go slow! That path is too steep for that speed."

Charles ignored him.

Herriott was an excellent judge of character, one of the qualities that had made him a good lieutenant. He had honed a clearer insight into people than Charles ever could. Now Herriott believed Sophia wished to marry him to become a countess.

As Lydia had.

Sophia had welcomed his kisses eagerly.

As Lydia had.

Sophia's kisses had thrilled him to the depths of his soul, stripping him of every logical thought.

As Lydia's had.

Was he making the same mistake again?

Lord, help me! he prayed over and over as he stumbled down the path toward the beck. He stopped at its edge, having no idea where to turn.

* * *

"There is only one place where they could be," Sophia said to her sister as Charles and Cousin Edmund rushed away in one direction and Vera and Mr. Bradby in another.

"Where?" Catherine still refused to meet her eyes, and her cheeks flushed each time either Sophia or Charles spoke to her.

"The stone with the dragon's face."

"But that is on the other side of the beck."

Sophia put her hands on her hips and gave her sister an ironic smile. "Do you think that small beck which can be crossed on a few stepping stones will stop two children who want to see the dragon's face? Did it stop us?"

"No."

"Then let's go!"

Catherine hung back. "But Lord Northbridge told us to search the top of the hill."

"We will." Sophia's smile became grim. "Only it will not be the top of *this* hill."

When her sister protested that Charles would stop them if they followed the path, Sophia walked around one of the huge stones and started down the sheer drop toward the bottom of the ravine. She did not like being deceitful, but Charles had refused to listen to her, acting as if she had nothing worthwhile to say.

Just as Lord Owensly had when he came to renege on his offer to take her to Almack's.

She scurried faster down the hill as if she could evade her own memories. Charles was nothing like Lord Owensly, who cared more about what others thought than he had about Sophia. No man could kiss her as Charles had and not feel something honest and true for her.

Or was she bamboozling herself?

By the time she and Catherine had reached the bottom and begun up the other side, the sunlight was being swallowed by gray clouds.

"It is going to rain," her sister said needlessly as they jumped over the slender beck.

Sophia's shoes sank in the mud. "Then we need to hurry even more." Pulling herself out of the mire, she clambered up the hill on the far side of the beck, sometimes gripping the grass to heave herself up the steep slope.

A shout resounded through the narrow valley. She whirled, hopeful, before she realized the voice had been Charles's calling to his children. His pain resonated through their names.

She crested the hill and ran toward the massive stone that resembled a dragon's head. Would the children have seen the likeness, or would they have gone on? The Bridestones covered a vast area on either side of the beck.

Her breath burned beneath her ribs as she reached the dragon stone. She shouted the children's names.

Giggles.

"There!" Catherine tugged on Sophia's arm and pointed to the next Bridestone.

Sophia ran to it and discovered an open space beneath one portion of the huge rock. A space just the right size for two small children. They looked at her, then each other, and giggled again.

"Come out," she ordered.

"You found us!" Michael squeezed out and bounced to his feet. "You hide now."

"This was even more fun than when we play in the nursery," added Gemma with a wide grin.

Catherine asked, "This was a game for you?"

"A fun game!" Gemma danced along with her brother. "Can we play again?"

A quick check told Sophia that both of them were fine. Putting her hands on her hips, she said, "You two know better than to run off without telling anyone where you are bound. Playing in the safety of the nursery is one thing, but you could have fallen on these steep hills and hurt yourself."

Michael was in no mood to listen to reason. He twirled around in his excitement. "We see dragon!"

"Are you mad at us?" Gemma grasped Sophia's hand.

"I am not happy that you took off as you did, but I am glad you are safe," she said, brushing dust out of the little girl's red hair. "Let's go. Your papa is very worried about you."

"He was not going to let us see the dragon." Gemma pouted.

"We see dragon!" Michael took Sophia's other hand.

Deciding that she needed to let Charles decide what to do now that the children had been found, she hoped he had learned enough in the past weeks to understand that the children had meant no real harm. She sent her sister ahead to let the others know the children had been found and followed at a pace Michael's short legs could manage.

Sophia could not help stiffening when they reached the beck and she saw Charles standing on the other side. His friends, her sister and Vera were behind him. Even before he spoke a word, she felt fury billowing off him. She steeled herself to defend the children from his wrath.

As soon as she swung both children across the beck and into waiting arms, Charles said in the coldest voice she had ever heard, "Your sister tells me the children believed they were playing a game you taught them."

"Yes."

"How could you?" he shouted as he grabbed the shocked children's hands. "You filled their heads with nonsense, and now look where it has led."

She needed to persuade him to listen to her. "Charles—"

"Miss Meriweather, you have nothing more to say that I wish to hear." He spun on his heel and pushed past his friends.

The children looked back, dismay and hurt on their faces, as he marched them up the hill in the direction of the carriage.

Sophia stared after them in disbelief. Charles had not heeded her feelings any more than Lord Owensly had.

Chapter Eighteen

Sophia was not surprised to find her sister and Vera in Papa's book-room the afternoon of their return to Meriweather Hall. They were waiting for her.

Unlike Charles. He and the children had arrived at the house before the rest of them. They had not left yet for Charles's home, but she guessed it was a matter of time. She wanted to see him, but what good would it do when he was furious with her?

It did not help that she was disappointed with herself. She should have let the children know the hillside was no place to play hide-and-seek. She had expected Charles to be upset, but not irate.

"We knew you would come here." Catherine embraced her as gently as if Sophia were a fragile china figurine. "This is your sanctuary." Releasing her sister, she tried to smile. "I never have understood why you hide with dusty old books or why Vera hides with dirt and seeds and bugs."

Vera sat by the hearth. "We each have our way of seeking the quiet to hear the small voice of God within us when we don't know where to turn."

"Maybe," Sophia said, "if we listened to His guidance before we find ourselves in a tough place, we would not need a haven."

"That voice can be very soft when chaos erupts around us." Vera's eyes filled with tears. "Or when one's heart's desire is standing right in front of one."

"You need not worry about that any longer as far as I am concerned." Sophia sat heavily on a chair in front of the hearth. "It is quite clear I am no one's heart's desire."

"Stop it!" Catherine's sharp tone startled Sophia. "You cannot believe Lord Northbridge's feelings for you have changed. If it had not been for you, he would have looked for his children much longer."

Vera took the other chair and leaned forward, folding Sophia's cold hands between her warmer ones. "You did not hear what your cousin had to say when he came out to instruct the footmen on where to take the various bags we packed in the boot."

"No, I didn't." She had not seen Cousin Edmund when she had run into the house as soon as she could get out of the carriage. She had hoped to see the children or Charles. The staff had informed her that neither Lord Northbridge nor his children would receive her. Lord Northbridge's rejection was as public as Lord Owensly's and in front of people she cared deeply about.

"Your cousin told us," Vera continued in the same calm voice, "that Lord Northbridge's temper is a direct result of him trying to protect what is his. Whether it is his children or a piece of ground that the French were trying to conquer, he sees it as a personal attack. When the battle is won, or in this case when the children were found safe and sound, that anger refuses to go away."

Sophia nodded. Her cousin had related that to her at Sir Nigel's assembly. "But Cousin Edmund said Charles was doing better since he came to Meriweather Hall." The words came out before she could halt them.

"As Mr. Fenwick would say," Catherine whispered, "that is because of the healing peace of Sanctuary Bay."

Sophia took one hand from Vera and clasped her sister's. Dear Cat! Her struggle with her faith was painful, but it was clear that she wanted to believe as she had before.

"It is sad," Sophia said, "that Charles's healing did not last long."

"Lord Northbridge vowed before God to protect his children," Vera said, "and he believes he failed both God and his children. His fury is eating him up inside, and he could not stop it from striking outward, too." Vera smiled sadly. "I doubt his feelings for you have changed."

"Vera is right," came a soft voice from the doorway.

Sophia jumped to her feet at the sight of her mother coming into the book-room. Since Papa's death, her mother had remained in her rooms. Sophia had not guessed that the first place Lady Meriweather would venture forth to would be her husband's beloved little library.

"Mother!"

Lady Meriweather kissed Vera and Catherine on their cheeks, then turned to Sophia. She held out her arms, and Sophia stepped into her mother's embrace. "I thought I might find you here, Sophia. Vera, will you excuse us while I speak with my daughters?"

Vera nodded and closed the door after herself.

After her mother selected one chair, Sophia sat in the other. Catherine drew out the chair from behind Papa's desk.

"I heard how you two found the children and what

Lord Northbridge said to you," Lady Meriweather said. "I am proud of both of you for making sure the children were safe, and I am sorry Lord Northbridge failed to see that. I suspect he is quite sorry now, but such a proud man will find it difficult to ask for forgiveness."

Sophia nodded, not trusting her voice to speak.

"I had hoped that this time you found a man who would truly love you," her mother continued. "Do not look shocked. You know that nothing stays secret long in Meriweather Hall, and the staff has been anxious if you will marry your cousin or the earl."

"Neither of them wants me." All her pain rushed out.

She thought her mother would offer her comfort, but Lady Meriweather asked, "Do you know why your father took you to London, Sophia?"

Her mother's question astounded her. "Because he knew no one in this parish would marry me. He hoped I might find a husband there."

Lady Meriweather's smile became sad. "Oh, my dear Sophia! That is far from the truth. You could have almost any man you wanted. Many men approached your father after you turned seventeen and asked permission to court you."

"What?" She was as shocked as she had been by Charles's frigid dismissal. She glanced at her sister. "Maybe Catherine, but they were not interested in me."

"No, Sophia. They asked permission to court *you*. Your father was a very wise man, and he said his permission was not what they needed, but yours."

"None of them ever—"

"Think, Sophia," her sister said. "You will remember many young men loitering near you at Sir Nigel's annual ball and at other events throughout the year."

"But not for me."

"That is where you are mistaken." Lady Meriweather gave her a gentle smile. "I did not realize, at first, that you thought you believed they were interested only in your sister. By the time I understood that, most of the young men were discouraged that you had nothing to say to them but commonplaces."

Sophia struggled to comprehend what her mother and sister were saying. She did remember the young men who seemed to be around whenever she and Catherine attended a social function or a church one. She had been sure they wanted only to speak with her sister, but she could recall several times when she had ended a conversation after Catherine was invited to stand up with an admirer. She had thought she was doing the young men a favor by offering them an excuse to take their leave to spend time with a girl who was not half a head taller than many of them.

But now she realized that most of those young men who had been shorter than she was had, in recent years, surpassed her height. Even so, she had dismissed their attentions as nothing more than courtesy until they no longer stood nearby.

"I had no idea," she said.

"I know." Her mother's smile softened. "When you look in a glass, you see the gawky, tall girl, not the lovely, graceful woman you have become." She put her hand on Sophia's on the chair's arm. "I know you are curious how I saw what you did not. It is because I once was a gawky girl who fell in love with a man who towered over everyone and was awkward himself until we both grew out of it. Unfortunately you encountered that boorish cad, Lord Owensly, before you could come to accept yourself as you are now."

It was almost too much for Sophia to take in, so she

returned to her mother's original question. "But if Papa did not take me to London so I could find a husband, then why did he insist on me going with him?"

"Because he feared for your safety here."

That answer surprised her sister, too, because Catherine gasped out a protest as Sophia asked, "*My* safety? I have always been safe in Sanctuary Bay."

"You were until you began asking questions about some people who would prefer you did not."

An icy chill cut down Sophia's spine as Catherine's face turned gray. "You are talking about the smugglers."

"Yes, and your father believed you were getting dangerously close to the truth about their leader. By the time you returned, that leader had been replaced, or so your father thought."

"Papa knew who leads the smugglers?" She wondered how many more shocks she could endure.

"I believe so." Her mother ran her fingers along her chair's upholstered arm. "No, I am sure he did, even though he never said a word. Because he knew their leader, he also knew that man would not hesitate to do what he must to protect his business interests in Sanctuary Bay. Sophia, you must promise me that you will not start asking those questions again. I could not bear to lose you, too."

Sophia did not hesitate, even though she guessed her mother was asking this of her now because Lady Meriweather assumed that Sophia would remain at Meriweather Hall for the rest of her life. As she saw the grim expression on her sister's face, she said, "I promise."

Herriott's rooms were grand as was appropriate for the lord of Meriweather Hall. Tall windows rose to a ceiling decorated with plaster flowers and garlands.

Fine art of even higher skill than the pieces on the ground floor hung on walls covered in red damask to match the draperies. Mahogany furniture was covered with ivory silk, and vases held freshly picked flowers.

Charles waited by the door for the footman to announce him to Herriott. He dreaded this conversation, but it must not be delayed any longer.

"Northbridge!" Herriott came through an inner door, his shirt hanging out of his breeches and his feet bare. "I did not expect to see you at this hour."

"I trust I am not disturbing you so close to dinner."

"No more than you ever have." Herriott's attempt at a smile failed, and his friend motioned for Charles to sit in a nearby chair. "My cousin thought it best if we each dined alone tonight, so trays will be delivered to our rooms."

Charles felt like his friend had struck him. As always, Herriott was trying to be diplomatic, but Charles heard what his friend was taking care not to say. Sophia did not want to chance that Charles would come down for dinner after he had berated her.

"I am glad you are here," Herriott said as Charles sat on a window seat. "I wanted to ask your opinion."

"On what? Why I am incapable of controlling my temper?"

Sympathy lengthened Herriott's face. "I thought you considered me too good a friend to say such things when you are in such a dismal state."

"But you think them?"

"I want what is best for you and Bradby…and for me." He closed his eyes for a long moment and sighed. "Pardon me. I am not expressing this well. I fear I have not had enough sleep in far too long."

Guilt pinched at Charles. "We should have known not to put my room so close to anyone else's."

"It is not your nightmares that have kept me awake."

His friend's words pierced the wall Charles had raised to keep any of his emotions from slipping out. "Are you having nightmares, too?"

"No. Dreams." Herriott sighed again. "I have been doing a lot of thinking since we stood by the beck in the midst of the Bridestones. I have realized some very important things that have left me heartsick, if you must know the truth, Northbridge."

Charles stared down at his clasped hands. If Herriott was about to ask him to leave and never return to Meriweather Hall, Charles would comply.

"Heartsick about what?" he asked, because he saw his friend wanted to talk to someone who would listen without censure. That was the least he could do for the man who had saved his life more than once. A man who had stood by him when the terrors of the past erupted into nightmares.

"The mistake I made. Do you remember what we spoke about while searching for your children?"

How could he forget anything about that conversation? The topic had been Sophia. Rather than ask that, he said, "Yes."

"Do not think me a horrible person when I say I was wrong to say what I did. I cannot allow myself to forget that many depend on me now that I am Lord Meriweather, and I must not shirk my obligations." Herriott stared past him to the unlit hearth. "Do you understand what I mean?"

"I believe so." That was a tepid evasion. He knew quite well what Herriott was talking about.

Sophia.

His friend continued to look at the hearth, his thoughts obviously focused beyond the room. It was clear Sophia was on his friend's mind…and in his heart. Herriott had been willing to step aside in order to make his cousin happy, but, now that Charles had destroyed any chance to have her in his life, Herriott was determined to do his duty. And Sophia would accept her cousin's proposal…to do her duty.

Charles ignored the pain squeezing his heart. He came to his feet and put his hand on Herriott's shoulder. "You are my friend, so I will step aside." He walked toward the door.

"Step aside?" Herriott blinked and stared at him as if he had been so lost in his thoughts that he had forgotten Charles was there. "Northbridge, wait!"

Charles did not slow. There was nothing more to say.

The message the footman brought to Sophia was simple. Lord Meriweather would like to speak with Miss Meriweather in his rooms before dinner was brought up.

Thanking the footman and asking him to inform her cousin that she would be there immediately, Sophia paused long enough to look into her glass. Her face had reddened from her time in the sun while she'd searched for Gemma and Michael. Maybe that was not a bad thing, because she would be spared from having her cousin see her flush if he read her a scold for being discovered in Charles's arms among the Bridestones.

Only now was she realizing what a humiliating moment that must have been for her cousin. He had said nothing on the hill, and he had rented a carriage to take the women to Meriweather Hall so he could go by horseback and avoid talking to her.

Would he ask her to leave? Would he insist that

Mother and Catherine go, as well? Her cousin must see her kissing his friend as a betrayal. If he did ask them to leave, she would find some place to take her family. Perhaps to Sir Nigel, who had asked kindly about her mother. The eccentric man made her uncomfortable, but he would not turn them from his door. Certainly Vera and her brother would welcome them, but the parsonage was tiny and cramped for the two Fenwicks. The situation would not be hopeless. Dire, yes, but she would trust that God had a plan for them.

Sophia gathered her composure as she raised her hand to knock on her cousin's door. She had not met or heard another person while she'd walked from her bedchamber to his. Not even in the wake of her father's death had the house been so silent. It was as if everyone held their breath waiting for Cousin Edmund to chide her.

When her cousin called for her to enter, she did. She scanned the room, looking for any changes he had made, but save for a few personal items, the sitting room looked identical to the last time she and her father had discussed where they would travel after the war was over.

She was startled that she could not recall the last time she had thought about visiting the Continent. Before her cousin's arrival—before *Charles's* arrival—that grand tour of Europe had been a dream she revisited each day.

Cousin Edmund wore a dressing gown over his shirt and breeches. His feet were bare. She wondered why he had sent for her when he was *en déshabillé*. One glance at his face warned her that he was very troubled.

As she walked toward him, he added, "I may have done a horrible thing." He sat heavily on the chair behind him.

She sat on the ottoman beside his chair. "I find that unlikely. You have been good to my sister and my mother and me."

"The one I have acted badly to is you, cousin."

"Me?"

He nodded and stood to pace from the door to the hearth. "I have made a muddle of everything when I thought I was finally making the right decision." He slammed his fist into his other palm, then winced. "I cannot make a single decision any longer. When I try to force one, it creates a disaster like now."

Unsure which statement to respond to first, Sophia rose. She put her hand on her cousin's arm as she had on Sir Nigel's terrace. "Cousin Edmund, you must allow yourself time to recover from the war."

"You are good-hearted, dear cousin, but you may not feel the same toward me when you hear what I have done."

"What have you done?"

"I believe I have convinced Northbridge that I intend to marry you."

"And do you?"

"No." Cousin Edmund smiled shyly. "It is not that I don't have affection for you, Sophia. The affection of one cousin for another."

"The same as I have for you."

"And I want you to know that you, your sister and Lady Meriweather have a home within these walls for as long as you wish."

Tears flowed down Sophia's cheeks, and she leaned her head against his arm. "Thank you."

"I know the widows and children of the previous barons have always retired to the dower cottage, but I need your help, Sophia, as I learn how to run this estate. I have not been educated to this life." He gave her a sad smile as she straightened. "And you know I need help with making decisions. Until I can do that again, I will need to depend on you."

"I shall be happy to help in any way I can."

"And I wish I could help you."

His words puzzled her. "Me? How?"

"I know you love Northbridge, but he is too much a gentleman to speak up now that he believes I wish to marry you." His gaze shifted away. "He seems to have taken my words about duty to this estate and its residents to mean that I intend to ask you to be my wife." The full impact of his words crashed over Sophia. Charles would never hold her again or kiss her because he believed her cousin had decided to marry her. A sob burst from her as she sat on the ottoman again. With her face in her hands, she wept for all she had lost before it even was hers.

Cousin Edmund patted her shoulder awkwardly, but paused when a knock was placed on his door. He turned, then hesitated.

She motioned for him to go. Hastily she wiped the tears from her face and knew she must apologize to her cousin for discomforting him.

As soon as he opened the door, Nurse Alice rushed in. "Is Miss Meriweather here?"

"Over here." Sophia stood.

The nurserymaid ran to her. "Miss Meriweather, we have looked high and low in every corner of Meriweather Hall. We cannot find them!"

"The children?" she asked, the familiar sinking feeling in her stomach.

"They are gone!"

Chapter Nineteen

Charles sat by his window and stared out at the sea. Night had blackened the sky, but faint flashes of light bobbed with the motion of the waves at the far edge of Sanctuary Bay. Smugglers. Herriott had spoken of them during the ride west to the Bridestones, because he wanted to rid the bay of them.

"Good luck with that," Charles mumbled as he pushed himself to his feet. But then, Herriott had a greater chance of halting the smugglers than Charles did of winning Sophia's heart.

As he walked past the hearth, his eyes were caught by a pair of china dogs on the mantel. They cavorted, frozen in a playful moment. The sight of those dogs sent a wave of nostalgia over Charles. He'd had two similar-looking dogs when he was a child. Their descendants still lived at Northbridge Castle, and he looked forward to introducing Gemma and Michael to them.

At least he had one thing to anticipate among his regrets that had sent him to his knees last night. He had prayed, struggling to keep his promise to God and yet find a way not to hurt Sophia more. The sight of her face, blanching as he bellowed at her, had kept him from sleeping for the past two nights.

He had overreacted by the beck. Even then he had known it, but could not control the beast that had begun to claw its way out when Herriott mentioned Sophia would prefer to be a countess rather than a baroness. He had not asked her if Herriott was right. He simply had given in to his pain and rage. He had hoped when he was honest with Sophia that he could keep the fury under control.

But you were not honest with her about Lydia.

Shame surged through him as he sat by the hearth. The very idea of telling Sophia about how foolishly he had fallen for his late wife's lies frightened him more than facing a French cannon. What would she think of him then? Would her admiration turn to distaste?

He would never know, because he had driven her away before he could find out the truth.

Charles jumped to his feet when his door opened, slamming into the wall behind it. Sophia ran in with others following. He paid no attention to the others as he drank in her beauty. Her golden hair streaming behind her where it had fallen from her prim chignon.

She stopped in front of him, reached for his hands, then quickly drew hers back. "Charles, the children are missing again."

"What?" he shouted. He was appalled when his warrior's instincts rose within him again. He would not surrender to that rage. Not again. His anger subsided, astonishing him. He had controlled it and let it seep away rather than explode out of him. No time to think of that now. Lowering his voice, he asked, "Do you have any idea where they went? When?"

Nurse Alice crept past Herriott. "My lord, I tucked them in their beds, but when I came back later to check on them, they were gone. It was no more than an hour later."

"But where would they go in the middle of the night?"

"The dower cottage," Sophia said.

He nodded, remembering that his son wanted to see the bats. He wondered why his daughter would have agreed to go in the middle of the night. He scowled. Gemma would go simply to vex her father.

"Herriott," he said, "we cannot be certain they went there."

"Sophia has already dispatched the staff to check the stables," his friend said, "and she suggests Bradby and I search the beach from here to the village."

Again Charles nodded. He wanted to offer his friend sympathy, because, even when the children might be in danger, Herriott could not make a decision.

"Let's go." Sophia halted his argument by adding, "You will never find the cottage on your own in the dark." She grabbed his arm, and he ran with her from the room.

Sophia hoped *she* could find the cottage after dark. During the day it had been easy to follow the faint path through the woods until she found the more well-used one.

"Thank you," Charles said from behind her.

"For what?" She glanced over her shoulder, but looked quickly forward when branches tangled in her hair. She struggled to free herself.

He reached around her and drew her hair away from

the branches. "For all of this. I know you did not expect to be chasing after my children again, especially after how it ended last time. I am sorry that I treated you badly."

"Charles, I know your temper is a war wound like your scar is," she said as she continued on among the trees.

"But my scar has healed. The other…"

"It takes time for our hearts to heal. Mine is beginning to, because once I believed that the only chance for me to be happy was to be far from here, seeking adventures. But I have found that I enjoy adventures with you and your children, whether the adventures are dancing together on the terrace or playing cat's cradle." She paused to let him catch up with her in a clearing. "Now you need to let us help you heal your heart."

"How?"

"You must forgive yourself for your wounds as you have forgiven Cousin Edmund and Mr. Bradby. I have seen you quietly helping my cousin make a decision, and you have laughed at Mr. Bradby's jests when I know you tire of them. You forgive them because you know they are still healing. Now you must forgive yourself so you can find healing."

"I don't know how."

"Yes, you do." She wove her fingers through his. "Trust God. Put your pain and fears in His hands. He brought you home to your children. Now let Him bring your heart home, too."

"To you?"

Love danced within her heart, but she said, "If that is what you want."

Charles released her hand as the trees surrounded

them again. She could not see his face as he asked, "Sophia, will you answer me honestly?"

"I will always be honest with you."

"Why would you want me in your life?"

"Because I love you." What a joy it was to speak those words at long last.

"Any other reason?" he asked, pain scraping his voice raw.

"Because I love your children."

"Any other reason?"

"I am sure there are other reasons," she said, "but why are you asking? Isn't loving you and the children enough?"

"It was not for my wife."

Sophia faltered, and he walked past her. Hurrying to keep up, she said, "But I thought you and Lydia had a wonderful marriage. My cousin has mentioned that often."

"Because Herriott does not know the truth. No one does, other than me and now you."

She said nothing as he explained how Lydia had married him solely to obtain his prestigious title. Her plan to give him an heir had been thwarted when she'd given birth to a daughter. When he had bought a commission to join the fight against Napoleon, Lydia had been furious because how could she give him a son if Charles was on the other side of the sea?

"After I went home during my last leave, she acted like the loving wife I believed her to be," Charles said sadly. "Then I returned to battle. When she wrote to share the tidings that we would have another child, she also told me that I need not bother to return to England. She had my title and was certain she carried my heir.

She no longer needed me. In fact, she let me know that she would prefer to be the dowager countess, the widow of a war hero."

Sophia wanted to protest that no woman would be that coldhearted, but she could hear the truth in his voice.

"The only thing she wanted," he went on, "was to go to London and rejoin the social swirl she adored far more than she ever did her husband or children. And, fool that I was, I had believed she loved *me*. I boasted about it to anyone who would listen, but I was wrong. She never loved me. She loved being a countess and aspired to a place among the powerful at Almack's to repay those who once had snubbed her." He grimaced. "She loved being a countess so much that she never dallied with another man, though she made eyes at them."

"Oh, Charles, I am so sorry." She ran her hand along his stiff back as she recalled Gemma talking about her mother flirting with men.

"No. I am the one who should be apologizing." He turned and caught her by the elbows. He drew her closer. "When we were searching for the children, Herriott said, half joking, that you would rather marry me than him because what woman wouldn't rather be a countess than a baroness?"

She drew in a sharp breath. "He could not have known what those words would mean."

"Of course not. I don't blame him for me losing my temper, but that showed me, my beloved Sophia, that I must be the master of my temper. I love you too much to inflict it upon you again."

"You love me?" she whispered.

"I have since the moment you splashed water in my face down in the bay. I—"

Sophia clamped her hand over his mouth and murmured, "Lights. Behind you. Coming this way."

He slipped behind a clump of tall ferns. She followed, crouching beside him. She held her breath as the lights moved closer. Dark lanterns, she guessed, because the light appeared and disappeared as they came nearer.

"...and you know where to take the brandy." A man's voice reached her ears.

"Smugglers," she whispered.

Charles tensed beside her before he pulled off his dark coat and slipped it over her shoulders to conceal her pale gown that could betray them if light caught it. He draped his waistcoat over his own shoulders to hide his shirt.

"Right. Any other instructions from the boss?" asked another man.

"Not for the likes of you."

Several men laughed.

Charles drew his dark coat more tightly around her, guiding her hands up to hold it closed. "Stay here," he hissed in her ear.

She seized his arm to keep him from moving. The men were only yards away.

"No," she whispered. "This is not your war, Charles. Your war is over."

"But—"

She pressed her lips to his to silence him as the men walked past their hiding place. His arms slid up beneath the coat, and he pulled her up against his chest. As he deepened the kiss, she lost herself in it. Only when he raised his mouth did she realize the smugglers had gone past without noticing them. He smiled at her, stroking her face gently.

They waited a full minute—the longest of Sophia's life—before leaving their hiding place and continuing toward the cottage. Neither of them spoke in their urgency. Sophia wanted to believe that none of the villagers would hurt the children, but the smugglers were determined to keep anyone from stopping their illegal trade.

The cottage looked deserted when Charles opened the door. Crates filled the ground floor. She opened her mouth to call out the children's names, but Charles put his hand on her arm and shook his head. He was right. They could not guess when the smugglers might return.

A soft sound came from overhead. Charles ran to the stairwell door and yanked it open so hard the hinges broke. He put his foot on the first riser, and it cracked beneath his step.

"Let me," Sophia said. "I am lighter."

He put his hands on her waist and lifted her to the second riser, steadying her as she put her weight on it. The board held, and she went up the stairs, testing each board before she stepped on it. The third from the top broke. It clattered down into the space behind the stairs. The sound was like a gunshot. If any of the smugglers were nearby, they must have heard it.

"Gemma! Michael!" she called, knowing there was no time left to lose.

"Sophia?" came a fearful squeak from the right.

She looked over the top of the stairwell to see two small shadows moving toward her. "Yes, your father and I are here." She held out her arms and gathered in Michael.

She handed him to Charles, then assisted Gemma over the edge of the stairwell and down the stairs.

"Someone is coming," Charles said as Sophia jumped over the lowest step. "Is there another door out of here?"

"No, but the window in the back room is large enough."

He scooped up Michael and ran around the crates to the other room. Sophia followed with Gemma. Charles had the window open by the time they entered the room. He climbed through, then held out his arms for the children. She handed them through, then grasped his wrists as he pulled her outside. She left pieces of her dress and skin from her elbows on the window's rough edge. She ignored the scrapes as she edged beneath the trees with Charles and the children.

Two smugglers rushed into the cottage, shouting for the interlopers to come out before they shot.

Tugging on Charles's ripped sleeve, Sophia motioned for him to follow. They reached the edge of the wood more quickly than she expected, but, even there, Charles scanned the open gardens before he allowed them to step out from beneath the trees.

A footman came running as they walked into the house. Sophia sent him with the message that the children had been found. Then she sat on a bench in the foyer when her knees collapsed beneath her. She put her arms around the children and hugged them close.

"Why did you run away again?" she whispered. "You scared us."

"We did not mean to scare *you*." The defiance had returned to Gemma's voice as she glowered at her father.

He must not have seen it because he sat beside Sophia and said, "I owe you another thank you, Sophia.

I know helping us was not a duty you expected when you opened your door to your cousin."

"I have heard enough about duty!" She set herself on her feet.

He stared at her in astonishment as he stood, too. "Pardon me?"

"You heard me. I have heard enough about duty." She held up her hand and counted on her fingers. "My duty to my mother and my sister to keep them from having to live in the dower cottage. My father's duty to protect me, even if it meant letting me believe that taking me to London was the only way a tall woman like me would ever find a husband."

"Protect you from what? The smugglers?"

"I told you. That is not your war. Nor is it mine. I am safe, and I have promised my mother to do nothing to change that." She held up a third finger. "And, last but hardly least, there is Edmund's duty to marry a woman he does not love as more than a cousin."

"Are you sure of that?"

Sophia nodded and smiled when she saw Charles's surprise. "I am very sure of that. He loves me as his cousin. Nothing more. He wants my help to learn how to become a good lord for Meriweather Hall. That is all."

"And I have heard enough about your duty to these children." She looked at Gemma and Michael who were listening with uncharacteristic silence.

"I vowed to God—"

"To provide for them, to guide them, to teach them of the Lord's blessings, but no earthly father can keep his children from ever being hurt again." Her voice softened. "Just as he cannot prevent himself from being hurt."

"But he can learn not to hurt others."

She nodded.

"Especially the ones he loves." He cupped her chin and kissed her lightly. Turning to his children, he said, "I see two young people who are up far past their bedtime. Let's go."

"No!" said Gemma. She folded her arms over her chest and glared at him.

"No!" said Michael, copying her motions.

"Children," Charles began.

"No!" they shouted in unison.

Sophia put her hands on their shoulders. "Please do as your father asks."

"Why should we?" asked Gemma.

"Because he wants what is best for you. You are his children, and he loves you."

"I don't want him to love me."

"Me neither." Michael hesitated, then said, "Maybe a little."

"No, you don't," Gemma argued. "Do you want him to yell at you like he yells at Sophia?"

The little boy shuddered. "No, not like that."

"Then you don't want him to love you. He will yell at you and then leave you. That is what he has always done. That is what Mama said. That is what Grandma says. He yells and then goes away."

Sophia put her hands on Gemma's trembling shoulders as color faded from Charles's face, making his scar more pronounced. "Is this why you have been trying to make him angry? To see if he will leave again?"

"Yes." Gemma choked back tears. "And we don't care if he does. Right, Michael?"

The little boy glanced between her and his father, torn in his loyalties.

"Gemma," Sophia said softly, "you don't mean that."

"I do!"

Charles squatted down in front of his children, so they were eye to eye. From the surprise on their faces, Sophia guessed he had never spoken to them from that position. "I am sorry you believe that, Gemma and Michael. I had to go away because of the war, but I don't intend to go away again anytime soon."

"But if we are bad and you get mad..." Michael's eyes glittered with tears.

"If you are bad, I may get mad, but only because I want to make sure you never do anything that will hurt you. Even if I am mad enough that steam comes out of my ears, I still will not leave. You are wrong. There is nothing you can do that would make me love you less and not want to be with you. Nothing!" He paused, cleared his throat, then said, "But I have been wrong, too."

"You, Papa?" asked Michael who had been trying not to grin after Charles mentioned steam coming out of his ears.

"Yes, me. I have said that I would die for you. I don't want to die for you. God listened to my prayers and brought me back to you. Now I want to live with you, to be with you until long after you grow up and have children of your own. Will you let me do that?"

Michael did not hesitate. He threw himself into his father's arms. Gemma hesitated for only a second, then whispering, "Papa!" flung her arms around Charles's neck. He cradled them both as he looked over their heads at Sophia.

She let her tears of joy fall. So much healing was still needed, but it had begun.

When his children released him, Charles winked at them, then said, "As long as I am down here…" He shifted to be on one knee and smiled at the children. "Will you give me your blessing to marry Sophia?"

They squealed their excited agreement.

Sophia held her breath as he looked up at her again and asked, "Will you marry me, Sophia? I will not be an easy man to live with, but I will do my best with your help and God's to find the healing my soul needs."

"Yes," she said, her heart trilling out her joy. "Yes, I will marry you."

The children danced around Sophia and Charles as he came to his feet and took her hand.

Michael asked, "Will you be our mother, Sophia?"

"Forever and ever." She kissed his cheek, then looked at Gemma. The little girl snuggled up against her, and Sophia understood how lonely the little girl had been for someone to love. Now she had discovered her father loved her and that Sophia did, too.

They all had been too lonely for too long, but that was over. Charles had told her once that they could not allow the pain of the past to taint their futures and that a tough lesson was worth the pain if they learned from it. And she had learned to trust that Charles truly loved her. As she gazed into his eyes, she knew joy awaited them as husband and wife and as the parents of his children and any other God gave to them.

Charles waved his children toward the stairs. "Go and tell Nurse Alice that you will be staying awhile longer."

They paused only enough to give both their father and Sophia a hug, then ran up the stairs.

"I hope you know what you are letting yourself in for," he said as he brushed her hair back from her eyes.

"A lifetime of adventures with you and the children we will share." She locked her hands behind his nape and smiled at him. "I thought I would have to travel the world to escape the jeers about my height and to obtain my heart's desire, but all I needed was to wait for you to find your way to me."

"You are right about that, my love, but you were mistaken about being too tall." He tilted her mouth toward his. "You are exactly the perfect height…for this."

* * * * *

Dear Reader,

I hope you enjoyed reading about beautiful Sanctuary Bay. The setting was inspired by Robin Hood's Bay in northern England. It is a spectacular location with a long history of smuggling and piracy. Visit my website www.joannbrownbooks.com to see pictures of the bay and village.

Wandering the village's steep main street, my husband and I were enthralled by the peace, and the wind and waves against the cliffs. I knew I had to set a story there. I decided, because of my military experience, the stories would focus on three men who fought against Napoleon and were dealing with the aftereffects of war's horror. They do not realize they can find healing in Sanctuary Bay, but in the beauty of God's creation, it is possible. Watch for the next Sanctuary Bay book, available in December 2013, from Love Inspired Historical.

Wishing you many blessings,
Jo Ann Brown

Questions for Discussion

1. Charles feels betrayed by his late wife. Have you ever felt betrayed by someone you love?

2. Sophia is bothered by her height. What aspect of your appearance bothers you?

3. Sophia and Edmund are both determined to do their duty to their family. Do you find it easy to be dutiful, or is it difficult for you?

4. With his children, Charles can be overprotective. How much freedom do you think a child should have?

5. Michael finds it easy to forgive his father while Gemma can't. How easy is it for you to forgive? Is it easier to forgive a stranger than a loved one?

6. Everyone joins in with the "clipping of the church." What activities do you enjoy with your church and/or community?

7. Which character in the story is most like you? Why?

8. Sophia is expected to marry her cousin. What expectations have you had placed on you? How did you react?

9. Charles and his friends travel throughout North Yorkshire in England. Do you enjoy visiting new places?

10. Sophia believes no young man wants to court her and then she discovers she is wrong. Have you ever made a wrong assumption? How did you feel when you found out you had assumed mistakenly?

11. Both Charles and Sophia struggle to trust each other. Is trust easy or hard for you?

12. Regency England was a time of fashion and flirtations. Would you have liked to have lived then?

REQUEST YOUR FREE BOOKS!

2 FREE INSPIRATIONAL NOVELS
PLUS 2
FREE
MYSTERY GIFTS

Love Inspired
HISTORICAL
INSPIRATIONAL HISTORICAL ROMANCE

YES! Please send me 2 FREE Love Inspired® Historical novels and my 2 FREE mystery gifts (gifts are worth about $10). After receiving them, if I don't wish to receive any more books, I can return the shipping statement marked "cancel." If I don't cancel, I will receive 4 brand-new novels every month and be billed just $4.74 per book in the U.S. or $5.24 per book in Canada. That's a saving of at least 21% off the cover price. It's quite a bargain! Shipping and handling is just 50¢ per book in the U.S. and 75¢ per book in Canada.* I understand that accepting the 2 free books and gifts places me under no obligation to buy anything. I can always return a shipment and cancel at any time. Even if I never buy another book, the two free books and gifts are mine to keep forever.

102/302 IDN F5CN

Name	(PLEASE PRINT)	
Address		Apt. #
City	State/Prov.	Zip/Postal Code

Signature (if under 18, a parent or guardian must sign)

Mail to the Harlequin® Reader Service:
IN U.S.A.: P.O. Box 1867, Buffalo, NY 14240-1867
IN CANADA: P.O. Box 609, Fort Erie, Ontario L2A 5X3

Want to try two free books from another series?
Call 1-800-873-8635 or visit www.ReaderService.com.

* Terms and prices subject to change without notice. Prices do not include applicable taxes. Sales tax applicable in N.Y. Canadian residents will be charged applicable taxes. Offer not valid in Quebec. This offer is limited to one order per household. Not valid for current subscribers to Love Inspired Historical books. All orders subject to credit approval. Credit or debit balances in a customer's account(s) may be offset by any other outstanding balance owed by or to the customer. Please allow 4 to 6 weeks for delivery. Offer available while quantities last.

LIH13R

He was her high school crush, and now he's a single father of twins. Allison True just got a second chance at love.

**Read on for a sneak preview of
STORYBOOK ROMANCE by Lissa Manley,
the exciting fifth book in
THE HEART OF MAIN STREET series,
available October 2013.**

Something clunked from the back of the bookstore, drawing Allison True's ever-vigilant attention. Her ears perking up, she rounded the end of the front counter. Another clunk sounded, and then another. Allison decided the noise was coming from the Kids' Korner, so she picked up the pace and veered toward the back right part of the store, creasing her brow.

She arrived in the area set up for kids. Her gaze zeroed in on a dark-haired toddler dressed in jeans and a red shirt, slowly yet methodically yanking books off a shelf, one after the other. Each book fell to the floor with a heavy clunk, and in between each sound, the little guy laughed, clearly enjoying the sound of his relatively harmless yet messy play.

Allison rushed over, noting there was no adult in sight. "Hey, there, bud," she said. "Whatcha doing?"

He turned big brown eyes fringed with long, dark eyelashes toward her. He looked vaguely familiar even though she was certain she'd never met this little boy.

"Fun!" A chubby hand sent another book crashing to the floor. He giggled and stomped his feet on the floor in a little happy dance. "See?"

Carefully she reached out and stilled his marauding hands. "Whoa, there, little guy." She gently pulled him away. "The books are supposed to stay on the shelf." Holding on to him, she cast her gaze about the enclosed area set aside for kids, but her view was limited by the tall bookshelves lined up from the edge of the Kids' Korner to the front of the store. "Are you here with your mommy or daddy?"

The boy tugged. "Daddy!" he squealed.

"Nicky!" a deep masculine voice replied behind her. "Oh, man. Looks like you've been making a mess."

A nebulous sense of familiarity swept through her at the sound of that voice. Not breathing, still holding the boy's hand, Allison slowly turned around. Her whole body froze and her heart gave a little spasm then fell to her toes as she looked into deep brown eyes that matched Nicky's.

Sam Franklin. The only man Allison had ever loved.

Pick up STORYBOOK ROMANCE
in October 2013 wherever Love Inspired® Books are sold.

Love Inspired HISTORICAL

Eve Pickering knows what it's like to be judged because of your past. So she's not about to leave the orphaned boy she's befriended alone and unprotected in this unfamiliar Texas town. And if Chance Dawson's offer of shelter is the only way she can look after Leo, Eve will turn it into a warm, welcoming home for the holidays. No matter how temporary it may be—or how much she's really longing to stay for good....

Chance came all the way from the big city to make it on his own in spite of his secret...and his overbearing rich family. But Eve's bravery and caring is giving him a confidence he never expected— and a new direction for his dream. And with a little Christmas luck, he'll dare to win her heart as well as her trust—and make their family one for a lifetime.

Texas Grooms

A Family for Christmas

by

WINNIE GRIGGS

Available October 2013 wherever
Love Inspired Historical books are sold.

LIH82983